I0694337

UNDER THE THUMB
STORIES OF POLICE OPPRESSION

UNDER THE THUMB: STORIES OF POLICE OPPRESSION
Guest Edited by S.A. Cosby
Copyright © and ™ 2021

Guest Editor: S.A. Cosby
Additional Editorial Staff: Roger Nokes, Jay Butkowski, Libby Cudmore, Paul J. Garth, R.D. Sullivan, and Albert Tucher

With Stories by: Hector Duarte, Jr., James Queally, Bobby Mathews, Hilary Davidson, Joseph S. Walker, Keith Rosson, Tim P. Walker, Travis Wade Beaty, Mike McHone, Oluseyi Onabanjo, Jeffrey Eaton, James D.F. Hannah, Michael A. Gonzales, Preston Lang, Andrew Case, Zakariah Johnson, Jeff Soloway, Richie Narvaez, and Michael Downing

Cover by Heather Garth
Book design by Jay Butkowski

ISBN: 979-8-9852904-0-0 (Paperback)
ISBN: 979-8-9852904-1-7 (Hardcover)
ISBN: 979-8-9852904-2-4 (eBook)

Library of Congress Control Number: 2021950638

10 9 8 7 6 5 4 3 2

Published by Rock and a Hard Place Press, an imprint of Rock and a Hard Place Press, LLC, Woodbridge, NJ.
rockandahardplacemag.com
amazon.com/~/e/B08WPQG5YV

Printed in the United States of America

DEDICATION

For George, Eric, Breonna, Daniel, Philando, Sandra and too many others. You died under the thumb, but your memory and your stories carry on.

Proceeds from *Under the Thumb* benefit **Black Lives Matter NJ**

The **NJ chapter of Black Lives Matter** works to empower the black community via mutual aid, protest, and education.

Black Lives Matter NJ's principles:

1. Uplifting the most marginalized of marginalized black voices

2. We are owed reparations NOW

3. Abolition of mass incarceration and police

4. The rights of protestors must be respected and protected

5. Solidarity not charity

6. Equity not equality

7. The BREATHE Act

"It is our duty to fight for our freedom. It is our duty to win. We must love each other and support each other. We have nothing to lose but our chains." -Assata Shakur

WE GOT US

WHAT IS THE BREATHE ACT?

IMAGINE: Schools free of police and full of trained counselors and restorative justice programs, where all our children are kept safe, and their needs are met.

IMAGINE: Easy access to trained, trauma-informed interventionists who can be called on in domestic violence situations and who are equipped to facilitate long-term safety, healing, and prevention.

IMAGINE: 911 operators dispatching unarmed mental health experts instead of police in situations involving behavioral health crises, and callers being allowed to request responders that connect to the gender identity of the person in crisis.

The BREATHE Act offers a radical reimagining of public safety, community care, and how we spend money as a society. We bring 4 simple ideas to the table:

- Divest federal resources from incarceration and policing.

- Invest in new, non-punitive, non-carceral approaches to community safety that lead states to shrink their criminal-legal systems and center the protection of Black lives—including Black mothers, Black trans people, and Black women.

- Allocate new money to build healthy, sustainable, and equitable communities.

- Hold political leaders to their promises and enhance the self-determination of all Black communities.

Learn more at **BREATHEact.org**

CONTENTS

FOREWORD

S.A. Cosby

One day in the summer of my sixteenth year I was riding around my hometown in my best friend's car. It was a jet-black sports car with flashy rims and a spoiler wide enough to be an airplane wing. We were listening to music, talking about the girls we liked and the dreams we had as young black boys who were trying to learn the ways of men.

I was the one who first noticed the blue lights.

My friend didn't panic. We both knew he wasn't speeding. We weren't drinking and neither one of us smoked weed. He pulled over and lowered the window then put both his hands on the steering wheel. I put both of mine on the dashboard.

This was the way our parents had told both of us to interact with the police. The conversations had happened at different times, but the content was the same.

"Don't talk smart."

"Keep ya hands visible."

"Tell them you are reaching for your license."

"Do whatever they say so you can come home."

These words, delivered in quiet tones and hushed voices, had never actually seemed real to me. I hadn't had that many interactions with the police. I was a rambunctious kid, but pretty grounded. I was in many ways a nerd. I liked to write. I read voraciously. I even entertained becoming a private detective or an FBI agent. I knew—intrinsically, as most people of color or people below the poverty line know—that interactions with the police can only really go in one of two ways.

Very good or very bad.

But I still didn't think about those interactions in respect to myself as a black kid in the South. It wasn't real to me, in the same way mortality or infirmity isn't real to any sixteen-year-old. Those things are just words to the ears of the young.

The police officer came up to the window and asked for my friend's driver license. My friend obliged. Then he asked for mine. I asked what I thought was an innocent question.

"Why do you need my license?"

In the few seconds between when the question was asked and when it was answered I watched this officer, a florid-faced white man who I vaguely recognized as a someone who had gone to school with my older brother, transform before my eyes. His countenance went from mildly disinterested to enraged.

He screamed at us to get out of the car. In the middle of July, he made us both put our faces to the hot asphalt. He tore into my friend's car without asking for permission to search it. He accused us of being drug dealers, thugs, criminals of the worst order. When I protested that we were none of those things he got down on one knee and put the barrel of his gun against the back of my head.

"You're whatever I say you are."

In that moment, mortality went from just a word to a reality. As I lay there with dirt and gravel sticking to my face, I realized that this man who had barely graduated from high school, who still came to football games and hit on the cheerleaders, who expected and received free coffee and donuts at every gas station in town, who had, at best, six weeks of training held my life in his trembling adrenalized hands. He could shoot me; say I'd made a move for his gun and get away with it. And neither my mother's tears nor my father's cries would make a difference.

It's said by more than one person who seeks to address the issue of policing in this and other countries that we shouldn't focus on the bad apples. They repeat that adage again and again, but they neglect to finish it.

One bad apple can spoil the bunch.

The comedian Chris Rock has a routine where he talks about how there are some jobs where you just can't have a bad day. Pilots, doctors, and cops.

We are indoctrinated from an early age to treat police officers with awe and respect. We are implored to back the blue. Officer Friendly is a character in primary books. Television, films, and books are full of stories of heroic cops bucking a system that doesn't work and taking matters into their own hands, to hand out justice and uphold the law. Police officers lay down their lives to protect and serve. And in a perfect world that would be the end of the conversation.

But the world isn't perfect, and we all fall short of grace.

There are police officers who I truly believe want to do the right things. They want to help the community. Protect the innocent and do all the heroic things they imagined they would do when they first put on the uniform. Unfortunately, in most cases the deck is stacked against them . . . and us.

Many modern police forces arose out of the slave patrols of the 1850s. After the Civil War, police forces were organized to control not only former slaves but anyone the majority deemed unacceptable. As the years rolled on many police departments experienced a shift in their mindsets. For many, protect and serve became terrorize and subjugate.

The actions of police chiefs in the South like Bull Connor, or officers like Jon Burge of the Chicago Police Department, made a mockery of not only the law but basic human decency. These men and other officers like them killed, tortured, and embraced corruption with impunity.

There is a tendency to push back against this idea by those who would seek to defend not just the police as an entity but policing as a necessity. "Not all cops are bad" they will cry. And they are correct. But to paraphrase Mr. Rock, Just one bad cop is one too many. Just one bad cop who feels he or she is a warrior in a near mythological battle with evil or, worse yet, feels that they are not beholden to any rules is the most dangerous person on the street. More dangerous than anyone they might arrest. Because they hold our lives in their hands. And many times, they are not careful with that awesome duty.

I think the conversation around policing has to change. The current structure is breaking down under the weight of its own hypocrisy. To quote Yeats, the center does not hold. We cannot continue down this path of idolization and impunity. Too many have died, too much blood has been spilled. I won't pretend to have the answers, but I am fiercely committed to asking the questions. My life and the lives of too many others depends on it.

The stories in this anthology are an attempt to change that conversation. In ways both subtle and overt, they ask the questions we all should be asking. How do we reclaim our power as a people? How do we hold the police accountable? What does it look like when those to whom we give great power don't understand the great responsibility that such power entails? And how do we move forward?

I am so proud to have collaborated with **Rock and a Hard Place Press** on this collection. These stories are ferocious and introspective. Powerful and heartbreaking and harrowing. They are raw and honest and most important of all, they are fearless. They speak truth to power in a way that only the very best literature can.

In the words of French philosopher Voltaire:

"If you want to know who controls you, look at who you are not allowed to criticize."

Or more succinctly in the words of Malcom X:

"I'm going to tell it like it is. I hope you can take it like it is"

These stories encompass both ideals.

S.A. Cosby,
Guest Editor
November 2021

P.S.—that cop that pulled me and my friend over? He retired after twenty years with a commendation from the governor.

1

"I'm nervous. I don't know why. I've never been pulled over. My record is squeaky clean but for some reason, whenever a cop is behind me on the road or freeway, I'm jittery."

PROM NIGHT REBOOT

HECTOR DUARTE, JR.

W e're run off our feet and I'm pissed I have to work on a Friday. One of the curses of being a teacher is the amount of time taken from your already busy life. My wife, God bless her, sees the silver living in everything. During nuclear fallout, she'd look up at the sky and point out the beautiful colors.

We've only been married a little over one year and don't have any kids, so we don't have the luxury of calling out on Fridays like this when it's high school prom and administration needs chaperones.

Truth be told, I actually like this group of outgoing seniors. After six years in the classroom, they're the first group I honestly connected with. They didn't give me any major problems. No fights, no one mouthed off and called me a cocksucker (that was the year before). This group was actually enjoyable and I would miss them. This was the first school year where my wife—let's call her Aly—was shocked I wasn't coming home on the daily to bitch about one student or another. Administration wasn't even getting on my nerves, something unprecedented. That's how stress-free this school year had been.

When I asked Aly if she wanted to join me for prom night on the beach, free dinner and dancing, the optimistic fun-lover jumped at the chance.

Dinner was all right. What you'd expect: Chicken Kiev with potatoes and rice pilaf. Dessert was flan. Soon as the students were done eating, they made a big show of coming around to say hi and meet my wife who they'd inevitably heard about in passing, during lectures or random conversation. I try to keep my personal life personal but inevitably a phrase like, "Me and my wife were watching

. . ." sneaks in. You'd laugh at how some of these kids' eyes would bug out in surprise that I have a life outside of the four walls encasing Room 227.

Kelsey Hollingsworth was the first one to come around that night, grip Aly's shoulders in a tight squeeze, and say, "Our class loves your husband so much. Is he as cheesy at home as he is in the classroom?'

Aly looked at me, winked, and said, "Worse."

Kelsey placed her hand over her chest, cocked her head back, and laughed. Seeing her in full makeup and dressed to the nines shifted my perspective. She was an attractive woman. Seeing them in uniforms every single day, not really trying to impress anyone by highlighting certain features, dulls them, makes me see them as just kids. Yet here was Kelsey Hollingsworth, acting like the adult she is, hamming up my wife, whom she had around her thumb and knew it. In a few months she'd use that same sass and charm to navigate herself around a college campus, ingratiating herself into a niche she'd make her own. My work with her, all of them, was done. She'd be just fine.

"It's so nice to meet you, Miss. Hope to see the two of you dancing out there later." Kelsey walked off bopping her hips left and right like a pendulum.

When she was well out of earshot, Aly leaned over and whispered, "Someone has a crush on you."

I scoffed. "No way. She's always making fun of how bad my jokes are and how boring my class is."

"She'd better be careful before I come over there and regulate."

"Please."

We danced a little bit but mostly made the rounds of the Miami Beach hotel lobby, sweeping the bathrooms to be sure no one was vaping or starting the after-party early. I caught Dennis Benitez (Every graduating class has one. Think John Bender from *The Breakfast Club*, only more burnt-out) sucking on something berry-scented. Turning pale white, he offered rapid-fire apologies in two different languages.

Now at liberty to speak to him candidly, I told him to, "Get the fuck out of here," and thank Yoruba I wasn't reporting him.

On his way out, he turned to clarify Yoruba were a people.

"Pa' fuera," I yelled.

"Thank you, Mister. Good year."

Tears were shed over the last song (Green Day's "Good Riddance," of course). By the end the entire senior class, forty-eight in total, gathered in a circle, hugged, and swayed back and forth. Even Dennis Benitez dabbed tears.

It was nice to see them turning into adults right there before my eyes, sad to know these carefree days were dissipating, soon to be replaced with real-world worries that would pile up and pile up until their entire lives were consumed with worry and cynicism. Green Day's "Good Riddance" would sound much different then.

She grabbed my arm, leaned on it, and asked whether I remembered my high school prom.

"I never went."

"You never told me that," she said with a tone like I'd just admitted to cheating.

"You never asked."

On the way out, we were greeted by students and administration alike thanking me for a wonderful year, celebrating its end, and, hallelujah, all we have left is graduation.

Advanced Placement Math teacher Charles Innis, face brightened in the dark by his phone's blue light, warned us the Forty-first Street Causeway was shut down. "Real bad accident."

"Jesus. South Beach is going to be rammed by the weekend warriors," I said.

"Best go by way of Sunny Isles," Innis said with a nod.

I grumbled. "That's going to add almost an hour to our drive."

"It's okay, baby. More time we get to squeeze out of our prom date." Aly pulled me in for a hug.

The night had felt like a prom date with the prettiest girl on campus on my arm. Me, the guy who never went to prom because no one asked or agreed to go with, so I'd stayed home with my stoner tribe, pulling bong hits while *Dazed and Confused* played on constant loop in the background. At the end of the night, instead of Green Day, we ate mushrooms and listened to *Grateful Dead Live in Europe*.

Aly laughed as I finished relaying the story. "Aww, that's so sad, baby," she said, tickling the tip of my elbow.

"We weren't all blessed with being head cheerleader."

Aly scoffed. "Who said I was?"

I knew she wasn't. I did know for sure she was second in command. I'm not sure what it's called in cheerleading world but basically an understudy. Where if head queenie was sick or could not perform, in came Aly. I loved ribbing my wife for it. I'd noticed in the five years we were married that she always made it a point to downplay her popularity in high school as a kindness to me. We both knew I was a mutant and I constantly denigrated myself for it, but she was cautious never to do it herself. Perhaps knowing how sensitive I was when others pointed out my foibles.

●

Easing onto the Sunny Isles Bridge, red and blue lights dance side to side in my rearview mirror. Just as I process the lights are meant for me, the officer's siren yells woop-woop.

"Shit."

"Just ease over soon as you can, honey."

"Pull over at the bottom of the bridge, sir," The officer says over his loudspeaker. I immediately hear an accent that's reminiscent of Dennis Benitez. I always played that scenario in my head. What if I randomly encountered these students again five, ten years down the line? How would that go? In what capacity would we cross? Would they recognize me now that I was a very small blip in the radar of their lives compared with how much their universe had expanded since?

I'm nervous. I don't know why. I've never been pulled over. My record is squeaky clean but for some reason, whenever a cop is behind me on the road or freeway, I'm jittery.

On the side of the road, we keep our seat belts on. I put my wrists atop the steering wheel and track the officer as he saunters over, crossing in front of his car to my passenger side, away from traffic, hiking up his beige pants against the weight of a Batman-esque utility belt.

He taps the glass and smiles at Aly, indicating to lower the window. "Sabes why I pulled you over?"

I shrug, hands still on the steering wheel.

"You can take your hands off el timon, sir. You were speeding."

"Really? I thought I was going forty."

"Not at the entrance to the bridge. Te grabe at fifty there."

"Really?"

"License, registration, and seguro, please."

"Sure. I have to reach into my pocket for my license and glove compartment for registration and insurance. Is that okay?"

"Of course."

I give him the three cards.

"Wait right here." He saunters back to sit in his car. It rocks under his bulbous weight.

"Fuck. I really hope we don't get a ticket."

"I think we're fine. You're record is clean and he smiled at me."

"Smiled?"

"A lot."

"Now?"

"Yep. When you were reaching for the cards."

"What the fuck is that about?"

The officer slams his door shut and back tracks like a raccoon toward Aly.

"Doesn't matter, just please don't make a thing of it," Aly says. "Just be nice and let's—"

The officer taps on the window again. I look at his tag. BACA. Replace the B with a V, it means cow in Spanish.

"Your record is good, hijo. Why were you speeding?"

The tone in my voice is different from when I first spoke to him. I must keep things civil. Aly's in the car.

"I didn't see the reduced speed sign, sir. I must have been distracted. I apologize."

Baca extends his arm, holding the cards for me. He stares, and smiles, at Aly. "I can see why you were distracted."

Aly keeps her eyes on the road ahead and smiles politely, not genuinely. As if someone took the corners of her mouth and pulled them apart despite her best efforts.

I forcefully pull the cards from Baca's grip.

Now he's looking at me. No smile on his face. "Hay algún problema, hijo?"

"Yes, sir. I don't understand why you have to make eyes at my wife like that."

"No entiendo."

"I think que tu entiendes perfectly well, Officer Baca. You've been smiling and checking my wife out since you pulled me over. Now, if that's the thing that's going to get me out of this ticket, you'd better write one up right now because I don't accept that."

Baca pulls his hand from atop the car door, takes a step back and hooks his thumbs atop his utility belt.

Aly faintly whispers, "Shit."

"I'm going to have to ask you to get out of the car, hijo."

"Stop saying that. I'm not your son."

"Step out and walk to the back of the car, *sir*. Slowly."

Aly rolls up her window and with ventriloquist lips says, "Please just get us the hell out of here. Don't fight with the guy. Please." Her voice cracks, on the verge of tears.

What the fuck am I doing? I've never had to stand up for my wife. I've never had the opportunity to be the protector for someone else. Since high school, I've just been a pack of one. If not now, when? If Dennis Benitez was destined to become an officer in the future and this, Baca, is what he became, then fuck him.

Baca leans on the trunk of my car facing his.

"Comfortable?" I say.

"Oye. What is your problem?"

"What's yours?"

"You know I could bang you up against this trunk right now and haul you in for resisting arrest?"

"On what grounds, officer? Standing up for my wife who you're ogling?"

"That's a serious accusation."

"That's a serious offense."

Faster than I'd ever give his fat ass credit, Baca pins me with an arm bar up against the trunk.

The thud causes Aly to spin around. She unlatches the seatbelt and cracks the door.

"No," I yell to her. "Stay in the car."

"Si, mija. Quedate en el carro."

This fucking guy's got my wrist twisted in a way that, with a couple more ounces of pressure, will snap it.

"Hi-jo. You better think about how these next few seconds are going to go down because I can change your lives in ways neither of you want."

"You better think," he says.

And do I.

I hear Dennis Benitez calling me a cocksucker. I hear my dad saying never to argue with authority and if I do, prepare for the consequence because what else do you expect? I see myself tripping balls on prom night with my dateless friends, laughing our heads off. I remember Vice Principal Cuntas giving Aly the eyeball top to bottom just a few hours earlier. Kelsey asking if this is my wife like she's surprised someone so beautiful could be married to me.

I think about my teaching certification. The fact that Aly will have to drive home, or to the station, alone. Following this asshole. What the conversation will be like when I'm not there. I think on how fucking hard we've been trying to conceive over the last eight months. Three miscarriages down the toilet. I stop thinking and I look through the rear window at Aly, her shaking hand over her mouth.

A car blares its horn as it speeds past.

I hope it's a fuck you aimed at the officer. It could be a death knell.

Fuck.

"Disculpa, officer. Everything's fine. I thought you were looking at my wife and I just . . ."

"Forgot you were speaking to an officer of the law?"

"Yes, sir."

"¿Quieres que te haga soplar?"

"No, sir. I'm not drunk."

Baca lets go of my arm. "Make any sudden moves and I swear to God I'm going to embarrass you even more." He straightens me out, shoving me lightly against the car. "I know you're not. Lucky for you you're not drunk."

I stand there motionless. Unsure if this is a ruse or a pardon.

"Vete de aqui, maricon. Y mas nunca speed on my bridge again."

I nod my head and slowly walk back to the car.

I can't look at Aly. She doesn't say anything, but I hold up a hand to silence her anyway as Baca pulls off the shoulder. I follow his taillights until they disappear into the Sunny Isles darkness and away from our universe.

I slowly continue on Collins as cars speed past and honk, drivers screaming out their windows for me to, "Hurry the fuck up."

Just before the 91st Street Causeway, our way off this forsaken island, the bridge looks infinite, taller than Mount Olympus. My throat closes and fists tighten on the steering wheel. I slowly pull over and start crying, like Aly did on each of the miscarriages.

And I didn't.

Each punch of the steering wheel comes with a sob. One, two three.

Without a word, Aly gets out and walks around the back of the car. Like a child, I slide across to the passenger side, sniffling and dropping salty-wet drops on the center console. I cry all the way home to South Miami, thirty minutes without traffic. Still staring out the window because I can't face my wife.

We're home from prom night. She goes into her room, and I go into my office. It started as an office, anyway. Somewhere I could escape and pretend to be a writer, though I haven't put thoughts to paper in eight months. The office is a place to retreat.

I don't know what to do with the night behind me. If I drink, the anger is going to eventually peak. How do I rid myself of it, then? I log on to YouTube and stream *Grateful Dead Live in Europe*. I have it on vinyl but listening to it holistically like that feels corrupted right then. I don't have mushrooms.

All for the best because I'd give myself a bad trip anyway.

Like my first stab at prom, this night ends with me listening to records. Tripping balls with friends, you're ultimately alone, so that hasn't changed.

This prom night reboot, though, sees me with a beautiful date, who's in another room processing a night in which I failed to make her feel protected, safe, armored.

I don't know what she's thinking and for these next few hours, I don't want to know. Don't deserve to know.

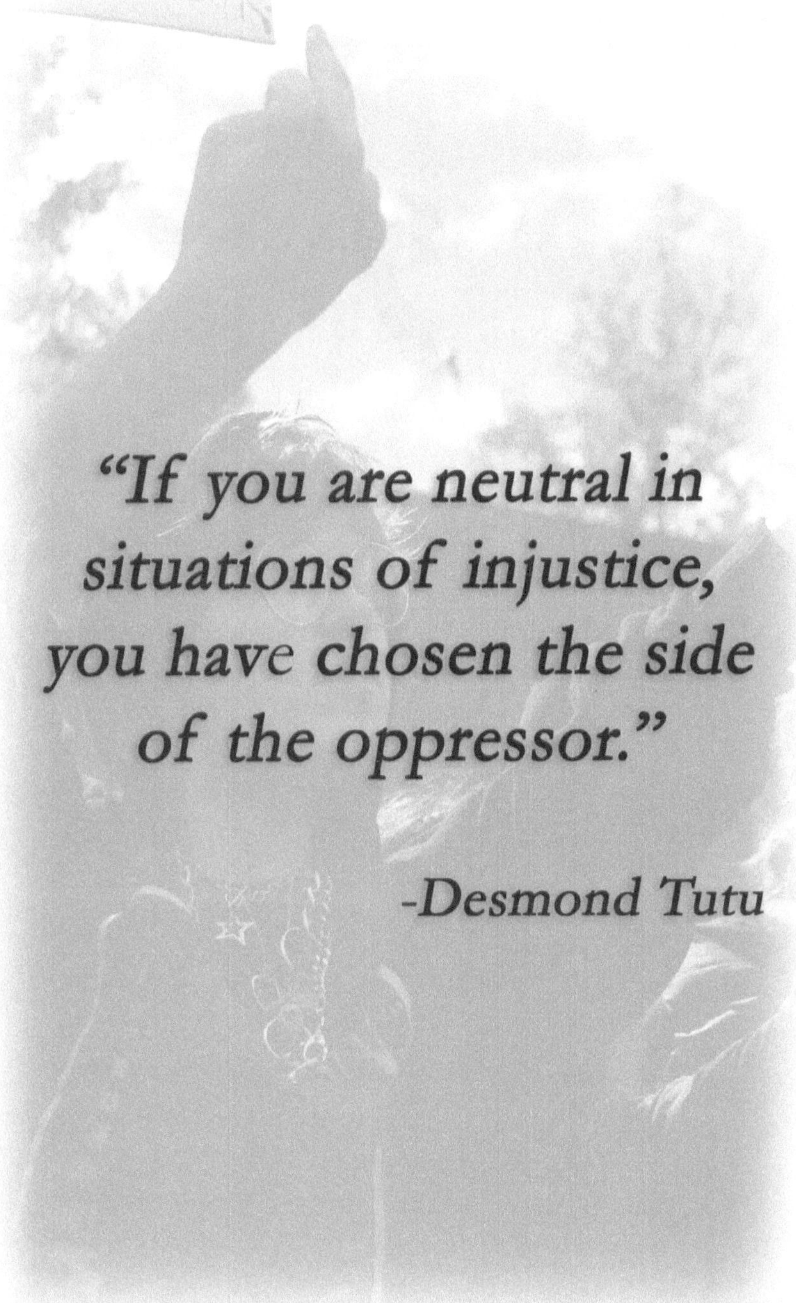

"If you are neutral in situations of injustice, you have chosen the side of the oppressor."

-Desmond Tutu

2

"Two officers closed in from her left. She noticed the zip-ties hanging from their waists. They'd expected this. Or planned for this. Hoped for this?"

Fit the Description

James Queally

For someone who'd never committed a crime, Traci Bridges was all too familiar with the men and women of the NYPD's 120th Precinct.

Innocence never spared anyone from being arrested. Detained. Questioned. Subjected to a field inquiry. Any of the phrases ripped from police policy manuals that didn't adequately describe the terror of all the times Traci had been told to stay put or else.

The times someone else gained control of her life for no good reason.

The times she had to choke her own voice for fear that detention might become an arrest. Or a charge. Or a death sentence.

Traci studied the cops assigned to the protest she'd staged inside the Staten Island Ferry terminal, scanning faces and badges for bad memories. Officer Donlan was gripping her baton as firmly as when she'd swung it, unprovoked, at Traci a month earlier during a demonstration in Clifton. A Universal Soldier looking cop stood next to Donlan, eyes as intense now as they were when he pointed a "less-lethal launcher" at Traci's face on Bay Street.

Behind them was Sgt. Patrick Reedy, whose presence was an implied "fuck you" to Traci and every protester around her. A video of his decision to treat a homeless man's mental health crisis with a TASER and a body slam in the terminal two weeks earlier had sparked Traci's latest call to action. Now, the NYPD had left Reedy holding the leash of officers who might want to use the same tactics on the protesters in front of them.

Traci locked eyes with Reedy, glaring at the brown irises pinching the nose of his doughboy face. She thought about the way the NYPD described his actions.

Less Lethal. Categorical Use of Force. More policy bullshit. More ways to say, "we beat the fuck out of you, be thankful you'll live to maybe get beat on another day."

Traci spoke their language. But the rest of the terminal, hell, the rest of the Island, wasn't fluent. Most people think of New York City as just one more blue metropolis, but that stereotype only applies to four of the city's five boroughs. Staten Island was an angry, red, rock largely populated by people who carried badges or wanted to. When someone in the Bronx or Brooklyn saw Reedy's YouTube debut, they asked what the cop's problem was. When people on Staten Island saw it, they echoed the mantras of their shithead cop neighbors: If you comply, you won't die.

Another boat arrived from Manhattan. People rose from their seats and turned toward the water, ignoring the protest. Not a single reporter had shown up.

The Staten Island Advance knew where to find Traci when they needed a quote slamming the cops, usually describing her as a "frequent critic of the NYPD and co-founder of the protest organization Shaolin Future." but they rarely attended her rallies. They weren't concerned with her message, just the conflict porn that might follow.

"You hold that line, boys," said a voice Traci fantasized about strangling silent daily. "Remember most of this Island loves its cops, no matter how many signs her little Scout troop holds up."

Wearing a Thin Blue Line shirt as he yelled at Traci from behind one, Richie Biongo was a bloated, wide-eyed bullfrog of a man who could shout himself into an asthma attack.

Part-time podcaster, full-time unhinged, Biongo led a group called Defend S.I. Traci only had to look in the mirror to know who they wanted to defend the Island from. Three-quarters of Staten Island's population was white. Three-quarters of those people wished that number was higher.

Defend S.I. was a cross between a beer league softball team and a dime store militia. Its trademark outfits looked like Yankees jerseys designed by the Fraternal Order of Police, complete with a misappropriated Punisher skull logo. Despite their idiotic attire, and the fact that Biongo looked like a pre-rehab Artie Lang, they were still dangerous. Disillusioned white men tended to hurt people at protests.

The more time Traci spent organizing, the more time Biongo spent on air trashing her. The more his fans slid into her DMs with racial slurs and death threats. Biongo had made Traci the very angry, very Black face of everything his followers thought was wrong with "their" Island.

"You gonna enlighten us, Miss Bridges?" Biongo asked. "Explain how we'll all be safer once you abolish the police. Or how you're going to be safe when they're not standing between us."

The cops didn't even flinch at the threat. The sky is also blue.

Traci turned to check on her crowd. Despite what the papers said, Shaolin Future was a banner to rally under, not an organization. She didn't have a roster, knew people more by face than name. The guy with the soul patch from the transport bus after the New Dorp vigil for Breonna Taylor. The girl who always did her makeup for marches, even in a New York summer with mascara-melting humidity.

But there was a face Traci was worried about, the one responsible for most of the new ones.

Ra was at the center of the Shaolin Future crowd, her bird-like frame near invisible except for the shock of pink in her hair. The girl wore fingerless gloves, a tight black hoodie, and a backpack with a 90s X-Men logo ironed on.

"You alright?" Traci asked.

"Punisher killed cops," Ra spat back. "Their uniforms are stupid."

Traci hadn't had much use for the word "Blerd" before she met Ra.

"You sure that's all you're worried about?" Traci asked, feeling the little quakes in Ra's body. "When these idiots show up, shit tends to get bad. I understand if this is too hot for your first time out, lil' hacker."

Traci smiled at Ra, who rolled her eyes. The girl normally helped Shaolin Future from behind a laptop. She managed their social media, and her ability to earn likes and follows had boosted the crowds at Traci's last few actions.

"I'm not a hacker, old head," Ra replied, forcing a smile, the quakes visibly calming in her.

Traci was 26, but Ra wasn't wrong. She was organizing protests behind a Wu-Tang Clan reference. Wu-Tang was for the kids, but maybe not kids in 2021.

Still, Traci remembered the panic of her first protest, the anxiety and uncertainty. Maybe Ra needed to see the power of their voices.

"Say his name!" Traci howled, marching toward the cops.

"Willy Watkins!" a few people responded.

"Say his name!" she shouted again.

They did, and the identity of the homeless man Reedy battered echoed through the terminal.

At 5'4 with a body thick and squat like a cannonball, Traci found herself looking up at most officers. But it was decibel level, not size, that put them on the same footing.

"Who did this?" Traci shouted.

"Pat Reedy!"

The sergeant chewed his lip hard enough to draw blood. Traci turned and found Ra, fist up, mouth wide, voice loud like it needed to be.

Traci would have taken a second to be proud, if Biongo's group hadn't started moving around the police line. A Blue Lives Matter chant erupted, ferocious and fevered. Traci tried to split her focus between the Defend S.I. idiots and the police. One of Biongo's goons got too close to Ra and bumped her.

That was when the yelling started. Traci saw Reedy pull a radio to his mouth. She'd been in this situation before, knew what it felt like just before the match was struck.

"Back up," she shouted, coaxing her people away from the cops, turning and hoping to catch Ra's eyes in the process.

It wasn't retreat. It was strategy. The cops didn't need a reason to arrest protesters, but it made their jobs easier when you gave them one. If anyone was gonna put Traci in chains, they'd have to work for it.

The group started moving back in slow, choreographed steps. One. Two. One. Two.

Then a bottle flew overhead, shattering at the feet of the officers.

It might as well have been a starter's gun.

Reedy ordered the cops to advance. Traci had heard this song too many times before. It didn't matter who threw what, the cops would treat whoever they grabbed first as an assault suspect.

She turned to run, bursting through the doors back to the Terminal's lobby, heavy footfalls that had to be cop boots right behind her. Traci took a hard right, looking for the exit toward the Yankees' minor league stadium. But three cops were marching up from outside, so Traci spun back the other way.

Two officers closed in from her left. She noticed the zip-ties hanging from their waists. They'd expected this. Or planned for this. Hoped for this?

She hit the brakes hard, digging her toes into the ground, going from 60-to-0 so suddenly that both cops stumbled. The stutter step created enough space that Traci slipped through and ran for the stairs toward the bus platform.

Halfway up the second flight, a shoulder blasted into her chest. Traci got her hands out and broke her fall, skidding on her ass toward a window.

She looked up to find Biongo smiling his idiot grin, lips curled in a way that made them an inviting target. Traci hopped up, right fist balled, but something in her brain held up a stop sign, reminded her where she was and what the cost of clocking this racist shitbag would be.

"Do it," Biongo shouted, too happy about the prospect of getting hit in the face.

Traci looked up to see Reedy coming down the stairs behind Biongo.

Biongo smiled one more time, right before Reedy put a baton in his rib cage.

"Officer in need of assistance," Reedy shouted into his radio as Biongo collapsed, coughing louder than the shot he took required. Traci would know. She'd taken it for real before.

Traci turned to run, feeling the snare tighten. But two uniforms appeared behind her, funneling her toward Reedy and his handcuffs.

They fit the same, no matter what you did or didn't do.

✺

As they led Traci through the 120th Precinct on a lie, she replayed the last few minutes in the terminal, saw the framework that would stand up the fiction and make it more believable than her truth.

She'd started shit with Reedy. Then Biongo's people started shit with hers. The bottle flew. It would have been easy for a Defend S.I. clown to slip behind her people and toss it. It'd be even easier for the cops to find a concerned citizen who saw the bottle come from where "the protesters" were standing.

Then she'd gotten herself trapped in a space with no witnesses except two people who saw her as a threat to their community, to their way of life.

Then they saw a chance to take her off the board.

Traci felt the snare tighten again. She wanted to scream, kick, shout. Punch the bars until her knuckles split and the rage dripped out. But she wouldn't give any cop the satisfaction of watching her act like the animal they wanted her to be.

Especially not the cops in the 120th precinct. Not Danny Pantaleo's bunkmates. Not the people who slapped him on the back the day he choked the life out of Eric Garner.

I can't breathe. The words that got her off the sidelines. The words that got her up every morning.

They killed a man for selling loose cigarettes, like every corner store on the Island wouldn't bust a pack open if you had 75 cents. Like half those stores didn't break federal laws and buy cartons out of vans driven up from Virginia.

Eric Garner wasn't dangerous. But he was big. And he looked like her. That was when Traci learned that was all it took to earn a state-sponsored street execution. That was when she decided any day not spent calling that out as completely insane was a waste.

The snare tightened again the next morning, after a two-minute car ride from the One-Two-Oh to Richmond County's criminal courthouse.

Sat next to a public defender who looked exhausted by the assembly line of clients shoved her way that morning, Traci listened as a judge read the charge against her. Second-degree assault with a deadly weapon. Punishable by up to seven years in prison. Nearly a quarter of Traci's life.

Before the enormity of that could set in, the judge asked the prosecutor about bail. The white woman opposite Traci's attorney offered an absurdly high number in a disinterested voice, like she was ordering coffee instead of setting a price on someone's freedom.

Traci was stunned by the figure. She was even more shocked when her public defender said they could post bond immediately.

"I don't have that kind of money," Traci whispered.

"Your friends do," the lawyer replied.

Slunk along the back wall was Ra, apparently getting more comfortable now with being out from behind her computer screen.

After an hour of forms, forms and more forms, Traci walked out of the court-house to find Ra smoking a cigarette, staring at the ferries traversing the Hudson.

"You secretly a rich kid?" Traci asked.

Ra shook her head and held up her phone, pointing to a GoFundMe page before opening Twitter and Instagram. Someone had filmed Traci being led away in handcuffs by Reedy, and Ra shared it from Shaolin Future's accounts, calling for supporters to help set Traci free.

"Why?" Traci asked. "You barely know me."

"You're innocent," Ra said, like anything was ever that simple.

"Doesn't seem to matter in there," Traci replied, pointing toward the court-house.

"It does if we can prove it."

"And how are we gonna do that?"

Ra twirled her phone in her hand, like it was a magic wand.

●

Ra laid out what she saw as Traci's path to freedom, one tweet and screengrab at a time.

Traci jabbed a fork into the goat curry she'd ordered as soon as Blaze opened, savoring the best Jamaican food she could find outside Brooklyn, assuming her meals would be subject to state budget constraints for the next seven years.

Between bites, Traci studied the scrawny, light-skinned girl she'd known less than six months. The girl who'd been too scared to put her body on the line at the Terminal one day, but had a plan to unravel an NYPD scheme to frame Traci the next.

Traci hadn't trusted Ra when they first met. People on the sidelines have little to lose. But Ra's fear of public clashes made more sense once she explained her odd nickname. It was a reference to the Egyptian sun god – Ra liked the idea that her web wizardry shined a light on things – but it was also a nod to the juvenile rheumatoid arthritis she'd suffered from since she was 15. Compromised immune systems and crowds didn't mix.

Ra's social media skills had drawn more bodies to Shaolin Future's protests in the last few months. They were probably the reason Traci wasn't on a transport bus to Riker's Island. Trusting Ra's ability to use a smart phone as a magic wand had worked out well so far.

The image on Ra's phone was a celebration of a recreational league softball championship. Traci recognized the two faces closest to the dollar store trophy as the last two she saw before the handcuffs went on: Reedy and Biongo.

Ra swiped right. The two appeared together again, this time in suits, sandwiching a third guy, the groom at whatever wedding they were attending. Biongo looked younger, 15 pounds lighter. Reedy's hair was fuller. Ra kept swiping. Images of Traci's twin tormentors kept appearing together in pictures spanning years.

"I file a public records request for the NYPD's roster once a year," Ra said. "Then I friend request as many as I can find."

She tapped the phone again. A profile belonging to an almost cartoonishly curvaceous woman filled the screen. A mixed-race Jessica Rabbit.

"Almost never get declined," Ra said.

"You're shitting me," Traci replied.

"I read something once about how cops use these fake profiles to monitor gang members and street racers online," Ra said. "It's always the same character. 20-something. Bi-sexual. All I did was use it against them."

"That's impossibly stupid," Traci said.

"The U.S. Capitol almost got toppled by a bunch of angry Dads who let memes and a pillow salesman convince them the election was stolen," Ra replied. "Internet illiteracy is the new common cold. And that's how we're gonna save you."

Traci smiled, but it was mostly because of the curry.

"You can show my P.D. all those pictures. How they're friends. How maybe that means they schemed to get me arrested. But you know where you live, right?" Traci asked. "We're in New York City by way of Alabama. This Island hates us. Why you think you only see Black folks on the North Shore? Like the rest of the Island's a sundown town or some shit? If this gets to a jury, most everyone who gets a vote will hear the people who serve and protect testifying that someone who doesn't look like them beat on someone who does. That don't end well for me."

"The pictures aren't enough. But like I said. Internet illiteracy. You saw how many of those Capitol idiots filmed themselves committing federal crimes, right?" Ra asked. "You think someone as loud as Biongo didn't talk about this over text, Telegram, any of the other apps that archive everything you say? If we get into his messages . . ."

"I thought you said you weren't a hacker," Traci said.

"I'm not, old head," Ra replied. "We're gonna get his phone."

"You wanna add robbery to my charges?" Traci asked. "The guy framed me for a felony. I can't just walk up to him."

Ra rapped her fingers on the screen. A flier appeared, Biongo's face red from shouting "what the media won't tell you." The words "Refund the Police" hung above him in all caps. The event advertised a live recording of his podcast. All proceeds headed to the New York City Police Foundation.

"He'll be in public. Distracted. Drinking," Ra said. "I know it's a little desperate, but like you said, if this goes to a jury . . ."

Traci looked out Blaze's window. At the part of Victory Boulevard that turned into Bay Street. Around the corner from the stretch where Eric Garner took his last breaths. A short walk from the courthouse where they let the cop who did it walk free.

"Why are you doing all this?" Traci asked. "I appreciate it, but you've known me six months. You like me that much?"

"You got me off the couch," Ra replied. "Made me stand up for myself. Not enough people like you on this Island, Traci. People who make the rest of us brave. If they put you away, maybe less people are brave. Maybe I go back to the couch. Maybe when the next Reedy goes after the next you, no one does anything about it."

⬤

It was easier than it should have been for Traci to disappear into the crowd at La Tourette Golf Course.

The hundreds of men populating the lush greens outside the course's antebellum style clubhouse were largely white, largely loud and largely offering opinions most people at least pretended to disguise before 2016.

A heavyset Italian man with one of those "swallow every word as you say it" Staten Island accents complained about how DeBlasio only governed for "them, his wife's people," like the unpopular mayor's policies were solely born of having a Black life partner. Two men laughed after one promised to call ICE on his contractor if he didn't offer a discount on a kitchen remodeling project. Traci noticed the comedian was Indian and winced.

She wanted to tell the man that being "one of the good ones" was pointless. That all it took to go from model minority to supervillain was one New York Post headline about someone you vaguely looked like.

But she couldn't risk it. Despite being one of the only Black faces in the crowd, she'd stayed invisible by virtue of a dress shirt and slacks. By ironing her hair straight. Ra had looked up the catering company La Tourette normally used, and now Traci was costumed in their standard attire. The best way to move among a crowd that hated her was take on a role they were comfortable with. The server. In her place.

Besides, Traci couldn't afford to be recognized with what was about to go down.

The "Refund the Police" event was a combination charity golf tournament and barbeque. While some guests explored LaTourette's course, 18 holes divided by Richmond Hill Road, most of the roughly 300 people Biongo had drawn were drinking or eating near the clubhouse.

He stood on a small wooden stage at the center of a grass circle near the clubhouse entrance, microphone clutched in his left hand. The podcast recording sounded more like a sermon, Biongo warning his flock of multicultural fire and brimstone.

"And these politicians, these city councilmen . . . sorry, I guess I have to call them councilpersons, don't want to assume anyone's gender," Biongo said, rolling his eyes. "These councilpersons want to appeal to these woke voters. What they need to do, is wake the hell up. Crime is surging, but they want less of you on the street. Less resources for the people who protect this city. They want to invest in services, whatever that means. We all know what this really is, right? Hug-a-thug! Give some punk Mets tickets so he'll show up for court. But what do they do for the officer on midnights who hasn't seen his kids in a week? For the law-abiding citizen? Nothing! They bow to the media, to Black Lies Matter, to anyone who edits a cell phone video to make you the bad guy. But we know the truth!"

Traci didn't choose to ball her fists up. They did that on their own as she listened to the man who framed her for a felony rant about manipulating facts. As she watched the crowd bark louder for Biongo's dog whistles. As she counted the number of concealed firearms on the hips of off-duty officers in the crowd she was wading through with a tray of cheeseburger sliders.

Traci was beyond outnumbered. Even if she got near Biongo, there were still three bodies hovering near the stage like security. Two of them were in their Defend S.I. baseball jerseys. The third was in an NYPD polo, badge visible on his hip. Sgt. Reedy.

Why hide their relationship? They were on their home turf. They thought they were safe.

They were wrong.

Traci headed for a serving station stocked with coffee and pastries. She dipped her tray toward a trash can, clearing space before loading up with a carafe and some mugs. Her phone buzzed. A simple message from Ra.

Now.

Traci saw the cars pulling up on Richmond Hill Road. Some people in Biongo's flock took notice, but it was already too late. Ra sent out the call to action on quieter channels: Discord chats. Reddit threads she was fairly certain the cops weren't monitoring.

There'd be no skirmish line this time. No pre-planned police presence.

Just a level playing field.

The cars emptied. People from Shaolin Future, Move Forward S.I., and other groups who'd shared space with Traci at past protests stepped onto the golf course. Dozens of bodies morphed into a swarm, signs and fists held high.

Biongo faced the crowd and shouted into the mic, but Traci wasn't listening anymore. Some of the cops and Defend S.I. members pushed to the front of the stage, blocking the protesters, thinking they were protecting Biongo, unaware of the real threat.

Biongo pulled his phone out and started filming. Traci and Ra had counted on this, figured he couldn't resist the chance to inflame his following just a little more. As he yelled something about Antifa over what Traci assumed was the beginning of a livestream, a frozen water bottle sailed toward Biongo's head.

It missed, but it sent him scurrying off stage. Back toward what he would perceive as a confused and scared waitress carrying a coffee tray.

When they collided, Traci made sure to flip the tray so the coffee flew right into Biongo's chest. She'd checked to make sure it was warm, but not scalding. Enough to hurt but not disfigure. Biongo fell to the ground, his previously boisterous voice reduced to a whine.

His iPhone 9, the one Ra had found more than a few pictures of him holding at other events, went airborne. Before it hit the ground, before Biongo could realize what was happening, Traci plucked his device out of the air and dropped a water damaged version of the same phone on the ground, one Ra purchased from a friend at a local repair spot in Stapleton.

"Oh my god, I'm so sorry," Traci said, going full code switch, becoming the deferential waitress she was cosplaying as. "Let me get you some towels."

"That's the least you could fucking do," Biongo growled, holding up the dummy phone, staring at Traci but clearly not seeing her. "If you broke it, your boss is gonna hear about this."

Traci bowed her head in fake apology as she frantically banged her thumb against Biongo's real phone, making sure the device stayed active and unlocked.

As Biongo turned his attention to the protest, Traci moved for the clubhouse, walking fast but careful not to break into a run.

She opened Biongo's Facebook. His texts. His emails. Less than a minute later, with access to every way Biongo might talk without using his mouth, Traci ducked into a bathroom stall and called Ra.

One-by-one, Traci pulled up the e-mail addresses and aliases Biongo used to enter each app, and Ra started trying to login from her end. Each time, Ra "forgot" Biongo's password. Each time, Biongo's phone pinged with a verification code for a new one, which Traci sent back to Ra.

As they played pitch and catch with Biongo's personal information, Ra started archiving. Traci started reading.

There was never any doubt that Biongo helped the NYPD set her up, that the department would go to these lengths to de-legitimize her. But seeing it laid out in plain English still felt like getting hit in the chest with a hammer.

Biongo and Reedy had talked about the exact ferry terminal stairwell to chase her into. They'd argued about where exactly Reedy should hit Biongo with his nightstick ("not the face," Biongo had cried). They'd even talked about the exact type of bottle to throw at the skirmish line officers to create the appearance of an unlawful assembly.

Not once, did they refer her to by name. Traci was "the bitch who needed to shut up and choke on some gangbanger's cock," according to the NYPD sergeant. The "cunt" and "monkey girl," per Biongo.

And that word. The word she wouldn't even give them the satisfaction of thinking. Over and over.

Traci's fists balled up again. Like they had in the terminal. In the jail cell. Rage as a survival instinct.

She wasn't a person to them. Just an obstacle. An enemy. An animal.

They deserved for her to act like one. For her to strike back with teeth and claws.

"I got it."

The voice snapped Traci out of the phone. She blinked three times, surprised by the warmth under her eyes.

"Traci," Ra said, the voice coming from her personal phone. "I got it. We can prove they set you up. I'm gonna call everyone off. We got what we needed. We won."

"OK," Traci said, taking a calming breath that did very little to calm her. "OK."

"Traci, you alright?" Ra asked.

She wasn't. But she'd deal with that later. In the gym or somewhere else. She just needed to get out of there. And she was halfway when she heard his voice again in the clubhouse lobby.

"This is what they get for hiring these clumsy fucking apes," Biongo growled as someone preened over him with a towel, helping him out of his coffee-ruined shirt. "Goddamn Negress. Goddamn . . ."

Traci had to leave.

Ra had proof of the frame job.

Soon, her public defender would too.

Reedy would be exposed. Biongo would be humiliated. The world would be a better place.

But he kept saying that word.

Traci's fists balled up one more time.

She was only human. Even if Biongo didn't think so.

Traci imagined using her fists to ruin Biongo's jaw line. Envisioned cradling the back of his head with her left hand and raining down blow after blow with her right, her knuckles warmed by the blood leaking from his face. She thought about how Biongo would never regain his alpha male status in front of his pack of hyenas after someone filmed him getting thoroughly beaten and dominated by a woman who knew her way around a squat rack.

"Traci," the voice in her ear said again. "Scanners are lighting up. They're sending uniforms from the 122. If one of them recognizes you, a whole lot of people just wasted their time."

Ra was right. Whatever beating Biongo deserved, the movement deserved better than to see Traci taking the L reserved for the NYPD.

She kept on walking.

●

Considering the treasure trove of digital fingerprints Reedy and Biongo had left on their frame job, the case against Traci Bridges should have collapsed in less than three days.

It took nearly three months.

Traci brought what she'd found on Biongo's phone to her public defender the day after her trip to the golf course. The overwhelmed lawyer submitted it as part of a motion to dismiss within 48 hours. Notified of the potentially headline-inducing hell Reedy had engaged in, the NYPD quietly acknowledged it would start an Internal Affairs investigation into the sergeant, while the Defend S.I. goons started to become more and more scarce at Traci's actions. While Traci would have enjoyed the chance to greet Biongo with a glare that said, "I have your balls in a vice and I don't mind squeezing," not having to hear his voice was enough of a reward on its own.

But for weeks, the D.A.'s office remained silent. Traci's public defender was less and less responsive to phone calls. She was sympathetic, sure, but she had other clients whose cases weren't frozen by the sudden appearance of damning impeachment evidence.

In the meantime, Ra tried to push the scandal public, sending snippets of what they'd taken off Biongo's phone to the Advance through a mixture of Signal and proton mail accounts. One reporter nibbled – last name Hart, seemed eternally pissed off at everything – but ultimately, he told Ra there was no way to prove the authenticity of the messages. Traci wasn't surprised and knew that answer probably came from way above the reporter's pay grade. The paper rarely went after cops 'cause it didn't want to print stories that half its subscribers would threaten to cancel over.

It wasn't until the week of Traci's grand jury proceedings, when a gallery of Staten Islanders would decide whether or not to hand down an indictment that would slingshot her toward a trial, when prosecutors finally relented. Grand jury hearings weren't public, but the transcripts could be eventually, according to Traci's public defender, who said she doubted the NYPD wanted anything they had learned about Reedy and Biongo on an official piece of paper.

That night, Traci told Ra to wear something she wouldn't rock at a comic book shop and to be ready by 8. Pushing back on cops on Staten Island would make Sisyphus feel like he was shoving a pebble, so the rare wins needed to be celebrated. The plan was dinner, maybe a drink.

Traci was staring at the steps to the apartment building whose address Ra had given her when someone appeared in the doorway in a navy-blue romper, one that cut a skinny frame, showing off a neckline and caramel skin Traci hadn't paid too much attention to before. When the girl wore makeup instead of a tee-shirt reading "Magneto Was Right," Ra had something working.

Traci laughed to herself. More to Lil' Hacker than met the eye. The plan was now dinner, maybe a drink, maybe more.

Traci got one more good look at the makeup applied to Ra's mischievous little face before it was washed out in blue and red. The chirp of a cruiser filled Traci's ears just in time for her to turn around and see two blue-and-whites fill the space behind her.

She wasn't double parked. She wasn't speeding. And she'd made damn sure both her taillights were working before she'd left home.

Which meant she knew exactly what this was.

Traci kept her fingers wrapped on the steering wheel, shaking her head at Ra once before turning her eyes forward. When the officer got to the window, he confirmed her worst fears.

"Evening Miss Bridges," the man said in a voice dripping with the kind of confidence that only comes from legal invincibility. "Our sergeant says good evening as well."

Traci turned her head to the officer just once, locking eyes with his body-worn camera. The green dot meant to confirm it was recording wasn't blinking. Because of course it wasn't.

She hadn't done anything wrong. Other than fight back. Other than drive through what she called her neighborhood but had always been occupied territory. Traci didn't know what they'd try next but given what she'd had to do to get clear of Reedy the first time, she didn't love her odds of pulling off the same magic trick twice.

Sometimes you fit the description.

But it's not that hard for them to find a way to make the description fit you.

3

"I didn't have time to figure it out. The cops were on me by then, and they drove me back down to the asphalt, putting my face in the ashy, salty, smudgy surface."

TRAP HOUSE

BOBBY MATHEWS

They came swarming in the front like blue-jacketed ants, 'POLICE' scrawled across their ballistic vests in reflective white letters that looked three feet high in the gloom, so I broke a window out the back of the trap house and went through it with a little more than my share of the cash.

The shattered glass hitting the cracked and patchy blacktop wasn't too loud. Besides, nobody in this part of Birmingham was gonna notice another window gone, and that's a fact. The houses are mostly empty, but they're close together here on the west side, creating a warren of alleys with lots of corners to dodge past. The neighborhood used to be a town of its own, but the so-called Magic City annexed the place back in the 1980s, and had ignored it ever since. I made two turns before I felt them behind me, running in heavy jump-laced boots that kept them from turning an ankle on the buckled and warped sidewalks.

I didn't have that kind of protection, so I had to pick my way along while I listened to the bastards gaining on me. It wasn't fair. Any kind of fair race and I'da been half a mile ahead and lost inside a labyrinth of deserted streets and shadows where even someone with a badge would hesitate to go.

Fingers flicked the back of my collar, grasping. I put on a burst of speed, a last-ditch effort to get some distance and fade into the night. The cops could sit at the bar and tell tall tales about me, like old fishermen talking about the one that got away. They were yelling, but their words were lost to the rush of wind in my ears. I gained one step, and then another. A half-block ahead, the black and yawning mouth of an access road beckoned with a promise of dark salvation. My legs and arms pumped harder, my head leaning forward, tucked away from those grasping hands.

I hit that pothole at the speed of light. That's what it felt like, at least, while I was tumbling through the air with no idea what body part would hit the ground first. The blacktop took skin off my elbows and shoulders, bit and bloodied my knees and shins. I rolled forward and up to my feet automatically, wondering how badly I'd been hurt.

I didn't have time to figure it out. The cops were on me by then, and they drove me back down to the asphalt, putting my face to the ashy, salty, smudgy surface. My breath exploded out in a long and ugly groan, and I instinctively tried to get back to my feet.

"Stay down," one of the cops said. He put a knee in the middle of my back while he twisted my arms behind me to put the cuffs on. I could see his partner, wearing tactical gear—hard kneepads, a riot helmet, heavy black leather gloves. The partner had one hand to the radio unit on his shoulder. It partially covered his mouth, so I couldn't hear what he was saying, but I had been arrested enough times by then to know that he was probably calling in our location so one of those big-ass white BPD Expeditions could swoop in and transport us back to the trap house.

And then to the jail.

"You're holding," the cop said. It wasn't a question. I tried to shake my head, tell him no, I wasn't down like that.

"No," I finally managed, but by that time he was already patting me down. He pulled my genuine imitation leather wallet from my back pocket; found the ID badge the jail gave me on the day I got my release. There wasn't much else in there: Arende's expired EBT card, a couple faded pictures, an appointment card with a date and time scribbled on it that I'd probably never get to keep.

The cop rolled me over, and the hard steel cuffs bit into my wrists and lower back. I put my shoulders on the pavement to try to arch my back a little and take some of the pressure off my spine. My lungs were still working to get back most of the breath I'd lost, and the weird position left me uncomfortable and exposed. The other cop saw what I was doing and chuffed a little laugh, like it was the funniest thing he'd ever seen. He took one long diagonal step toward me, like a field-goal kicker on a sixty-yard try, and booted me right below the ribs.

I puked. I couldn't even remember the last thing I'd eaten, but whatever it was came up like a geyser. Old unfaithful, that's me. Some of it came back down in my mouth and went down my throat. I tried to spit it out, but couldn't. No breath, no nothing. Just blind panic. Spots swam in front of my eyes and a rising black sea threatened to take me down into darkness deeper than midnight. From far above me, I could hear the cops yelling.

"... aspirated, get him turned ..."

Rough hands rolled me onto my side and held me fast, but my chest and throat felt locked tight, suctioned closed.

"Goddamn it," one of the cops said. "Hold him still."

Another jackbooted toe found my abdomen, this time about two inches above my navel. This time, everything I'd eaten over the last decade came out and splashed against the wavy, uneven pavement, and suddenly fresh air whooshed in and burned its way down into my lungs. Snot and drool trailed from my face to the ground, and I could feel tears hot and fresh on my face. I hated myself for crying, hated hearing the sound of my sobs echo against the ugly siding of the houses that loomed close over us, like giants spying on the games of children.

The cop who kicked me the first time stood back from me, his face turned away. I couldn't tell if it made any difference to him that he'd nearly killed me just to get his jollies. I probably wasn't the first defenseless arrest he'd kicked or punched or otherwise taken advantage of.

That's how the police play the game.

"Hey."

The cop squatting next to me snapped his fingers in front of my face to get my attention. I turned bleary, red eyes toward him.

"You okay now? Breathing all right?"

I breathed in and out a couple of times, gingerly, like I was testing it out. Then I nodded at him.

"I'm gonna stand you up, go through the rest of your pockets. You got anything sharp in your pockets? Anything that's gonna stick me?"

"No," I said. "I got a Swiss Army knife. Right front pocket."

With him supporting me by one shoulder, we managed to lever my body into a sitting position. The kicking bastard cop came over, ran his hand under my other shoulder and helped his partner pull me to my feet.

"I get stuck by a needle, you ain't making it to jail."

I didn't even acknowledge the words, just stood still. The frisk was fast, professional. He found the knife I'd promised, and the wad of money I hadn't said a word about. He undid the rubber band I'd wound around the cash to keep it tight and fanned the green out in his hands. It was a lot of money.

"Hey hey," he said. "What's this? Mark, shine a light over here."

I didn't say anything. I knew better. It was the best part of five grand, enough to pay off what I owed. A bundle for a fresh start so I could maybe give my kid the kind of opportunity that I never had and never would. And now it was going away from me like water disappearing down a drain. The first cop, the one who wanted to act like a nice guy, shook the money in my face.

"How much were you there to buy? Too much for just you, am I right?"

He had his mind on that money, and not on me. If I'd had my hands free, maybe I could have done something. But they had me cuffed good, and I was still shaking and exhausted from the boots to the belly.

"You owe me, you know," Mr. I'm-an-Alright-Guy Cop said. "How much you wanna give me for saving your life? All of it? That's very kind of you." He paused, staring me down, as if he were waiting for me to say something. He wasn't, though. He was acting. Just playing around. I knew he was gonna keep my money. He knew he was gonna keep it. We all knew. I knew better—I've always known better—than to talk to the cops, but this time I couldn't help myself.

"That's my money," I said. "You can't just take it."

Officer Nice Guy laughed in my face, fanned himself with all my money.

"We can confiscate drug money any fucking time we please, kid."

"That's not drug money," I said. "Come on, man. It's for my kid."

That didn't even move him, not that I thought it would. Cops want to think they're the good guys. They'll go right on thinking that while they smile and put you in the fucking ground.

"Please," I said. "I gotta get it back. It's for my kid. My boy, he's six. You saw the picture in my wallet, right? I took it out to help a buddy. I just got it back tonight. I wasn't even supposed to be there."

"Right," Officer Alright Guy said.

He divided the money, took half of it, and gave it to his partner. The guy looked at the stack of green in his hand, grinned so hard I could see the cavities in his back molars, and stuffed the cash in his own pocket. Maybe he could use some of my kid's money to fix his teeth.

Now he came forward and I flinched away. I'd had enough of him already. But the truth is that I preferred him to the Alright Guy. At least this one knew he was a piece of shit. The guy who frisked me and took my money would never think about it again. He'd think he deserved a medal for saving my life after his shitkicker buddy nearly ended it.

"You could be a help with this other thing," the cop who first kicked me said. His partner had called him Mark. He fished in his pants pocket for a minute, and

I tensed. I knew he was going to bring up a throw down piece and start shooting, and there was nothing I could do about it. The idea was so visceral that I could see it happening in my mind. I tensed and started moving away, ready to break into a run no matter how useless it might be, until the Alright Guy grabbed my arm and held me still.

Officer Mark held a burner phone in one black-gloved hand. He pushed a button on the side of the phone and lit it up, illuminating his face like he was the man behind the curtain. Oz the great and powerful.

Yeah, right.

He tapped the contacts on the phone. Of course there weren't any. No voice-mails or texts, either. But there were five numbers on the recent calls. I didn't recognize any of them.

"Who do these numbers belong to?"

I lifted whatever part of my eyebrows hadn't been sanded off by my spills on the blacktop. If my arms had been free, I would have shrugged. "How am I supposed to know? I've never seen them before."

Officer Mark grinned at me like a hyena stalking helpless prey. He held the phone up to my face so that its brightly lit screen made me squint.

"Those numbers, you know who those guys are, right? If you don't know now, you could find out. You're a bright guy, got a kid you wanna put in college, right?"

I closed my eyes, shook my head. "Hey," I said. "Don't fuck with me about my kid."

I never saw the slap coming. Mark probably didn't hit me as hard as he could, but it was close. I rocked back on my heels, would have fallen down and busted up what was left of my head, but Officer Alright Guy was there holding me up. Constellations that no other person could see in the night sky were wandering around in my vision.

"Uncuff him," Officer Mark said.

"You sure?"

"Yeah," he said. "I think we can work something out here."

The cuffs clicked free. Warily, I brought my hands around in front of me, chafed my wrists to restore some circulation.

"Wrong place, wrong time tonight, huh?" Officer Mark said. "I get it, I get it—you're a good guy, just trying to protect your family. Just trying to do right by your kid. Right?"

Now that my hands were free, I was getting pissed. It didn't matter, though. Officer Alright Guy was close by, his hand on his Taser. I wasn't going anywhere, even with the cuffs off. And the sooner I recognized that, the sooner I could maybe get myself out of this. As soon as those words went through my head, I shook them off. I knew that I was going to jail. To think anything else would just be believing in fairy tales, and I gave those up a long time ago.

"What do you want," I said. Maybe it was supposed to be a question. I don't know.

"You're gonna know those numbers," Officer Mark said. "Nick's gonna turn his body cam on, and then we're gonna find the phone when we search you. Got it? Eventually, we're gonna tell you who the digits belong to, and you're gonna pass that to the detectives who interview you. When it comes to trial, you're gonna stand up and point the finger at the guys we tell you. Get me?"

I got him. What I didn't know yet was what I was going to get outta the deal. So I didn't say anything for a while. Officer Mark's radio squawked a couple of times, and he radioed in that he'd found a suspect and what our position was.

"Quick now," he said, "before they get here."

"Why should I?"

Officer Nick, the Alright Guy, slapped me hard across the back of the head.

"We'll make sure your kid gets the money, you dumbass. Now choose. You gonna be helpful or not?"

I thought about Rodney, six years old and living with his grandma. That money could get me out from under, it could help me get him away, get up and out of Birmingham one day. It could help me, maybe help him eventually. He could go somewhere better. God, I hoped he could at any rate. So I said yeah, I'd help them out. Shrugged my heavy shoulders and said, "Of course I know those numbers. I know all about it."

They handcuffed me again, only this time it was looser. When that bright white BPD ride rolled up on us, I slid into the back seat, behind the chicken wire that separated me from the driver, closed my eyes, and tried to get some rest.

I didn't want to think about what came next.

"I'm sick of watching 'Blue Lives Matter' supporters idly stand by any police officer simply because he wears blue, ignoring the facts that should make them cringe in disbelief and horror. Police brutality is systemic, not anecdotal."

-Seph Lawless

4

"Day or night, the thought that pricked at her heart was, *Why would anyone murder my daughter?*"

ANOTHER HOOKER

HILARY DAVIDSON

It was only after the funeral mass was over and her daughter's body was rendered to ashes that Leanna Dowd began to ask questions. At first, they came to her unbidden while she was at home alone. *How long did it take Sophie to die?* flitted through her mind when she was washing dishes. *How much did Sophie suffer?* flashed on a loop while she brushed her teeth. Day or night, the thought that pricked at her heart was, *Why would anyone murder my daughter?*

The little that Leanna knew was almost too much to bear. The police officer who'd driven her from Queens to the Manhattan morgue had warned her the crime scene had been a gruesome one. When the medical examiner lifted the sheet covering Sophie's body, he'd tried to hide her throat. The man who'd killed her had almost taken her head off.

Leanna would've done anything to wipe that image from her mind. Her small, tidy house was filled with framed photographs of her only child. There was Sophie as a smiling baby, a toddler, a first grader. There was daredevil Sophie, riding a bike and holding both her hands in the air. The photos were mostly of a grinning, happy child, with the exception of one taken after Sophie's father died suddenly when the girl was nine. In the photos after that, Sophie still smiled, but Leanna couldn't tell how genuine the cheerfulness had been. It was too painful to walk into Sophie's room, so she kept that door closed, but she found herself staring at the photos while time slouched by. No matter which image she gazed at, a vision of Sophie's corpse crept into her head. *Had she known she was going to die?* Leanna wondered. *Did it happen too quickly to call for help?*

Leanna kept her dark thoughts to herself until the day she found herself crying in the middle of the bank where she worked. Her manager told her to take the rest of the afternoon off, but instead of heading home, Leanna took a train into the city. One of the detectives investigating Sophie's death had given her his card, and it led her to a gray stone fortress on West Fifty-Fourth Street.

When she walked into the police station, it was a surprise to herself as much as it was to the cops. Someone got her coffee and brought her into a small room with metal furniture. It didn't take long for a pair of detectives she recognized to walk in. Mark Grennell had been the name on the card. He was in his late forties, heavyset with iron-gray hair and a heavily creased face. His partner was O'Keefe, a decade younger with cold blue eyes and a bored demeanor.

"How have you been keeping, Mrs. Dowd?" Grennell asked.

"It's been hard," Leanna answered, her voice so quiet she could barely hear herself. "I think about her—about Sophie—all the time. I still can't believe she's gone."

"No mother should go through what you're going through," Grennell said.

"I keep thinking about how she died . . ."

"There's no good in thinking on that," Grennell interrupted. "I know it's not much consolation right now, but we got the bastard who did this to your daughter. He'll never do this to anybody again."

"You said he confessed." Leanna stared at her hands in her lap before glancing up. "But no one ever told me what he said."

"His reasons don't matter." O'Keefe leaned back in his chair. "Javier Castro is a junkie scumbag and a murderer. People like that don't have reasons."

"The important thing to know is that he's being held without bail," Grennell added. "He won't get out of jail."

"Sociopaths should be locked away for good." O'Keefe shook his head. "Piece of shit like him never should've been out of jail in the first place."

A chill ran through Leanna. "He's been in jail before?"

"He killed another hooker a few years back," O'Keefe said. "He never should've gotten out after that."

Leanna's mouth opened and shut. *Another* hooker, the cop had said. Meaning that he thought her Sophie was one, too. "My daughter was not a prostitute," she said.

"Mrs. Dowd, I can't tell you how many parents we meet who don't really know what was going on with their kids," Grennell said.

"Do you have children?" Leanna demanded.

"Three crazy rugrats," O'Keefe said.

"A son," Grennell said.

"He's as much trouble as a dozen rugrats," O'Keefe threw in, but the grin disappeared from his face when he caught the look his partner gave him.

"Every kid gets into scrapes," Grennell said slowly. "I'm sure your Sophie was a great girl, but I also know she had secrets from you. We investigated thoroughly. Sophie rented the Airbnb where she was killed. She wasn't lured there. She rented the place for the weekend. It was where she saw her clients. She had rented it, and places like it, before."

Leanna chewed the inside of her lip to keep from crying. Sophie was a student who lived at home to save money, but she liked to spend weekends in the city sometimes. There was nothing wrong with that. "You're telling me this man who murdered her . . . was her client?"

"No. It was a case of wrong place, wrong time," Grennell said. "Javier Castro thought the apartment was empty and broke in. He was high, and . . . well, you know how things ended."

"I do." There was nothing else to do but get up from the table, even though Leanna's legs were wobbling underneath her. "Thank you," she murmured, wanting to be polite even though her throat burned with acid. It was how she'd raised Sophie. Be polite, no matter how you feel.

Outside, it was sunny and warm. Even the weather mocked her, Leanna thought. She headed for the subway, but once she got to her stop, she turned in the opposite direction from her house. She knew someone who'd have answers. Madison had been Sophie's best friend since they'd met in a gymnastics class for toddlers.

Madison greeted her at the door with a hug. "Sorry I haven't called since the funeral," she said.

"I know you're busy with school," Leanna said. "But I need to ask you something about Sophie."

"Is there something new?" Madison asked, leading her inside. "I thought they caught the guy?"

"They did. But I'm still . . . I'm trying to process everything. The police say Sophie was working . . . that she was a prostitute. I don't believe it, but I'm her mother. What do I know? Will you tell me the truth?"

Madison regarded her with sad eyes. "I don't know what to say."

"You're saying it's true." Leanna's heart crashed through the floor. Her baby. How could she not know?

"It's not like that," Madison said. "Sophie always needed money, even though she worked hard. She joined one of those websites, the kind where you look for a sugar daddy."

"She . . . what?"

"A lot of girls did it," Madison said quickly. "I did, too. But you learn pretty fast that most of the guys on there are cheap as hell. They give you a little cash and think they're doing you the favor. A lot of the guys aren't even rich, they're middle-aged accountants."

"How many men did she meet?"

"I don't think there were a lot. Sophie got close with one guy, Walter. She saw him one weekend a month. I don't know his last name, but he flies in from California."

"Do you think she knew the man who killed her?"

"That Castro guy?" Madison looked aghast. "No way. Sophie steered clear of druggies. She didn't even drink."

By the time Leanna got home that night, her heart was even heavier than it had been at Sophie's funeral. For the first time since the morning of the funeral, she opened the door to her daughter's room. It smelled of roses and sandalwood. Sophie's phone was missing from its stand on the night table—the police still hadn't returned it—but everything else was tidy and neat. Leanna stepped in and closed the door behind her. She sat on the pale pink bedspread, staring at the images on the wall. Sophie had dreamed of being an urban planner, and the images she'd tacked up were of global metropolises instead of the boy bands Leanna had idolized when she was young.

Leanna had never been one of those mothers who invaded her child's privacy, but she suddenly felt like she had to. Meticulously going through Sophie's desk and dresser and nightstand, she found nothing of note. It was a shoebox at the bottom of Sophie's closet that held her secrets: a diamond tennis bracelet she'd never seen Sophie wear, bundled cash—a quick count came up to $8,000—and a small gun that gleamed silver.

What was Sophie doing with a gun?

That question made Leanna's heart pound. At the bottom of the box was an embossed business card with the name *Walter Ostrander* and an address in San Francisco. Without thinking, she dialed the number as she nudged the shoebox under the bed with one foot.

Leanna told the receptionist that Sophie Dowd was calling. A moment later, she heard a sharp intake of breath.

"Who the hell is this? Because I know this sure as hell isn't Sophie."

"It's Sophie's mother, Leanna. I just found your card in my daughter's room."

There was a long exhale. "I'm really sorry about what happened. She was a special girl."

"Someone told you she died?"

"I was supposed to see her the night she died, but my flight was late," Walter said. "When I got there, the place was crawling with police. She was already dead."

"I found a gun. Do you know anything about that?"

"She actually got it?" Walter sounded surprised. "She'd talked about it. There was a guy she was afraid of, kind of a stalker. I told her to call the cops, but she said that would be a waste of time."

Leanna took a breath, thinking about how quick the police were to write off her daughter's death. How mean they were, calling Sophie a hooker. How careless they were. Sophie had been right: contacting them was a waste of time.

"What was his name?" she asked.

"No idea. She hadn't mentioned him in a while. I thought he was history."

The phone call didn't make Leanna feel better; if anything, she felt sick. Sophie had been in danger. The police had told her Javier Castro was on drugs, but that didn't explain why he'd attacked Sophie so violently. *If Javier Castro had simply been planning to rob the apartment, why had he murdered Sophie? He could've fled, couldn't he? Why had he practically hacked Sophie's head off?*

The more time that passed, the more she wondered how this man could've done what he did. After a series of sleepless nights, she made a decision. There was only one way to learn the truth: she would ask Javier Castro herself.

Leanna had never visited anyone in jail. Whatever TV-fed ideas she had about the matter were dashed by the Department of Corrections website, which informed her that in-person visits were still suspended because of the pandemic. But there was another option: a virtual visit. She filled in the request form immediately and filed it online.

When she went to bed that night, there was only one question on her mind. *Why did you choose to kill my daughter?* That was what she needed to ask. But when she got up early the next day, there was already a message back from the DOC: *Request denied.*

There was no explanation why.

She sat down and poured her heart into a letter. She didn't know how it all came out as it did—recalling moments when Sophie was growing up, how good and kind she had always been—but she poured it into a pair of double-sided handwritten pages, stamped an envelope, and walked it to the mailbox down the street. *Why did I send that to a murderer?* she wondered as she walked back to her house. She couldn't explain it. All she wanted was for Javier Castro to understand what he had done. Maybe in prison, off drugs and alone with his thoughts, he'd be ready to answer.

She went back to staring at pictures of Sophie, as if she could communicate with her dead daughter. *I would've taken on another job*, she told Sophie. *If you'd told me what you needed.*

She went back to work and tried to push the pain from her mind. Couples came in looking for mortgages on little houses just like hers. They were hopeful, as she had once been. She felt pained dealing with them. *Just wait*, she thought. *Wait until you see what life has in store for you.*

A week after she mailed the letter, she got a collect call after eight in the evening. She almost hung up when the automated voice told her it was from a jail. Then she realized who it was and took a deep breath. "I accept the charges."

There was a crackle and a pause on the line. Then a man spoke. "Leanna Dowd? This is Javier Castro. I got your letter and it... it broke my heart. I'm sorry about your daughter."

Leanna stood stock still, holding the phone to her ear. "You're sorry?"

"I am. I truly am."

"I need to ask you something," she said. "You could've run away. Why did you kill her?"

"I didn't," he said.

"You did. The police told me you confessed."

"I made a confession. But it wasn't the truth." He took a deep breath. "You have no reason to believe me, I understand that. But I never met your daughter."

"The police told me you killed another girl," Leanna said. "Are you going to say that's a lie, too?"

"No, but that was an accident. We got high together. I never meant for her to overdose."

"Overdose?" Leanna repeated, feeling faint.

"Heroin."

"I don't understand. Why would you say you killed Sophie if you didn't?"

"Because I made a deal. It'll get me out of prison faster than the drug charges they arrested me on. Look, it's light's out here soon, so I have to go. But I had to tell you the truth. I'm going to set things right."

Leanna didn't sleep that night. How could anybody set things right with Sophie dead? She felt like a sucker for listening to Javier Castro's story. Of course he would claim that he wasn't responsible. What else would he say to a grieving mother?

When she went to work the next day, she pretended to review a stack of applications, but she couldn't concentrate. Her phone rang and rang and rang, compounding her headache. One of the tellers popped her head into her cubicle.

"Did you talk to that reporter yet?" she asked.

"I don't want to talk to any reporters."

"He said the man who murdered poor Sophie killed himself last night," the teller said.

"Javier Castro is dead?"

"I guess maybe this reporter thought he was giving you good news?" The teller's sweet face was sympathetic. "I know it doesn't bring Sophie back, but . . ."

Leanna stood up. "I need to go out."

She took the subway to the police station. On her phone, she looked up Javier Castro online. There were a couple of short items about his apparent suicide. What he'd told her about the other girl was true; he hadn't been a violent killer. He'd dealt a lot of drugs and a prostitute he traded some to had overdosed when she was with him.

There was no point in going to the police station, yet Leanna went anyway. At the front desk, she asked for Detectives Grennell and O'Keefe. They were on their way out, but they greeted her with broad smiles.

"You heard about Javier Castro?" Grennell asked. "Must've made your day."

"Good riddance to bad rubbish," O'Keefe added.

"Actually, it felt like horrible news," Leanna said. "He called me last night. He told me he didn't kill Sophie."

"Of course he said that." O'Keefe rolled his eyes back into his head. "You can't believe a junkie jailbird."

"What could he possibly say that he convinced you he was innocent?" Grennell asked.

"He told me he made a deal."

"A deal." Grennell's face was blank. "What kind of a deal? And a deal with who?"

"He said it would get him out of jail faster." As Leanna spoke her mouth felt dry. If Javier Castro had made a deal, it could only have been with the police.

Grennell gave her an ironic little smile. "So you're saying this was a man willing to make up a different story for everyone. Of course he lied to you."

"Sure." She nodded as if she believed them. Questioning them wouldn't lead anywhere. They were slippery as quicksand and just as deadly. The cops had lied about her daughter and now they lied about the man they'd set up. "That makes sense. Thanks."

She hurried out, because the police station seemed like a bad place to be.

When she showed up at Madison's door, her hands were shaking. "I need to ask you one thing," Leanna said. "You told me you and Sophie met all kinds of guys on that sugar daddy website. Were any of them cops?"

"No," Madison said. "We never met any cops that way."

"Oh." Leanna's heart sank. For a brief moment the puzzle pieces in her daughter's murder seemed to come together, but it was a mirage.

"The only cop Sophie went out with was this guy she met in a club," Madison added. "He was an asshole."

"What was his name?"

"I don't remember. This was, like, a year ago? It didn't last long."

"Can you describe him?"

"Big. Military haircut. Clearly worked out a lot." Madison shook her head. "I only saw him once. He came into the restaurant where we were working, shouting at me about Sophie ditching him for a rich guy. He really was an asshole."

An ugly idea was snaking around Leanna's brain. She found photos of Grennell and O'Keefe on the NYPD's website. "Was it one of them?"

Madison shook her head. "I don't think so. They both look old."

It had been a long shot, Leanna knew that, but she also knew that Javier Castro's sudden death was unnatural. If he'd been telling the truth about confessing to a crime he hadn't committed, someone had shut him up permanently.

The problem was, there was no one she could report that crime to.

When she went to bed that night, she couldn't sleep. She lay there, thinking about Sophie and the formless, nameless man who'd terrified her. The cops were involved, and not just as investigators. Why would they want Javier to confess to another man's crime? Her mind circled around that question, unable to see a way past or through it. She could've wept in frustration, but that wouldn't get justice for Sophie. Or for Javier. She drifted off, feeling trapped on all sides.

The sound of a door closing snapped her awake. She glanced at the clock. It was after four in the morning.

Someone was in the house with her, and it was no ghost.

When she sat up in bed, she realized a hulking silhouette was blocking her doorway.

"You killed my daughter. Now you're here to kill me." Leanna's voice was strangely calm.

"That's not what happened." It was Grennell's smooth voice; she recognized it with a jolt.

"I know the truth," Leanna said. "Sophie broke up with you, and you couldn't handle it. You killed her because she didn't want you."

"I didn't kill her."

"You're a liar. You got another man to confess. Then you killed him. You're covering up your own tracks."

"You asked me at the precinct if I had kids," Grennell said. "I have one. A son. And he's done some things he shouldn't have."

Leanna remembered what Madison had told her. "There was a young cop Sophie dated. That was your son?"

"She didn't want anything to do with him because he didn't have money."

"Or maybe she didn't want anything to do with him because she sensed he was the kind of man who'd hack her head off if she said no to him."

"I'm not justifying what he did," Grennell said.

"He murdered Sophie. What about Javier? That was you."

"You would've done anything for your daughter, wouldn't you? Well, I'd do anything for my son."

"The apple didn't fall far from the tree," Leanna said. "He's a killer, just like his dad."

"I hope you satisfied your curiosity," Grennell said. "Because that's what killed you."

"You're determined to pretend none of this is your fault." She reached out for the bedside light switch. Grennell winced, but the gun he held was steady. "You're going to shoot me? Don't you think that'll look suspicious?"

"I was going to make it easy on you," Grennell said. "Overdose, a painless way to go. No surprise that a grieving mother would want to exit like that."

"That would be better than being shot. But I'd want to be in Sophie's room, surrounded by her things."

Grennell thought about that for a moment. "Okay," he said finally. "But no sudden moves. And only if you swallow this pill."

"What is it?"

"Doesn't really matter, does it?"

"Okay," Leanna agreed, slowly sliding out of bed and wrapping herself in a robe. Grennell handed her a pill and she popped it into her mouth. He kept his gun pointed at her head as he followed her across the hall. "I'm not running anywhere."

"It doesn't matter if you do. My partner or another officer would catch you. We take care of our own."

Sophie's room still smelled like her, that lovely mix of roses and sandalwood. Grennell turned on the light.

"I'm going to say a prayer," Leanna said, falling to her knees at the side of Sophie's bed. She hadn't swallowed the pill, but it was dissolving in her mouth and already making her woozy. "Maybe you should pray for your son."

"A little late for that."

"Where's Bluebell?" Leanna asked. "That's Sophie's bear. He should be on the bed." She glanced under the bed. "There he is." She reached into the shoebox, put her hand on the small silver gun, and prayed that it was loaded.

Grennell didn't realize what had happened until she pointed it at him and fired. His gun was already on her and he shot back, hitting Leanna in the shoulder. She fell back against the bed, watching his big body sliding down the doorframe. She'd had beginners' luck: she'd shot him in the head.

The room spun around her, and she spat out the tablet he'd given her. Leanna had known she couldn't save herself from Grennell. The best she could do was take him with her.

She heard a door crash open and heavy footsteps stampede toward her. Leanna knew the cavalry wasn't coming to rescue her. Grennell had been truthful at the very end of his life: he and his brother officers cared only about protecting each other.

"Mark, did you shoot her?" called a hoarse voice she didn't recognize. "The paperwork is gonna be . . ."

The uniformed cop gasped as he reached the doorway. As he crouched to take Grennell's pulse, Leanna aimed the gun again. The man screamed and fell backwards. She prayed she'd hit him, but her heart sank as his heavy footsteps clattered back down the hall and he shouted for backup.

Grennell was dead, but it didn't feel like enough to Leanna, not after what they'd done. The police had covered up her daughter's death and killed an innocent man to keep the secret. How many others had they destroyed to protect themselves?

Whatever Grennell had poisoned her with was coursing through her bloodstream, draining the life out of her. Leanna's body was so numb she couldn't even feel the bullet wound anymore. She was barely tethered to the world. Her vision dimmed as her life played out before her eyes, the good and the bad zipping past in two painstakingly slow heartbeats. There was a voice in the room with her—maybe more than one—but it didn't matter anymore. Nothing did, except for Sophie's warm presence opening her arms and welcoming Leanna into the darkness.

5

"The queers sat against the wall. The cops stood around, watching nothing and everything at the same time. We all waited to see if someone was going to pay the tax tonight."

Everybody Pays a Tax

Joseph S. Walker

Jason, who gives me physical therapy three times a week, is probably in his late twenties, but I can't help thinking of him as a kid as he wheels me from my room—I'm sorry, my *suite*—to the big rec center, talking all the way. He's good at his job, cheerful, always polite, even when the exercises get me mad enough to curse him. He called me Mr. Harper for months, even after I told him anybody that familiar with my body can call me Toby.

Jason wears a bright little rainbow pin every day. Hanging in his office is a picture of him and his husband on a beach somewhere in Mexico, hoisting drinks the size of their heads. His husband. Right there on the wall, where everybody can see it. When I was his age, I couldn't have imagined the life he's leading.

But then, he probably can't imagine the life I led.

●

When I first got to this city, men were *everywhere*. Yearnings I'd barely had words for in the small town I came from, could now be met as easily as picking up a loaf of bread. There were men cruising at the Y, men cruising in bookstores and libraries, men cruising in train station restrooms. Quiet men in understated three-piece suits, sitting in lounges with dark wood paneling, and the beautiful, dangerous street queens in their wigs and tied-off blouses. Burly dockworkers lingering near unused piers, and long-haired students sprawling on blankets in secluded nooks of the parks. There were bars where men could buy each other drinks and hold hands. There was a club where we could dance with each other.

Back home, I spent four years trying to concoct a reason to touch Robbie O'Neill, our high school's pretty basketball hero. I'd been in the city less than two days when Andy K pulled me behind some bushes, in the small park near my rattrap apartment, and became the first man to kiss me. I didn't even know his name yet. When he pulled my hand to the front of his pants and I hesitated, he laughed softly.

"Here's a rule I live by," he said. "It's the things you don't do that you end up regretting."

●

Most of the time, being in the city felt like I'd been set free. The times when it didn't feel that way were mostly because of the cops, who could be the ruin of one night if you were lucky, or a few weeks if you weren't. More than one shift commander padded his arrest stats by sending his best-looking young officer out in civilian clothes to collar any man who so much as winked at him. Andy K taught me things to look for. An undercover almost never had hair that looked right, and most of them rushed things, or used slang terms stiffly. Still, it was easy to get tripped up. You let a guy in a bar buy you a beer, or followed him into a bathroom stall, and next thing you know he's slapping cuffs on you. There wasn't much you could do at that point. Hope you're not holding anything that will add to the charges. Hope Lily Law is just looking for the easy arrest and you'll be out by breakfast. Hope you don't end up getting ground through the system for months, sharing cells with speed freak bikers who use you to kill the time.

Andy K called it the cost of doing business. Street theater, so the papers could say the city was safe for decent people. Some of the political types went to city council meetings and bitched about entrapment. You can guess how far they got. We hated the cops, but we could manage them. They'd raid a bar early in the evening, a little money would change hands under a table, and by midnight it would be reopened, with the guys who got busted trickling back in as they posted bond. Mostly, cops were more an annoyance than a threat, and they didn't keep us from feeling like we had made the city ours.

But if a place feels like paradise, look around for the serpent. The snake in our garden was Lieutenant Francis Morelli, head of the city's Immorality and Indecency task force. Compared to the other cops, Morelli and his squad were very different beasts. Still pigs, but feral razorbacks. They didn't bother with entrapment, they didn't care about public relations, and they weren't just out to pad their numbers. Their game was catching gays in the act, and their goal was making anyone they got their hands on suffer.

I saw it for myself one night when they raided the empty trucks parked down by the docks. One minute everything was peaceful, guys pairing off to melt into the shadows or climb up into the empty trailers. Somebody had a little portable radio, and a few guys were dancing, the thin sound from the cheap speaker drifting out over the river. Then there were shouts, and a flying wedge of cops, nightsticks slashing out in every direction, blocked the main route back out to the streets. Morelli was in the lead, yelling for everybody to sit their asses down and motivating the slow with blows to the head. I fell to the ground and rolled into the filthy space under a van parked against a wall. From my hidey hole I watched feet scrambling around, listened to yells and curses.

A Hispanic man in a fringe vest fell to the ground ten feet away, bleeding from an ugly gash on the side of his head. His eyes were open and pointed right at me, but I didn't know if he was seeing anything. I thought about trying to pull him under the van, but before I could, Morelli himself was squatting by the man's head. Morelli was six and half feet tall. The short sleeves of his uniform strained against his biceps. His round stomach hung out over his belt.

"Sally Ruiz," he said. "I thought I told you to get your faggot ass out of my city." He bounced his nightstick solidly off Ruiz's elbow. Ruiz bit his lip but didn't cry out. I was sure now that he saw me.

"You don't listen so good," Morelli went on. "Looks like you get to pay the queer tax tonight." He grabbed Ruiz's long black hair and pulled the man up as he stood. I watched as he half marched and half dragged him around the corner. I kept an eye out for Sally Ruiz after that. I never saw him again.

⬤

Like Andy K, Morelli had a rule: sooner or later, everybody pays a tax. Most of the gay men he and his crew picked up on any given night just got arrested, which was bad enough. It meant hours, possibly days, of being run through institutions designed at every point to make you feel dirty, and small, and worthless. It meant sitting behind bars, hoping your cellmates weren't in a dangerous mood, while the cops on the other side sneered and spit. When Morelli got you, though, just getting arrested felt lucky. It was better than paying a tax.

Morelli's queer tax took a few different forms. It *could* just be financial, if you happened to have enough folding money in your pocket to catch his interest.

More often, the queer tax meant that Morelli and his thugs with badges took you into an alley or some dark corner and went to work with sticks and fists and feet. Their reports would say you resisted arrest. When you paid the tax that way, you went to the hospital, not jail, and you were there for a while, pissing blood into a bedpan.

If you really annoyed Morelli, or he remembered you from one too many previous busts, or he was just in the wrong mood, you paid a different queer tax. He dragged you into that alley all by himself, shoved you to your knees, and lowered his pants. He held his service revolver alongside your head, to discourage any bright ideas about biting. When it was over, he slammed the gun butt into your temple and left you stunned on the ground.

✺

"That fascist asshole is going to kill somebody," Andy K said.

I ran straight to his place after Morelli's crew cleared the docks, leaving me undiscovered under the van. Andy K's apartment was right across the street from mine, which was convenient, since he'd become my best friend. We fell into bed together once in a while, but often just hung out or went to movies.

When he was in elementary school, there were five kids named Andy in his grade, so the teachers added last initials to call on them. In Andy K's case it stuck. Even his severely uptight parents called him Andy K, when he called home once a week to mournfully report that he still hadn't met the girl of their dreams.

I shook as I talked about Morelli dragging Sally Ruiz away. Andy K gave me a joint, which didn't help much, and sat on the couch holding me, which helped some. For a couple of weeks after that I went straight home after work and stayed away from all the popular pickup spots. I couldn't walk toward a corner without imagining that Morelli was just around it, waiting for me. When I did start going out again, I was perpetually on alert, ready to run at the first sign of a raid.

I only wish Andy K had been as careful.

✺

I was out of the city the weekend it happened, back home for a cousin's wedding. After almost two years, seeing family members and friends from high school, some with their own spouses and wide-eyed pink babies, was surreal. I couldn't escape the feeling that everyone was wearing a mask. I wondered who and what they would be if they could really choose, as I had chosen. I couldn't wait to get back to my new life. My *real* life. I rehearsed in my head the report I would make to Andy K, the cutting lines I would use to preen about how completely I'd left that world behind.

But when I got back, Andy K was in the hospital. He was making out with an art student from Long Island, in that same little park where he and I first met, when Morelli and his crew swept through. Andy K was Morelli's choice to pay that night's queer tax.

I sat in a bright yellow plastic chair and held the hand that wasn't cuffed to the bed. There were four beds in the room, and the flimsy curtain pulled around us didn't allow me to forget the other patients and visitors. The way they had looked when I came in, their eyes flicking from me to Andy K. You could see them filing us away. Fruits. Faggots. Their faces were as cold as the cop guarding the door.

Andy K's eyes were swollen almost shut. He had a cast on one leg and every move he made was stiff and slow. I brushed hair off his forehead and spoke softly. "Somebody said you took a swing at Morelli." I'd heard that but didn't believe it. Andy K weighed maybe 140 pounds.

He nodded. "Got him," he said. His voice was a rasp. I held a cup of ice water with a straw to his mouth. After he sipped, he sounded a little better. "Right on the chin. Best punch of my life."

"Why would you do that? You're lucky they didn't kill you."

His chest jumped a couple of times, like he was trying to laugh and couldn't. "Things you don't do, you regret," he managed.

When he was able to get out of bed, they sent him away for six months. He told his parents he'd won a grant to attend an intensive actors' retreat that allowed no contact with the outside world.

✳

About a month after Andy K paid his tax, Morelli raided a bar I was at. I had no chance to run. His men sat me against the wall, lined up with a dozen others, under the watchful eyes of a couple of uniforms. In the severe glare of the overhead lights they'd turned on, the elegant martini-and-olive atmosphere dissolved into an ugly basement lined with stained curtains.

Morelli walked in front of us, looking closely at each face. He used his nightstick, not gently, to raise the chin of anybody who tried to keep their head down.

When it was my turn, I managed to at least look him in the eye. I was terrified, but I owed Andy K that much.

The queers sat against the wall. The cops stood around, watching nothing and everything at the same time. We all waited to see if someone was going to pay the tax tonight.

The last guy in line, the bartender, was older than anybody else in the room. He stared at his feet, stretched out in front of him. Morelli slammed his stick into the wall, an inch over the bartender's head. The bartender didn't flinch. He sighed and looked up.

"I've seen you before," Morelli said. "Work a lot of fag joints, don't you?"

"Money's the same color as yours," the bartender said.

Morelli shook his head. "You're lucky I'm in a good mood, Pops. I could make this the worst night of your life."

He was turning away when the bartender spoke again. "You wouldn't make the top ten, you limp-dick pig motherfucker."

I think everybody in the room stopped breathing. Morelli stood still for a long minute. He didn't turn to look back at the bartender. When he finally spoke, his voice was quiet and carefully measured. "Bring him," he said. "Get the rest of these assholes in the wagon."

I never knew exactly what Morelli did to the bartender. Somebody told me he had to move to Florida, where he had a sister who could tend to him. They said that the sister, like the bartender, had a number tattooed on her arm.

❋

Andy K was released from prison on a Saturday morning in April. A Department of Corrections van took him and a few others to a nearby train station, where he bought a ticket for the three-hour ride to the city. Then, ever playing the dutiful son, he called his parents. I don't know how long he talked to them. I know he tried to call me, afterwards, but I'd gone out for coffee and eggs. Andy K's call was answered by Miguel, a fantastically agile dancer I met the night before, brought home, and became so besotted with that I wanted to cook him breakfast.

I don't know what might have been different if I answered.

Andy K asked Miguel to take a message. "Tell Toby that Morelli called my parents," he said. "Just that. He'll understand."

Then he hung up and walked onto the tracks, directly in front of an arriving train.

I spent a week in bed, unable to do almost anything but cry. Sometimes it was angry crying, and I threw things around and fantasized about burning Andy K's childhood home to ashes. Mostly I just numbly stared at the wall as the tears came. I kept the blinds pulled down and the lights off. I barely ate. By the time I went back to work, I was so gaunt that nobody questioned all the days I called in sick.

I worked in customer service at one of the big downtown banks. I helped poor people open checking accounts and start quarter-a-week savings for their kids. I sent any customer with a more complex request, or seeming to have any significant money at all, to larger desks, manned by older men in better suits. It was dull, but most of the people I knew washed dishes or waited tables, so I didn't complain much.

About two weeks after I went back to work, I looked up and saw Morelli in the lobby. He was walking away from one of the teller windows, tucking an envelope into his breast pocket. He glanced in my direction, and I was too slow looking away. He saw the expression on my face. When I looked back, he was coming my way, grinning broadly. He stopped on the other side of my desk and looked down at me. "I know you," he said.

This time I couldn't look at him. I stared at his belt buckle. "I don't think so, sir."

"Sure I do." He rapped his knuckles on my desk. "That pansy joint in the basement, the one with the mouthy bartender. You were there. Never would have figured somebody like you worked in a classy place like this." He pointed at a desk a few yards behind mine. "That your boss?"

"No," I said.

"No, huh? Looks like a good conversationalist, anyway. You think I should go talk with him?"

I didn't say anything.

"Gimme twenty dollars," Morelli said.

"What?"

"You heard me." He raised his voice a shade. "Give me twenty dollars."

My face felt warm. My jaw clenched so tightly I don't think I could have talked again. I took out my wallet and found two ten-dollar bills. Morelli held out his hand, but I put the bills down on the edge of the blotter. He chuckled and picked them up.

"That's okay," he said. "You'll put it right in my hand next time, pervert. Won't you?"

❋

I like to think Andy K had something to do with what happened a few weeks after that. He was popular, and the way he checked out upset a lot of people. It's not like there was any shortage of other things to be upset about, though. Really, it was probably the heat as much as anything. It was the hottest summer anybody could remember, leaving everyone miserable and short-tempered. The city was in an ugly mood. It all boiled over one night when the cops raided the dance club, and the queers fought back.

I wish I could say I was there when it started. I've met a lot of guys over the years who claim they were. I doubt any of them were telling the truth.

My truth is that I was at a party Miguel was throwing, five or six blocks away from the club. I still wasn't in much of a party mood, but some friends got insistent, telling me I was letting Morelli win by wallowing in my room. I was half stoned when the phone rang. Miguel picked it up and waved at somebody to turn the music down. When they did, we heard what seemed like dozens of sirens outside. He listened, and got the kind of expression that makes everyone in the room freeze, waiting to hear what's happened.

"There's a fucking riot going on out there," he finally told us. He listened for another minute. "Reuben says the street queens are chasing cops around in the streets."

"Bullshit," somebody said.

"Maybe not," said a guy with John Lennon glasses. "I wouldn't cross those bitches. Every one of them goes around with a knife."

"Yeah, well, the cops go around with guns."

Miguel waved us to silence, his ear still to the phone. "Some kind of raid at that club across from the park," he said. "They're throwing rocks."

I stood up from the couch. "I wanna see."

Somebody tried to pull me back. "You don't want to be out there when the riot squads show up."

I shook them off and headed out the door, not waiting to see if anyone else followed. By the time I got to the street I was running, heading in the direction of the sirens and the yells.

It was well past one in the morning, but the streets were alive. A lot of people were going the same direction I was. We passed people coming the other way, some of them bleeding or limping. Pretty soon I could see that the street up ahead, between the club and the park, was thronged. A group on the sidewalk had their fists in the air, chanting something I'd never heard before: *gay power*. A police wagon halfway up on the curb was rocked back and forth by dozens of people, apparently intent on tipping it completely over. I skirted the edge of the park and grabbed somebody's arm. "Where are the cops?" I yelled over the racket.

"Pinned inside." He pointed at the club. The front door was closed. Some people were trying to break through the plywood the owners had put over the windows. Three guys ran right past me with a parking meter they'd somehow wrenched out of the ground and started pounding it against the doors.

It was already noisy as hell, then a bigger clamor broke out down the block. People on balconies pointed down and waved frantically. A couple of big police vans had pulled up at the edges of the crowd and cops in heavy armor and helmets were pouring out, starting to swing their nightsticks. The crowd scattered, but didn't break. I watched from the park as a group of the street queens, terrifyingly young and small, mooned the cops, then ran. The cops gave chase, but they were slower, weighed down by their equipment. The street queens turned into side streets, went around the block, and came up behind their pursuers, singing taunting songs and throwing rocks. The cops spun and started after them, and the queens did the trick again.

I was starting to feel ashamed of myself for lurking behind a tree. I was looking around for a rock to throw when I saw Morelli. He was in uniform, but he'd lost his hat. His thinning hair pointed out wildly in every direction. He must have gotten separated from the rest of his men, somehow. He was running across the park, away from the club, being chased by a crowd of about ten gays, some of them street queens.

Without a thought, I ran after them.

Morelli was faster than I would have expected. Maybe sheer terror made him faster than he'd ever been before. The group after him obviously knew who he was, and the things they were shouting would have gotten anyone's adrenaline going. *Kill the pig! Fuck his fascist ass!*

They were out for blood, and gaining on him. He turned into an alley. The small mob followed, me about ten yards behind the others. I turned the corner into the alley and skidded to a halt. Morelli had stopped in front of a set of garbage cans twenty yards into the alley. His chest was heaving as he tried to catch his breath. He was turned to face us, and he had pulled his gun. The crowd chasing him was stopped, halfway between me and him. I hovered at the mouth of the alley, waiting to see what would happen.

Morelli had his gun down by his side and his other hand up toward his pursuers. I think he was starting to say something, but before he could get it out, somebody threw a rock. Whoever it was should have tried out for the Yankees. The rock hit Morelli hard, directly in the forehead. He staggered back against the cans and fell. There was a victorious yell and we all started for him again, but at that moment a police cruiser turned into the other end of the alley. The driver hit the siren and lights and came toward us, accelerating. The mob wavered, then broke, running past me back out onto the main street. I ducked back around the corner and put my back to the wall. In a few seconds the cops came past me, turning to pursue the biggest group as they ran back toward the park. I doubt they'd even seen Morelli.

I went back into the alley. Sirens and shouts from blocks away echoed strangely off the brick walls. There was nobody else around. I felt weirdly detached from myself as I walked toward Morelli. He was on his hands and knees, swaying a little as he tried to get up. From ten feet away I could see his blood dripping onto the filthy pavement. His gun was on the ground where he had been standing. I picked it up.

I stood over Francis Morelli, one foot on either side of him, like I was going to sit on his back for a game of horsey. I clutched the back of his collar with my left hand and used the right to put the barrel of the gun against the base of his skull. He tried to reach back for me, but he was too weak and winded.

My father taught me about guns. One of his efforts to make a man out of me. "First lesson," he said. "You don't put your finger on the trigger unless you are going to shoot."

I tightened my grip on Morelli's collar and put my finger on the trigger.

It's the things you don't do that you end up regretting.

●

I look at the picture of Jason with his husband while he twists my body, trying to get my legs to hang onto whatever life they've got left. I guess I'm supposed to think it was all worth it, if it ends up with that picture on the wall. And I do. I just wish Andy K got to see it.

I don't have regrets. What I have are memories. Young people don't understand the weight memories carry. I didn't, until now, in this broken body, with so many friends gone. If everyone pays a tax, maybe mine is that weight, those fragments of a world I hope Jason never knows. In the middle of the night, I feel Andy K's delicate hand in mine. Rolling down the hall inch by inch, I see Miguel's lithe form spinning through the air. And sitting down to lunch, I hear the empty sack that had been Morelli, crumpling limply to the ground.

6

"Most of the city moved on; there was a sense of acclimation, of getting used to it. Resignation that the cops kept shooting people—mostly black people—and how it just seemed like that was the way the world worked.

"But some people didn't get used to it. The fucking protesters."

VIGILANCE

KEITH ROSSON

They took him when he was getting into his truck, parked in the rear lot of Twister's, a sports bar out in Lake Oswego. Wiles was buzzed and slow to react to someone behind him. They fucking tased him, right there on the back of the neck, and he just dropped. The idea of pulling his piece wasn't even a breath of a dream; it was like his whole world came undone in a heartbeat. He landed on the pavement next to his keys.

They scooped him up—two men—and put him in a van. Zip ties around his wrists, behind his back. Put a cloth sack over his head. He'd pissed himself: couldn't help it. They took his gun.

He threw up inside the sack—prime rib and tequila spilling down his collar.

"Fucking nasty," one of them said.

He was more in his body by the time they stopped. They marched him inside, down some steps. The rasp of cement against his shoes. The hum of overhead lights. They sat him down in a folding chair and lashed him to it with a single, endless hank of duct tape.

The sack came off and he squinted against the light for a while. His pants were still damp. The smell of puke on his collar, cement dust, oil. It was a windowless place—some kind of industrial basement. Huge steel pillars in the middle of the room, leaning stacks of plywood and rebar here and there.

Three of them. The two, plus a driver. They were dressed in black, masks on. One of them sat on a plastic bucket. The other two stood behind him, arms folded. One of the standing men was black, the other two white.

Wiles said, "You people have fucked up so bad."

"Listen to me," said the one sitting on the bucket. He pointed a gloved finger at Wiles. "You won't get many chances with us."

"Fuck you."

"Officer Wiles. Derek? Derek, listen to me."

That chilled him—that they knew who he was. That they had taken him *because* of who he was.

"You know you get life in prison for kidnapping a cop?" Wiles said.

"Nah," said one of the standing men. "We get life if we kill you, though."

"We want Kleeman," said the one on the bucket.

"I don't know who the fuck Kleeman is," Wiles said, and it sounded like a lie even to him.

"Man, this is where things go south. You think he'd hold out for you? Thin blue line and all that shit? You know what we could do to you right now?"

"You're not going to do shit."

"Maybe he doesn't know," said one of the standing men. "Maybe he's useless to us."

The one on the bucket stared at him. He had ice-blue eyes that terrified Wiles for their clarity, their utter lack of fear. "Is that true, Derek? That you don't know Kleeman? You've both been photographed at the protests. Shooting moms with rubber bullets and shit. Shoving people to the ground and walking over them. Firing at people from ten feet away, breaking their jaws. Did you know you did that, Officer Wiles? That you broke someone's jaw with a rubber bullet the other night? Because you did, my man."

The third one, the one that hadn't said anything yet, walked behind him.

The one on the bucket kept going. "You get to cover up your badges, isn't that right? And your unit commander gives you a four-digit number instead, to put on your body armor? You just put it on with tape, right? And sometimes that tape falls off, or the numbers are strangely illegible, right? So really, when you think of it, it could be *any* of you doing all this stuff."

Wiles tried to turn his head, to see what the one in the back was doing, but they'd really done him up with the tape. True fear was creeping in now. They had his gun.

"But you . . . we got pictures of you. Your number, Derek, is 4982. Kleeman's is 0479. That's who we want—0479. If you don't know him, or his number—if you can't tell us anything—that's fine. But without that, you're dead weight to us."

Wiles leaned his head over as far as he could and spat on the concrete. It cost him—his mouth was dry, his skull throbbing. His mouth tasted like death.

"Everyone knows who the fuck Kleeman is," he said.

The one on the bucket, his eyes went wide at this. "Oh yeah? Why?"

"Because he shot that kid downtown last week. It's what all the fucking protests are about."

"What kid is that, Derek?"

"Fuck you."

"What's the kid's name, Derek?"

"Fuck you," Wiles said again.

The one on the bucket leaned forward into a crouch in front of him. Wiles had been wrong at first: it wasn't a lack of fear in the man's eyes. It was mirth. A kind of joy at being there. "Tell Kleeman we're coming for him. And anyone else that is a danger to our community, you understand? We're done with this shit."

Wiles opened his mouth to laugh—in spite of everything, it was so fucking ridiculous—and the one from behind grabbed his jaw and held it open and they shoved something in his mouth that clacked against his teeth. They threw the cloth sack over his head again and cinched it tight with tape this time.

He could feel it in his mouth. A bullet.

He spat it out, and it hung there like a dark pill at his collar, trapped in the sack.

They cut him loose from the chair. He started to scream and they tased him again, before they dragged him to the van.

●

It was fucking huge, what happened to Wiles. The local FBI field office opened up an investigation into his abduction. A crew of other cops were put on a detail to keep tabs on him and Kleeman. The chief of police told all the precinct commanders to double up guys on patrols: no more solo shifts. Wiles was debriefed for fucking days over what happened. Where was he? How much had he had to drink?—not that anyone, the chief stressed again and again, was busting his ass—how far had they driven him in the van? Had he seen any graffiti or identifying things in the basement? The bullet they put in his mouth was indeed a 9mm round; it had come from his own gun, which was now missing.

Kleeman was pumped. He'd been catching endless heat—protestors clamoring for an independent review of the shooting, just like they did every time cops shot some fucking maniac or dope dealer—and this thing with Wiles painted them all as the hunted and not the hunter. A cabal of black-clad anarchists that hunted cops? It was perfect. A bevy of FOX hosts were shitting their pants with victimized glee. It was open season on the message boards.

The memorial for James Malkaley, the kid that Kleeman had shot the week before—a 19-year-old black kid who pulled out his phone after he'd been told to get on the ground—stayed fresh. New flowers and candles every night, freshly chalked messages on the dirty sidewalk where Kleeman had shot him nine times. Most of the city moved on; there was a sense of acclimation, of getting used to it. Resignation that the cops kept shooting people—mostly black people—and how it just seemed like that was the way the world worked.

But some people didn't get used to it. The fucking protesters.

Citizens—if you could call them that—mobilized nightly for Malkaley, usually in the hundreds, sometimes the thousands, in marches that wound their way through downtown and then focused on the federal courthouse. The mayor had petitioned the feds for help and had gotten it: over fifty DHS agents were brought into the fold. Every night the protests ended with black bloc anarchists and hardcore protesters knuckling down outside the courthouse, often hundreds of them, throwing paint balloons and taunts over the courthouse fence until the cops and feds had enough and started lobbing less-lethals and tear gas, then rolling out into the fray.

All for a guy who'd called Kleeman a pig and refused to get on the ground, then pulled out his phone from his back pocket. A guy who had roughly fit the description of the motherfucker they'd been looking for in the first place. Malkaley: suddenly the poster boy for a bunch of communist leftists.

●

Kleeman and Wiles and a bunch of other guys from the unit were getting beers at a bar not far from the precinct after they'd wrapped up at the protest. It was midnight when they'd rolled in after getting off-shift, all six of them rowdy as shit. Doing riot control always fired them up. Getting screamed at by a bunch of liberals, then the black bloc basement-dwellers sticking around afterwards to call them pigs and use leaf blowers to blow their own CS gas back at them. Every fourth asshole had a press pass, and you had to supposedly leave them alone, even when they got up with their phones right in your face. Kleeman wanted to just roll into the crowd and start swinging.

There was a couple at the window table, and Wiles flashed his badge and told them to beat it. He'd gotten real punchy in the weeks following that thing in the basement. Acting like a dude that had something to prove. Kleeman didn't mind—other cops kept telling him the thing with Malkaley was a clean shoot, that the review board would clear him in a heartbeat. And if, somehow, the DA pressed charges, there wasn't a jury in the world that would convict. But there was a part of Kleeman that liked being around Wiles now, who was acting every inch the loose cannon. Like the fear had gotten to him. Wiles acted like he had a target on his back now, and it took the pressure off Kleeman.

They had another hour before last call, the six of them pounding drinks. Loud, slapping the table, pushing each other around a bit. Some of the guys wore pieces off-shift, and the flashing of their guns in their holsters and their general raucousness cleared that part of the bar out.

It was when they started to talk shit about the DA, and how the DA's office had decided to stop prosecuting misdemeanor arrests during the protests, that Kleeman raised up his hands in resignation and went to take a piss.

As he began blearily making his way along the bar towards the bathroom in the back, he heard Wiles crow, "I just fucking arrest 'em anyway, and make sure they stumble while being detained, you know? Getting 'em in lockup with a bunch of charges, even if they don't stick, gets 'em out of my fucking face, right?"

The bathroom held a toilet and a urinal. A sink covered in stickers. Graffiti everywhere. The din of the bar seeping under the door. Kleeman had started pissing when the door opened, and someone ran his skull into the filthy tilework in front of the urinal. Piss ran down his leg, black stars exploding across his vision. He was tased on the jaw and fell in a heap on the piss-soaked floor, almost biting his tongue in half. He heard the man lock the door from the inside and then Kleeman was lifted up and dragged into the stall, where he was lashed to the toilet tank with duct tape, his face pressed against the plastic seat, arms wrapped around the bowl. Kleeman vomited, IPAs and blood frothing out over his ruined tongue.

"Say his fucking name," the man above him said.

Kleeman gagged in response, an animal sound.

"James Malkaley. Say it."

The man shoved something into Kleeman's jacket and walked out, left him stuck there, the throb of shitkicker music coming in under the door.

●

The mayor was apoplectic and talked about implementing a curfew, but City Council read the wind and shot that down. The DOJ appointed a federal Task Force, a combination of Homeland Security agents and local cops. They combed through footage of the bar and brought in large numbers of leftists and black activists for questioning. It got ugly.

Kleeman and Wiles were present for the interviews, standing there in plainclothes behind one-way glass. The Feds were good at leaning on these people: they kept the pressure on, were matter-of-fact, offering solace in trade for information. Kleeman had been drinking non-stop since the bathroom thing, percolating in a mixture of shame and rage, and his nerves were shot.

"What is this," asked the detective in the interview room, pushing a piece of paper across the table to the kid sitting there. The kid's name was Ragan; he had a number of arrests stemming from protest participation. Leftists considered him a "community leader." The few left-leaning CIs they had on the payroll confirmed he was a shot-caller in black bloc circles. But he also stood about 5'7", with arms that looked like bicycle spokes. No way he could have dragged Kleeman across the bathroom and cinched him up like that.

Ragan peered at the piece of paper. He wasn't handcuffed. They'd picked him up on a bullshit loitering charge and brought him in. He'd so far steadfastly refused to say shit, just demanding that he wanted a lawyer and was choosing not to speak. Kleeman was infuriated by his calmness.

"What is that?" the detective asked again, tapping the piece of paper in front of him.

"I'm not saying a thing."

"You can't read?"

Nothing.

"Where do you think we found that?"

"I want a lawyer," Ragan said. "I'm choosing not to speak."

The detective stood up and picked up the piece of paper, put it in its manila folder. He stepped out and entered the room where the rest of the Task Force stood in front of the glass. "We can hold him for a while longer if you guys want," he said to the feds, "but I don't think he knows anything." He tossed the manila folder on the table.

"They all know each other," Wiles muttered. "All those BLM guys and the fuckin' anarchists. They all share info."

"It's an organized operation," one fed said. "At least three men involved, and probably more. Logistics, all of that. Somebody knows something."

"I think we should be a bit more aggressive," Kleeman offered. "But quietly. Not involving the department."

"I would not be opposed," said the detective after a moment, and the fed nodded in agreement.

Kleeman picked up the folder, looked at the piece of paper the detective had brought in, the one that had been shoved into his pocket in the bar bathroom.

A list of people killed by local cops over the past decade.

It was a long list.

At the end: *James Malkaley.*

The fear in Kleeman started to bloom and take root.

❁

Protests continued; cops in Cincinnati shot some autistic twelve year-old, and then New York cops arrested a seven-year-old girl at school and fractured her wrist. Both of them were black. Streets nationwide heated up all over again.

Kleeman, Wiles, and two feds on the Task Force got in a white van Kleeman had rented from Hertz that afternoon. It was 10 p.m. and the streets downtown already held the distinct tang of tear gas. All four of them were armored up: no badges or names showing, no numbers. They circled the protest, and when they found a lone black bloc kid strutting down the darkened street, all the buildings graffitied and boarded-up around him, Kleeman screeched to a halt and the feds yanked him into the van.

A quick drive to the garage of the Justice Center, a few discreet punches to the kid's face and ears, and they hauled him into another interrogation room. They went through his shit. No ID, no wallet. A backpack full of spray bottles that they used to wash out tear gas from people's eyes. Bandages.

The four of them went into the room where the kid was handcuffed to a chair. They kept their masks on, armor on. The kid was weeping from fear and Kleeman felt strong.

"Who's doing it?" Wiles said, leaning over the kid. "Who made the list?"

The kid sputtered, and one of the feds slapped the table in front of him, making him jump.

"You think you can run us? You think you're in charge?" This was from the other fed. "We run the fucking show. How does twenty years in Guantanamo Bay sound, motherfucker? It can happen in a heartbeat. I say it, it happens."

Kleeman slapped the back of the kid's head and he cried out, and it opened some dam inside of him. He punched the kid in the back of the neck, hard, and then did it again until Wiles and the feds had to drag him back. The four of them stood there, panting, trying to push back against the thing that Kleeman had awakened—the fear that they weren't the ones in charge.

One of the feds took his own sidearm and laid it on the table in front of the weeping kid, who had drool hanging down into his lap. The fed spun the pistol around, and the barrel pointed at the kid's chest.

The fed leaned over the table. "Tell your crew that we are coming," he said quietly. "You're concerned about police violence?" He said it mockingly, sneering under his mask. "The violence hasn't even started."

They put him back in the van and pushed him out at the foot of the Burnside Bridge. They started over the bridge and one of the feds, with the van door still open, threw the kid's backpack into the river below, a dark shape tumbling in an inevitable arc.

❋

Wiles lived in Lake Oswego, a wealthy suburb outside of town. Not many cops actually lived in the city they policed in. Why would Wiles want to live in a shithole? Living among a bunch of lowlifes that he arrested? His place was nice; two bedrooms, a green swath of backyard. Patio with a nice grill set up.

He was divorced, his wife left two years earlier and moved to Bend. She had tried to take the house after claiming he'd beaten her multiple times, but every time a Lake O cop answered the disturbance call, Wiles was able to buddy-talk him out of doing anything, so her lawyer didn't have shit to go on. This was the thing people did not understand—there were cops and there were other people, and cops had a code. Back each other up, no matter what. He and his walked the line every fucking day, and other people just pissed and moaned and watched cop shows.

It was a lazy Sunday afternoon, and Wiles had the next two days off. He was alternating between grilling on the patio and watching the Timbers in the living room. He was wearing shorts and a gray OSU t-shirt and no shoes; the backdoor let in an occasional breeze tinged with charcoal. He and the Task Force guys had a plan to march with the protesters that night and take some photographs, see what they could see. Run any pictures they got against fed databases, slash some tires if any license plates downtown matched names of those associated with antifa or BLM. Just get shit done.

Wiles had a beer bottle in his hand when he stepped back out onto his patio. A man in a balaclava was standing next to his grill. He lifted a shotgun and shot Wiles in the chest with a bean bag round. The projectile hit the beer bottle he was holding and exploded glass into Wiles's face. He screamed and fell back. The shooter rabbited over the fence.

◉

Wiles laid in a bed in the ER, surrounded by uniformed cops, plainclothes detectives, off-duty guys, cursing and ranting in spite of the good dope they gave him. Annoyed nurses pushed their way through blustering men crowded in a too-small space.

Wiles's face was covered in stitches. Frankenstein's monster. He would lose the eye for good, most likely. A bandage and gauze over that half of his face, iodine and blood seeping rust-red through white.

It was an accident. They knew it, they figured it—the bottle had gotten in the way. Otherwise, Wiles would have caught the beanbag round in the chest, and who knows what would have happened after that. Probably more game-playing with the stupid fucking routine these people had started. More duct tape. More interviews, more pieces of paper.

But Wiles had lost an eye, and that changed everything.

Kleeman and the rest of the cops went buck wild that night; the news of Wiles being shot by some black bloc fuckwad ripped through the ranks. They marched and kettled and busted heads. A patrolman named Lee shoved a reporter and she fell backwards and cracked her head against the curb, and when street medics and protestors and legal observers in their stupid fucking green hats showed up, the cops pushed them back as the woman had a seizure. Another cop shot a CS canister from fifteen feet away into someone's hand, shattering four fingers. Buck fucking wild. *Protest injustices*, Kleeman thought, adrenaline coursing through him, sweat roiling inside his body armor, *here's your fucking injustice.* They made mass arrests, entire blocks clouded with tear gas, Kleeman firing less-lethals through the smoke indiscriminately because let's face it—if you're on the street past a certain point, you're one of them and you deserve what you get.

He went to bed that night with adrenaline hammering his veins, getting up three times to do a perimeter of his own house. He lived out in Milwaukee and slept with his Glock on the nightstand and a shotgun under the bed. Got shit sleep, had to be up and at the precinct at 8 the next morning. It sucked, but the protests were fantastic for OT, thank you, James Malkaley. Kleeman never thought about James Malkaley unless someone brought him up, unless he was in front of seemingly endless appointments with the IA review board. But beyond that, never.

But he couldn't stop thinking about the guy in the bathroom, and the way he'd bitten his tongue, the way it hurt to talk for a week afterwards. The helpless feeling of being lashed against the filthy toilet. The way all power had been taken away from him. He'd spent his whole life veering away from that sense of helplessness, had been willing to inflict that helplessness and worse on others so as to not have to feel it himself, and now he felt it like a viral load in his blood. It wouldn't fucking leave him alone, that fear. That lack of power. Checking the windows and doors of his house, it felt like he had a sign on his back.

●

Weeks passed. The protests continued through the fall and, to the surprise of everyone in the department, into the winter. Through the rain, sleet, cold-ass wind knifing through everything, people kept at it. They kept marching. And cops nationwide kept gunning people down, reigniting the rage.

There would be times where Kleeman was holding the line, bristling in his armor, shotgun across his chest, and some citizen would try to *reason* with him, try to get him to understand what they were doing and why they were doing it. He had that vacant stare, Kleeman, that unwillingness to engage. You weren't supposed to talk to them. So he stood there and held the line and listened as these people talked about all the young black men and women killed by cops. Black children killed by cops for running away, for nothing, when mass shooters—always white men—could gun down fifteen people in a Wal-Mart and get arrested, still alive and sieg heiling, and then get taken through a Wendy's drive-thru before they went through booking.

Couldn't he see that disparity? Couldn't he see the different ways black and white folks were treated by police in this country? In this city? Hadn't he seen it himself? How many times had he done a stop and frisk—even if it was called something else—because a black man just had that *look*? Or because he saw a black man hunched down low in a car, the seat pushed back? How often did he pull over white folks for that?

Once, bristling, Kleeman had said, "I'm not a racist," thinking of the other cops he worked with—Lee, who was Asian, and Potter and Jackson, two black cops in his unit. He held the line, seething, trying to tamp the fear down. That sea of angry, hurt faces looking back at him.

❊

For Wiles, winter meant navigating disability offices, doctor's appointments, all the shit that came with it. His face was pockmarked with dozens of tiny scars that showed up only under certain light. He spent a lot of that winter staring in the mirror, trying to discern shapes in the scars, like connecting stars in a constellation. He was trying to get disability payments through work, but he was stunned to find that the legal department was fighting him, saying that, since he wasn't on duty when the shooting took place, they weren't legally obligated to pay out his disability.

"I got shot because I was a cop," Wiles told his union rep over the phone. "I was targeted."

"I hear you," his rep said. "It's bullshit. We'll raise hell, son. This'll go to the Supreme Court if it has to."

He discovered that he missed the city. The din and clamor of it. The sense of closeness, the world pressed in like that. It came as a surprise, and he found himself taking the bus downtown a few days a week, walking around. Sleep was a joke, and he hoped to tire himself out. Maybe it was a kind of mourning, really. His old life decimated, and he was raking through the ashes. He'd sometimes walk by the precinct on his way to one appointment or another and occasionally another cop walking by would recognize him in his plainclothes and dark glasses. The cop would do a double take so minute as to be almost imperceptible. But Wiles always saw. Even with one eye, he still caught that look.

He'd pass through the corridor of downtown where the protests still happened every night. Once he found a blackened tear gas canister in the gutter. He resisted the urge to pick it up.

He walked and walked and thought of the bullet they had put in his mouth those months back. *We're done with this shit.* He thought of the list they had put in Kleeman's pocket, and how Kleeman had looked at him since losing his eye.

Like Wiles was some weak link. Like it was his fault the bottle had exploded in his face.

Like he was lesser than, now that he wasn't a cop.

Walking across the bridge, the river below was a loveless steel gray. Gunmetal gray. He remembered the kid's backpack they'd hurled into the water. The inevitable arc of it.

The list had had so many names on it. Malkaley was the last, but there had been so many before, and some since, too. Entire columns. All these young black and brown men and women—children—lives stopped at the hands of cops like him. Lives ended, like shutting a book.

He walked the city endlessly with his one eye, the breadth and knowledge of what he had been a part of slowly beginning to unfold in front of him.

One January day he was crossing an overpass, the throaty bellow of I-5 below him, chin tucked down against the knifing cold, when someone called his name.

Wiles began to turn.

He felt someone touch his arm.

A bag was thrown over his head. He was pulled into a van.

The van took off, and in the dark Wiles was yelling, saying he wasn't a cop anymore, they didn't need to do this, he wasn't a cop.

"We know," someone said. "That's why you're here."

The van turned.

"Wiles," the voice said, "let's talk."

"A system cannot fail
those it was never built
to protect."

-Vann Newkirk

7

"*Lie to me*, those eyebrows seemed to dare. *Either way, I'll get a warrant and I'm going to come in.*"

C.C. + Joy

Tim P. Walker

The moment she stepped off the elevator, Joy heard the squawk of their walkie-talkies echoing from somewhere around the corner; a din of distorted, disembodied voices—their language a jumble of numbers and code words. By the noise alone, Joy figured that they had to have been two-thirds of the way down the hall, twenty-five paces from the elevator and squarely in front of the door to Room BL2 in Calvary Hall.

Her and C.C.'s room.

Shit, she mouthed as she froze. She closed her eyes, and her mind floated down the corridor, under her door, and into a desk drawer where she kept her stash—stems and seeds mostly—and a little stained-glass pipe that she meant to soak in a dishpan filled with soapy water. They smelled it. They must've. They had to be there for some reason, and they didn't seem to be leaving, either. Of course not. It was the one thing she learned listening to Grateful Dead lyrics—cops don't simply scamper off. Threats always lurk behind their maws to make you sit while they wait for a piece of paper that says they're free to pick your world apart. If they got a warrant, they're going to go in.

She took a deep breath and turned the corner.

They were standing exactly where she thought they'd be. Louder and more distorted, the radios clipped to their shoulders howled like a pair of hawks squabbling over prey. Head down, Joy pressed onward—no sense in turning around. The cops stared at her silently, their eyes as cold and rigid as their dark blue uniforms. Pitched stripes and patches embroidered with a silhouette of the campus chapel steeple adorned their sleeves. Their belts bulged with long clubs and flashlights. One of them was mostly bald with a brown furry caterpillar for a mustache perched on his face, its weight bending his lips into a permanent scowl. The other looked like a middle-aged Boy Scout. His complexion was bright, his face clean shaven, and he had the kind of haircut—parted, swept, gelled—that reminded her of that Jesus creep she ran into at the mini-mart next to the laundromat, the one who wore a plain white button-up shirt with a stop-sign-colored name plate over his breast pocket who'd trapped her for twenty minutes between the potato chip rack and the Gatorade cooler, pelting her with promises of salvation until she agreed to come to his church that Sunday afternoon.

Fishing her keys from her pocket, Joy kept her head lowered and forced a smile as she passed through their shadows. The cops towered over her. That creep at the mini-mart towered over her, too. Were they going to quote scripture and tell her how pretty her brown eyes were as well? The key was in the lock and the doorknob was half-turned when a hand landed on her shoulder.

"Pardon me, young lady," the haircut said. The name plate under his badge was slate black and read SHEPARD. "We're looking for Cassandra Canali. Are you her?"

Joy stood frozen with half an eye on the hand still on her shoulder and the man it belonged to.

"Cassandra Canali?"

"That's not her," the cop with the mustache mumbled. His name plate read DOBBINS.

"But she does sleep here, right?" asked Shepard.

Joy felt a tiny spark flicker in the back of her throat, and a tear formed in the corner of her eye as she fought the need to cough it out. Dobbins leaned in, his nostril hairs sticking out over his moustache.

"C.C.?" Joy managed to say. "She's my roommate."

"Is that what she goes by?" Shepard said. "I guess that's who we're looking for. She in? We've been knocking on this door for some time now."

"I don't think so," Joy answered sheepishly, her voice quivering.

"You should check first," Dobbins grunted, nodding at the door.

The burn in Joy's throat returned. She glanced down at her own hand wrapped around the doorknob, unmoving.

"Go on," Dobbins pressed, his voice coarse and curt.

Shepard lifted his hand to his partner. "What we mean to say is: Mind opening your door so we can be sure?" He gave a stiff nod of his own, as if to insist that he wasn't actually asking.

Her hands were already shaking as she finished turning the knob, so when the walkie-talkies suddenly screeched, every nerve in her body scattered in a million directions at once. Dobbins chuckled under his breath as the cops turned down the volume on their devices.

The room was empty—nothing stirring but dust mites dancing in a broken beam of sunlight streaming through the window. The red shag throw rug laid out in the middle of speckled gray tiles of cold linoleum made for a crowded dance floor.

Shepard ran his eyes all over the room—four cinderblock walls painted a fleshy color, two single beds, two dressers, two desks in each far corner, a bookshelf under a high window adorned with books and a small stereo, and two walk-in closets near the door, each with a body-length mirror echoing the dim emptiness of the room.

"Okay," Shepard said. "What time does she get back?"

Joy, still shaking, answered with a shrug.

Shepard glanced at the dry erase board clinging to the door just below the peephole and the room number. Scrawled at the top in marker: *C.C. + Joy.* "How about...," he started to say before his eyes darted between the board and Joy's chest.

"You must really be into bears, huh?" he asked.

For a moment, Joy forgot that the stickers running along the board's edges were the same daisy-chain of smiling rainbow-colored bears dancing across the front of her sky-blue tie-dye t-shirt, peeking out from underneath an unzipped navy-hued hoodie. "Oh yeah," she said. "Bears."

"What do those mean anyway?" Shepard asked, a sharp glint forming in his eye.

"Mean?" Joy said as a chill ran through her blood.

"Yeah, I see a lot of shirts with those bears on them. Kinda wondering what they're all about."

"I've seen them around, too," Dobbins added, crossing his arms. "Seen them stuck to the window of that one shop a few blocks over on Union Street. You know what shop I'm talking about."

Joy swallowed her tongue and felt herself shrink. The shop happened to be the very place she bought that stained glass pipe, the one she meant to clean.

Shepard grinned. "Just curious if the bears had any meaning is all," he said.

He knew of course. He couldn't have spent any amount of time patrolling a college campus without knowing what they were and the kind of students that wore them. But this was the game these guys play. *Lie to me*, those eyebrows seemed to dare. *Either way, I'll get a warrant and I'm going to come in.*

"It's . . . a Grateful Dead shirt," she answered wearily. "I like their music. That's all."

Dobbins shook his head and smirked. His moustache seemed to cross its own arms and smirk along with him.

"Of course," Shepard said with a wink. "Do us a favor then and jot down a note for your roommate." He gestured to the marker dangling from a string on the white board. Squinting at the writing just below the bear stickers—"Joy, right? Well, Joy, tell Cassandra to call either Sergeant Shepard or Sergeant Dobbins at Campus Police as soon as she can." He slowly spelled out both of their names, and Joy pretended not to have noticed their name plates.

They were just about to leave when she felt that spark tickling her throat. "Is C.C. in trouble?" she asked. For a moment, she thought she made a mistake when Shepard turned around and stared back at her.

"You ought to talk to your roommate about that," he eventually said. Neither of the cops said another word as they walked down the hall toward the elevator, the linoleum floor crunching under their footsteps as their walkie-talkies chirped to each other.

As soon as they were out of sight, Joy licked her thumb and wiped their names and the phone number from the white board. She'd tell C.C. herself. The rest of the floor didn't need to know their business.

She never went to that creep's church either.

⬤

It was nearly an hour later when C.C. scurried into the room, her backpack clutched to her chest. She was wearing the same baggy overalls she had on the day before and those thick-framed glasses she usually only wore late at night or those few Sunday afternoons when she was nursing a massive hangover.

Joy was sitting cross-legged on her bed, elbow deep in the Crusades section of her Western Civ textbook. She barely had a moment to set it down and say hello before C.C. blew across the room and switched out a book from the shelf for one in her bag.

"C.C., wait," Joy called out before her roommate could slip out the door again. C.C. stopped and half-turned her head.

"There were a couple cops here a little while ago." Campus cops, she clarified, not townies, though she did forget their names. "They told me to tell you to call them or something. Wouldn't say what it was . . ."

But C.C. was already gone.

Joy didn't see her again until after her evening classes. She looked for her in their favored section of the dining hall because it was Monday, and Monday was one of the days when C.C.'s off-campus gig working the cash register at Target didn't get in the way of them eating dinner together. But she was nowhere to be found.

Back in the room, Joy was piecing together notes for a Poli-Sci paper and losing herself in an everlasting piano solo on a Phish bootleg when C.C. returned, backpack clutched to her chest like it was earlier.

"Hey," Joy said, turning in her chair to face her roommate. Her roommate barely managed to move her lips to greet her back, but Joy saw the dark spots hidden behind C.C.'s glasses and realized that the backpack was far from the heaviest thing she was carrying.

C.C. dropped her bag in her desk chair and turned for the exit. For a moment, Joy thought she would vanish again; instead, C.C. opened her closet door and shut herself inside for a few minutes. When she emerged, she'd ditched her overalls for a tightly tied furry bathrobe the color of midnight. Shower caddy in hand, slippers on her feet, she stepped out of the room again and crossed the hall to the bathroom.

Joy felt that sting in her throat again, and it couldn't be coughed away. Nor could the itch in her eye be blinked out. The piano was still playing, but it no longer sounded like it was playing for her, so she turned the tape off and sat in silence. Just a week before, while Joy was listening to a Spanish language tape for a class assignment, C.C. found a whitehead on her rear. Instead of popping it, she took a blue ink pen and drew a nose and a mouth around it to make it look like a tiny face with one bulging eye growing out of her ass. She decided the tiny face needed to speak in a deep voice and roll its r's like Ramon Azteca. "You're a beautiful woman," the zit cooed as C.C. wiggled it in Joy's face. "I want for you to squeeze me 'til I go *pop*. Squeeeeze meeeeee!" it sang. Joy laughed and smacked her roommate's bare ass until the girl pulled up her sweatpants and carried her zit away to put it out of its misery.

Now C.C. was undressing in the closet, the campus cops were looking for her, and Joy just didn't know what anymore.

⬤

The next morning was quiet. Tuesdays usually were, especially in the fall and particularly on days that were gray and chilly. But silence hung around Joy like she'd spent an evening guzzling twelve glasses of it. C.C. was still in bed when Joy left for her early class, and unless the girl got up sometime in the dark of night, that would've made eleven whole hours she'd been asleep. After her shower the night before, C.C. slid right under her bed covers without uttering a single word to Joy. Joy quietly studied for another two hours before she turned in herself.

Coming back from class, Joy figured C.C. would be awake, but she wouldn't have expected her to be making the kind of noise that was echoing into the hall from their open door as she rounded the corner from the elevator. It didn't sound like any kind of music she'd play. It didn't sound like music at all. As Joy got closer, she recognized the squawk of disembodied voices and she realized who was in there. She walked faster; her mind skipped past her stash, past her pipe. She found her roommate sitting on her bed, clutching a pillow like it was the mast of a sinking sailboat. The mustache cop, Dobbins, stood by the window near Joy's desk. The one with hair like that creep, Shepard, sat on the edge of the other bed—Joy's bed—his hands on his knees.

He spotted Joy in the hall and gave her smile. "Come on in," he said, patting a spot next to himself on her bed. He then stood. "It's okay. You're not in any trouble. We do have a couple of questions we'd like to ask you, though."

Joy pulled the straps of her backpack tight as she hesitantly stepped into the room. "C.C., you okay?" she asked. Her roommate cast her eyes to the floor and gripped her pillow tighter.

"She's okay," Shepard answered. "Like I said, nobody's in trouble. Go on. Have a seat."

Joy did, and she could still feel the cop's body heat radiating from the spot on the blanket where his ass just was. He stood in the space between the beds, hands folded, seeming to hold back the light peeking through the window.

"Since you're here, Joy, I'll go ahead and ask," Shepard started. "Have you borrowed any of Cassandra —sorry, C.C.'s—clothing since Saturday night?"

The question was odd enough without having to listen to C.C.'s meek whine. Did they find a baggie in the pocket of something in her laundry? Was C.C. trying to pin it on her? What were they doing going through her laundry in the first place? Anyway, the only piece of C.C.'s clothing that Joy ever borrowed C.C.

was already wearing—those same baggy overalls she'd been wearing since Sunday. Shepard kept his gaze fixed on Joy, awaiting an answer.

"I . . . don't think so. What is this about?"

"So you haven't borrowed any of your roommate's clothing since Saturday night?"

"Stop it please," C.C. moaned.

Over by the window, Dobbins craned his neck to glance at the assorted bric-a-brac adorning the shelf above Joy's desk. He reached to pick up a piece: a small, stained wood box with a rose carved into its lid. Seeing this, Joy spoke up, her voice trembling, "Excuse me, sir, could you please be careful with that? That was my grandmother's."

"Joy," Shepard jumped in, snapping his fingers inches from Joy's face. "I need you to focus." Behind him, Dobbins cracked the lid and passed it under his nose. If old jewelry had an odor, it would've had its work cut out for it. The string of ash from the last burned stick of incense still sat in the wooden tray atop the bookshelf next to the nosy cop.

"Like I said," Shepard went on, "nobody's in trouble, but we have to be certain . . ."

"Stop!" C.C. spat as she lifted her head, her eyes glowing red through the lenses of her glasses. "Just leave her alone. I know where they are, okay? Please."

"So you do know where your clothes are," Dobbins pounced, slapping Joy's grandmother's box down next to the incense tray, knocking ash onto the shelf. "A minute ago you said you didn't."

"I just . . ." C.C. dropped her head again and squeezed her pillow. "I forgot."

Grinning, Shepard held his hand up to Dobbins. "All right, Rick, take it easy. Cassandra—C.C., I mean—would you mind grabbing them for us, please?"

C.C. let her pillow fall to the floor as she stood and stomped three paces to her closet door. She pushed past the half-stuffed mesh bag of dirty laundry hanging from the door hook, and, instead of closing the door behind her, dropped to her knees, and crawled further in. The sound of crumpled plastic echoed from the closet and for a moment it fought with the radios, both of which started crowing at once. When C.C. crawled out again, she had a large, mostly empty black kitchen-size trash bag tucked under her arm. Sneering, she dropped it on her bed and threw a cold look which Dobbins seemed to snatch out of midair.

"Hey, listen to me!" he snarled, throwing a finger at her from across the room. "You better adjust that attitude. I don't know what you think entitles you to act like that, but this is serious. Those accusations you made—those are serious. We're talking about someone's damn life here. Do you understand?"

"Take it easy, Rick" Shepard, still grinning, cut in. "Cassandra, it's great that you bagged your clothes for us, but we've got our own bags here that we use, so we're gonna need you to take them out."

Joy felt that scratch in her voice again. She could feel herself speaking her roommate's name, but not a sound came from her own mouth as C.C. opened the trash bag and dumped a t-shirt and skirt on her mattress. Shepard unfurled what looked like a Ziploc freezer bag and held it open.

"What I need you to do is fold up that shirt and slide it on in this bag."

C.C. stretched out her shirt, a pale blue number, and began to fold it, sleeves first.

Dobbins scoffed as he read the graphic aloud—the letters S-E-X-I spelled out across a wavy red, white, blue soda can logo. "Unbelievable. And yet it's always a mystery how . . ." The moustache seemed to clamp his lips shut at that moment and he shrugged it off.

She finished folding the shirt and stuck it in Shepard's bag. "Jeez," he said, "I think we might be able to fit that other piece in here as well. What do you think?"

She sighed and picked up the skirt, a denim number with a frayed hem.

"Hold on," Dobbins jumped in, the moustache twitching. "Why don't you hold that up against your waist for me a second."

C.C. didn't answer.

"Let me see it," he pressed, stepping closer. "You did it in the mirror at the Gap or wherever you bought the damn thing from, right?"

C.C. shook her head and muttered a curse to herself. Slouching, she slapped the skirt against her front.

"Goddamn," Dobbins snorted, "that is short. You musta been freezing in that thing."

"Language, Rick," Shepard told his partner, but then he clicked his tongue and shook his head. "No, that's not her Sunday best though." He shook the bag and C.C. quickly folded the skirt and tossed it in.

"What are we missing?" he asked.

C.C. sniffed and shrugged, but he asked again.

Joy tried to think back a few nights herself, but everything in that bag was everything C.C. had on when they left the room Saturday night except for a pair of sandals. She even remembered C.C. chattering her teeth loudly and rubbing her arms for warmth as they walked across campus.

"Undies?" Shepard asked. "Panties? Bra? Did you wear any of those?"

C.C. wrapped her arms around herself tight and pressed her legs together. Hanging her head, she said she didn't know.

"You don't know if you were wearing undies or not?"

"She was," Joy tried to say. She remembered full well. They were passing Joy's pipe between each other and listening to Bob Marley's "Three Little Birds" while C.C. danced around in a pair of panties and that SEXI top, scrunching her face at Joy. *What do ya think?* C.C. had asked, snapping the elastic band of the lilac cotton panties dotted with tiny teddy bears. *Too baby? Too slutty? What?*

Who's going to be looking at them? was Joy's response as she blew a plume of smoke up at the open window.

"I must've lost them," C.C. told the cops.

"Lost them? Lost them where? Alpha Theta house? Here?"

"Couldn't have lost anything at that Alpha house," Dobbins said. "I checked Corey's room. I checked the common area. I didn't find anything there that wasn't theirs."

"Well, think maybe you weren't wearing any undies?" Shepard asked, eyebrows raised, thumbs hooked to his belt.

"But she was," Joy spoke, her voice a tiny squeak.

Shepard barely looked at Joy as he held a finger up to shush her.

But that finger couldn't scratch the itch in her throat, which burned like it was being tickled with a lit match. Trapped in her windpipe, the damn thing was threatening to sear a hole straight through her neck, and there was nothing she could do but spit it out.

"She was wearing them!" she spat, the words tasting like ice water. "I know she was. I swear I saw them on her." Dobbins tried to jump in, but she kept on repeating what she saw, several times over and louder with each word.

"What does it matter anyway? It's not like it's anybody's business what she's wearing under her clothes!" Joy wailed. "And what difference does it make how short her clothes are? What difference? That's nobody's business either. And you haven't even said what the fuck you need her clothes for anyway."

"Hey!" Dobbins snapped, cracking his moustache like a bullwhip. "Watch your mouth."

Joy wouldn't stop. She turned to her roommate, who stood rocking on her feet, face buried in her hands. "C.C., I'm sorry, I don't know what happened. I really don't. Whatever it was, whatever it is, it's just—it wasn't your fault, okay? It can't be your fault. Please."

"Look, girls," Shepard cut in, "we've got a job to do here, so . . ."

Joy couldn't stop. The itch hadn't receded either; it merely spread to a spot in the back of her eye sockets. "C.C., you really should've told me," she said, her voice creaking as her roommate bent over and dropped to her knees. "I don't know what I could've done. I don't. But please, if you just tell me, I'm sure I can help you. I'm sure I can do something to make it better. I just . . ."

"Girls . . ." Shepard said.

"I don't know what I can do to help you," Joy growled, "but I do know it'd be a lot fucking more than what these . . ." The word *assholes* danced on her tongue. She didn't say it, but the cops smelled it on her breath anyway.

"Enough!" Dobbins barked. "I'm not asking you again."

"No, it's okay," Shepard said. He reached into his back pocket and pulled out a notepad. "Tell you what, Joy—since you're up for it, I do have a couple of questions for you." He plucked a click pen from his breast pocket.

He asked about the party at the Alpha Theta house. He asked if she went, and she admitted that she did. He asked if she went with her roommate, and she said yes to that, too. The place was crowded though, the loud club music gave her a headache, and she worried that if she bent over at any point to wipe the spilled beer from her sandals, she'd get trampled. By that point, she'd already lost C.C. in the crowd. So she told Shepard that she left alone.

"You mean you abandoned her?" Shepard asked, looking down at her over the spiral binding of his notepad. He clicked his pen twice, and the sound of it made Joy feel like it was stabbing the back of her tongue through her chin.

"No, it wasn't like that. I . . ."

"Well, both of you went together, and then you left by yourself—what do you call that?"

"I . . ."

Shepard clicked his pen a few more times, and Joy felt her tongue twisting around it like a spit over the hot coals coating her throat.

"That's not right!" Joy cried, and the heat from her throat was starting to make her eyes sweat. "How can it be my fucking fault?"

"Hey!" Dobbins growled. "I told you to watch your mouth." He pushed past Shepard and leaned over Joy, his nostrils leading the charge. "What, you think we can't smell it on you? I know you're hiding dope in here, girlie. You know we could tear this whole room apart if we wanted to. We could make life hell for you and her. You wanna know why? Because whatever we find in here is on both of you. You know that? You learn that in any of your classes? Any of your doper hippie friends ever tell you that?"

"Easy, Rick, we got what we need," Shepard said as he shook the Ziploc bag.

Dobbins turned and stood over C.C., who was still crouched next to her bed and peering through her fingers between sobs. "Corey Stone's a good kid. Heck of a ball player, too. He could go pro from what I hear. But you two don't even pay attention to any of that, do you? Do you know when the last time this school—your school—had someone make it to the pros? And the team he's on right now—they need him, too. They're playing Antioch in four days. How do you think he's gonna play with this thing hanging over his head? Huh? You want to screw that up for him? For the whole damn team?"

"Listen, Cassandra," Shepard cut in, "you ever go to church? Do either of you ever go to church? I know Corey Stone does. I see him there every Sunday. This very church." He tapped the embroidered steeple on his shoulder patch. "The one here on campus. He was there this past Sunday as a matter of fact, the night after you said he . . . Well . . ."

"Well, we know she wasn't in any church," Dobbins spat, pointing down to C.C. "She was up at the station. Weren't you? And this one . . ." He flicked a sneer at Joy, and she could feel every whisker on his lip fan the flames in her throat. "You don't go to church either, do you?"

"Easy, Rick," Shepard said, stepping in, folding his hands as he stood over C.C. and Joy. "Look, girls, if you knew anything about the Bible, you'd know that it teaches a thing or two about forgiveness. Cassandra, I don't know what happened between you and Corey. I don't." He lifted his hand like he was reaching to heaven. "But I know God would want you to forgive him for whatever you think his trespasses may be. And you know what? We might just cut you two a break and forgive whatever it is you guys have done in here, too. That sound fair?"

He nodded at both roommates, but neither of them said a word.

"Okay, we'll leave you two to think about it." He held up the Ziploc bag stuffed with C.C.'s clothes. "We're going to hold on to these for now. We're not going to send them off to the lab quite yet." He gave C.C. the side eye as he breezed past her. "Just in case you come to Jesus on this one."

Casting the parting glare, Dobbins followed Shepard out. As their footsteps receded, the cops' radios cackled their victory song in numbers and code words, the Lord's work done. C.C. curled up on the cold linoleum floor and chucked her pillow at the door to shut them all out.

Joy opened her mouth to speak, to tell C.C. that she was there, and she could reach out to her, and that she didn't need to worry and everything would be all right. But the fire in Joy's throat snuffed out, and she couldn't find the words in the ashes. And she never realized how wide it was in that room and how bitter the cold that radiated off the floor was until she stretched her hand out to her roommate.

C.C. was too far out of reach.

◉

The ball team beat Antioch the following weekend. They went on to play in some national tournament, and they even won a few rounds before getting knocked out the second weekend of December. Or so Joy heard. By then, C.C.'s belongings had long been packed up and cleared out of Room BL2. Joy came back from the brief Thanksgiving break to find half the room barren—the bed stripped, drawers empty, the desk bare. The throw rug remained, stretched across the middle of the icy floor, staring at the emptiness like an orphaned critter hoping against hope for its mother's return.

Joy expected to be assigned another roommate by the next semester, but C.C.'s side stood barren through half of February. Around Valentine's Day, she brought in a few blankets and a stack of pillows just to have something taking up space, generating warmth. The room stayed chilly straight through April. By May, Joy packed up her own things, then she left, too, and never looked back.

She left the message board on the door until then, and it still read *C.C. + Joy* just in case her roommate ever found her way back to the nest. But Joy never did see her again.

"Most middle-class whites have no idea what it feels like to be subjected to police who are routinely suspicious, rude, belligerent, and brutal. "

-Benjamin Spock

8

"Cops hate prophets. Always have. They arrested Jesus, for God's sake. What will they do to a man like him? Oh, right, they'll put his head on a silver platter."

The Prophet

Travis Wade Beaty

"Only a killer can hunt a killer. Are you emotionally, spiritually, psychologically prepared to snuff out a human life in defense of innocent lives? If you can't make that decision, you need to find another job."
—Lt. Col. Dave Grossman, Ohio police training seminar

Sadie rummages through the drawer next to the refrigerator in search of the kitchen timer, but instead finds Peyton's medicine box. Shoot! It's full of pills he ought to have taken all week. Oh, but this is not the end of the world. He's gone off before, and she's convinced him to get back on. Although, it takes so much nagging. He won't go along unless she presses and chides and bothers and perhaps refuses to make him dinner. He's like a rusted-out tin man who needs a bunch of oil in his joints and a swift kick in the rear to get on down that yellow brick road, but he does go eventually and with a big heart. He's her boy and so that's her job: to nag.

Not today, though. Today is his birthday so she won't hassle him about a thing.

She drops the pillbox back in the drawer and slides it shut. Out of sight, out of mind. Right now, she needs to find the timer so this cake doesn't burn. She's making his favorite: a yellow cake with chocolate frosting. She tries to keep him away from treats because he's gotten too big, but today is his 30th birthday, and that ought to be a big deal, so, by God, she's gonna make it a big deal.

First, they'll go for lunch at that Mexican place even though she can't afford it. And then they are going to the movies even though she absolutely cannot afford that either. She's going to let him choose the movie and she's not going to complain when it's full of gratuitous nudity and morons running around blowing everything up.

Now if she can only find the kitchen timer. Boy, she's made an absolute mess of the kitchen. She forgot all that goes into baking a cake. Did she really need to use so many mixing bowls?

She hears Peyton thumping up the basement steps and wonders if those poor creaking planks might give way soon. No, she's not going to complain about his weight or scold him for smoking or even look worried if he brings up the bugs.

✲

Peyton is aware that someone might see him in this state, red-faced, sweating, tearing the kitchen apart, and get the wrong idea. They might think he is Captain Ahab, come up in a fresh rage from his cabin to pursue vengeance on that which will consume him. But Peyton does not read *Moby Dick* for the white whale. He reads it for the sea. He reads it to feel the oar in his well-calloused hands, to feel the stinging spray of saltwater on his sunbaked face, to strain all the sinews of his body as he and his fellow whalemen thrust their boat through the boundless brine.

Also, there are no bugs when he reads. He woke up thinking about them and reached for his book, but it wasn't on his bedside table. Where the hell is it?

His mother looks at him and smiles as if she is not worried, but her eyes give her away. He is not Captain Ahab, and he has explained to her many times that he is not the man possessed by Legion. He is John the Baptist. He brings news! His head is possessed not by minions of The Enemy, but by a burning bush, a flickering flame that foretells the coming of a new breed of insect, worse than locusts; in great swarms, they fall on the cities of the north, working their way down from Canada, consuming everything in their path. He and his mother, and everyone in the town ought to move, ought to go south, away from the advancing swarms.

But he can't make himself understood. Every John needs a Jesus, a prophet who can speak truth to men's hearts, but, alas, Peyton stands alone, drifting in a stagnant sea, peering into the glare of the horizon hoping to search out a like-minded sail and finding only The Enemy, circling like a host of sharks.

And now they've taken his book. He had it last night before bed but now it's vanished. Damn it!

And why is the kitchen so cluttered, anyway? What in the devil has his mother gotten up to? Has she lost her mind? There's, like, every mixing bowl in the house out and some kind of white powder covering everything. How is he supposed to find anything in this mess? And, on top of everything, she hasn't even made coffee.

His ears buzz. Or is that the insects buzzing? How far away are they? And why are they so against *Moby Dick*? Is it the language? Do they, like his mother, take issue with so many chapters void of plot? A fair critique, but it's not about the plot, and he never demanded they read it. Melville is not for everyone. Why couldn't the bugs leave it be? They despise the sea, don't they? And why not? Its capricious breezes do merrily toss insects over to high-reaching waves, dampening their paper-thin wings, and leaving them to flitter miserably into the salty abyss where they become morsels for a vast and hungry host of ever-searching mouths.

Hark! Here is a prophecy: an ocean. Aye! He needs a shovel! A shovel and a garden hose!

✳

Sadie stands in the corner of the kitchen and watches as Peyton knocks mixing bowls off the counter and kicks over the trash can. A newly lit cigarette hanging from his mouth bobs up and down and sends thin tendrils of smoke swirling through the air. He can't find his book. She curses herself for not splurging to buy a spare copy. But it's such a big book. How could he lose it?

"No, coffee?" he asks, a slight whine in his voice. He's flinging open all the cabinets and sliding dishes around. He hasn't even said good morning to her, doesn't even seem to notice she was doing something unusual in the kitchen, something special.

She wants to say, "Really, Peyton, you think you need caffeine in this state?" But she bites her tongue.

Peyton picks up the pile of mail on the kitchen table for the third time to see if his book is underneath and starts to moan. Off his meds and moaning. This is bad. She wishes she could hold him in her arms and rock him back and forth. When he was little, he used to want hugs all the time. He was such a big, cuddly chunk of a boy. Not fat, just a little chunky. And he had all the hugs in the world for her. But she can't touch him now. He's all grown-up and doesn't like to be touched, especially when he's anxious.

One time, he had said her hugs felt like prison. She had thought that had been one of the meanest things anyone had ever said to her. She had gotten bitter and said, "You'd be in real prison if it weren't for me."

He'd said, "I'm sorry mom, I love you, but no hugs right now," and then he'd wept in his hands and she'd felt miserable.

She takes a deep breath and begins to tidy up behind him, picking up the trash can, closing the kitchen drawers, re-organizing the mail, praying she'll chance upon the book and end this tantrum.

"Stay here," Peyton says. "I have to go to the shed. Don't follow. Stay inside."

Oh crap, he's got an idea. That's worse than a tantrum because now he'll start doing things. Doing things gets him in trouble.

When he's outside, making a clatter in the shed, she calls the county mental health crisis hotline—just for peace of mind. They explain that she would need a court order to admit him. Of course, yes, she knows that. But it won't come to that.

They ask if Sadie is in danger.

"No, no," she says. "Is Dr. Wexler available? She was so good with him."

They explain Peyton would need to be admitted to talk to Dr. Wexler. Yes, yes, of course. She thanks the crisis hotline, hangs up and takes the non-emergency police number from its magnet on the fridge. Peyton, after much cursing in the shed, emerges with a shovel. He's somehow got a cut on his forehead which is bleeding down the side of his face.

"Peyton, baby," Sadie shouts out the kitchen window, "You're hurt, come in here."

"Are you in danger, ma'am?" the dispatcher asks. She can't remember dialing the number.

"Oh, no," she says, "I don't think so."

"Are you sure?"

She walks down the hall to look out the front screen door. Peyton has the garden hose. He's spraying the yard with it.

"He's, no, he's just . . ."

"I can send an officer."

She hangs up and runs out the front door to wipe Peyton's head with a wet rag.

"Peyton, baby, you're hurt. Come in. Stop that and come in."

"Hold on, Ma." He continues dousing the front lawn with the hose. He gestures at his cigarette, a new one that he's somehow managed to light in the midst of his mania, as if the cigarette will explain everything. She stands on her tip-toes and wipes the blood off his head.

"You need a band-aid for that. Come on inside. I'm baking a cake. We're going to go to that Mexican place and the movies. And then we can come home and eat the cake."

"We can't afford a restaurant," he says. He throws the hose down and picks up the shovel. He stabs the grass with it and pulls up a clod of dirt.

"We'll be fine," Sadie says, trying to keep the warble out of her throat as she watches him dig. He could tear up the whole yard if he had a mind to, couldn't he?

"It's your birthday, you know?"

"It is?"

"Yes, you silly goose, now come on inside. You're ruining the yard."

"Just let me finish this smoke, okay?"

"Is this about your book? I'll find your book, okay? It's in the house some-where."

"They took it," he says, his voice rising and incredulous.

"Who took it, baby?"

She notices Cynthia Miller standing on her front porch across the street in a purple house dress. She's got that same old scowl set in that same old wrinkled face. She's staring at Peyton, her cordless phone gripped in both hands.

"He's okay," Sadie yells out. "We're gonna head out in a minute. We're going to the movies! He's just getting something out of his system. He's okay."

Cynthia doesn't say anything. A few months ago, Peyton knocked on her door to warn her about the bugs. He didn't go into her house or anything. Nothing worse than what a Jehovah's Witness might do, and Cynthia had tried to file a restraining order. The judge threw it out of court, thank God.

"Don't need to call anybody, Cynthia," Sadie yells out. "He's okay."

"He came over here and sprayed my yard again," Cynthia yells.

"Protects against the bugs," Peyton yells back.

"He's just trying to be helpful," Sadie says. "But, Peyton, don't mess with their grass, okay? You just keep it in our yard."

Cynthia shuffles back into her house.

"Peyton," Sadie says. "You need to get back inside, baby. You're still bleeding."

He ignores her and begins filling the long shallow trench he has dug with water.

Okay. Get a bandage for his head. Find the book. He'll go back to reading and they can go out to lunch. Just need to find the book.

●

"Remain humble and compassionate; be professional and courteous—and have a plan to kill everyone you meet."
—John Bennett, patrol lieutenant, Charleston (IL) Police Department, "How Command Presence Affects Your Survival"

"What are you doing there?" a man says. He has materialized out of thin air, perhaps fallen straight out of the sky. The man is a cop, short and compact, with a buzz cut and a triangle for a nose. His hands are on his belt as if to signify this is the most important thing about him.

"What am I doing?" Peyton says, trying to stay calm. Cops hate prophets. Always have. They arrested Jesus, for God's sake. What will they do to a man like him? Oh, right, they'll put his head on a silver platter.

"Making an ocean," Peyton says.

"An ocean?"

"Yeah."

The cop slides one hand around his belt with mechanical precision until it's resting on a holster. Peyton admires the amount of detail put into this well-oiled automaton. But who would send such a thing? Who would want to stop his ocean-making?

"How did you get that wound?" The cop asks as he points to Peyton's head.

Peyton feels his forehead. He pulls back his hand and is surprised to see his fingers are slick with bright red blood. He smiles at this trick. Here is The Enemy at work. Here is when Peyton is meant to be intimidated and shaken from his path. But the wound is nothing. Peyton knows men are made of more than flesh and blood.

"Can you put the hose down and step over to the sidewalk?" the cop asks.

"Why?"

"I'm asking you to put your hose down and step to the sidewalk."

"I don't want to."

❋

Sadie gives all glory to God as she finds Peyton's hardcover. Her blessed cookbook was sitting on top of it the whole time! *Moby Dick, or The Whale* is so worn out it nearly splits at the spine as she picks it up.

"Peyton!" she yells. "I found it. I found your book!"

She can smell the cake's about to burn and so drops the book, grabs the potholder, swings open the oven door, takes the cake out and, wow, it's perfect, with the steam rising off and the sweet golden aroma filling the room. She'll cool it in the fridge and ice it when they get back from lunch and a movie. Peyton needs to get in here and clean himself up so they can go.

"Peyton!" she shouts. "Get in here! I found your book!"

❋

"Put the hose down and put your hands in the air. I need your hands up."

The cop is talking too fast. Talking like a crazy person.

Peyton drops the hose and watches to be sure the water continues to fall from its mouth into the trench he dug. He's made a little ocean of salvation, just big enough for him to lie down in when the bugs descend.

"Keep your hands up! Do you have any weapons on you?"

"I have a pen I take notes with."

"Don't reach in your pocket! Keep your hands up. Right now, I'm going to search you for weapons, okay?"

Peyton puts his hands up. "Okay."

The cop comes over and does not search Peyton for weapons. He takes Peyton's hands and pulls them down behind his back.

"Are you arresting me?"

"Hold still."

"Stop, man! I just have a pen, that's all."

Peyton tries to pull his hands free, but the cop only tightens his grip. Peyton has been here before. He was arrested for shoplifting three years ago. And he'd let them put the cuffs on because he'd done the crime. Fair is fair. But this? This is some bullshit.

"I haven't hurt anyone!" he says.

He twists his body and drops to the ground, bringing the cop along with him. Free from the cop's grip, Peyton rolls into the muddy trench. The cop jumps on his back and Peyton screams as he feels the cop's knee ram into his spine. With a roar, Peyton manages to turn himself over, but the cop stays on top of him. Blinded by the muddy water splashing up, Peyton runs his free hand up one of the cop's arms and finds at its end a thing of metal, a machine with a barrel and a trigger. He holds tight to it, but the gun slides free from his grip.

Gunshots blast his eardrums.

Peyton recognizes the searing pain pulsing from within his muscle and bone. It is the dread he has so long felt finally piercing through the veil of his mind and into the flesh. The bugs have come in all their rage. They dance murderously within him, buzzing, stinging, burning. When his eyes finally blink away the mud, all he can see is the endless blue sky above. It seems to be falling down on him, and he seems to be rising up to meet it. The next moment, the whole world flips. Instead of rising, Peyton falls into the sky, which has become the sea. The sun is a golden beacon shining up from Neptune's deep, watery abode, and as Peyton reaches out for it, the flames in his head do one more little jig before they flicker out.

●

"If you do the rationalization and acceptance ahead of time, if you prepare yourself and immerse yourself in the lore and spirit of mature warriors, past and present, then the lawful, legitimate use of deadly force does not have to be a self-destructive or traumatic event."
—Lt. Col. Dave Grossman, *On Combat*

Having dealt with the cake, Sadie grabs the book off the floor. The spine gives way and the book splits in two. Oh, well, shit. She should have gotten him a new one for his birthday. That's what he really would have liked. Maybe they ought to stay home tonight. Going out will only set him off more, won't it? They'll order pizza. Eat the cake. Watch whatever he wants on TV.

"Peyton, baby, I found your book!"

She hears him screaming on the front lawn. Oh, lord, she prays, don't let him be screaming at Cynthia. She hears a gunshot, and another, and another, and another, and another.

She leans to see down the hall. Through the front screen door, she can see someone lying limp on the front lawn. She exits her body and floats up to the kitchen ceiling, tucking herself into a corner, behind the refrigerator. She listens as if at any moment she'll hear him cry out, "Mom! Mom!" And then she'll go back to her body and run to him.

She hears the crack of a police radio and the sound of muffled staticky words. She opens her eyes and finds herself in the shivering mess of her body.

She grips the book in her hands as if it were the only thing keeping her from sinking into the tile floor. She takes a step back toward the stove. She won't go forward. She won't go out there. She'll stay here forever with the cloying scent of Peyton's freshly baked cake in her nose and the yellowed, nicotine-stained pages slowly sliding apart in her hands.

9

"'It happens. It's going to happen again. Maybe not to you, but to someone else. That's why I'm always telling you, make yourself invisible, mi hijo.'"

THE LESSON OF THE LAMP

MIKE MCHONE

S
he may as well have sucker punched you. It would've made less of an impact.

"I want to introduce you to my aunt and uncle," she told you. "Let's go say hi," she said, grabbed hold of your hand and walked you over to the folding table, one of a dozen in the backyard. You saw the face of her aunt first, a little woman with a cotton ball head and a denture-filled smile, but you only saw the back of her uncle's head, that close-cropped crewcut above the collar of a red checkered shirt. But when you stepped closer you saw who it was.

Him. Of all people.

Panic snapped your nerves to attention, turned your legs to spaghetti, worked your lungs like a bellows. You stopped. No . . . Maybe you were seeing things, maybe you were confused. No, you thought, it can't be him. There's no way. No goddamn way.

But here you are, now, standing here, looking at him, his profile, the curve of his nose, the jut of his chin, the mole on his cheek, the lines in his face, and realization slaps a lifetime of sense into you that, yes, one-hundred-thousand fucking percent, yes, it's him. Of all people. Him. Your girlfriend's uncle. Her relative. Her blood.

"Uncle Frank, I'd like you to meet my boyfriend, Stephen," she says.

He turns. His face. More wrinkles than you remember. More gray at the temples, the eyebrows bushier. Liver spots dot his forehead. He looks like he's aged thirty years in the past ten. He didn't have that gut back then. You never noticed that American flag tattoo on his forearm. Of course, back then, it was covered by the sleeve of the uniform.

Jesus . . . How can it be him? Whatishegoingtodosaydotoyousaytoher?

Relax! Breathe! Your heart's about to pound out of your chest. Let your hands hang loose, for God's sake. You're clenching too hard.

"Stephen, this is my Uncle Frank."

He looks at you. Those eyes. Those pale blue eyes, like little circles of slate. A decade ago in those eyes. A part of your life in those eyes. He smiles. You never knew his first name, but you're well acquainted with his last. Dodson. Frank Dodson is smiling at you. Former Sheriff's Deputy Frank Dodson is smiling at you, and he is your girlfriend's uncle. He extends his hand. Your stomach is quaking. "Pleased to meet you," he says.

Pleased to meet you? Like it's . . .?

He doesn't remember.

His hand is out. Shake it. Now.

You raise yours. You take his and grip it. Not too tight. Give it a firm pump. Two shakes then pull away, just like dad taught you. "Nice to . . . meet you," you say into those slate eyes. He releases your hand (The cuffs. Remember the sound of the key sliding in, the feel of the bracelets unhooking? Remember what he said? "I'm releasing you." Yeah. Releasing you. Like a fish back into the water after you'd been baited, hook-jammed, and held onto by some asshole who decided that you weren't worth keeping. Or killing.).

"And this is my Aunt Laura," Marlene says.

The old woman stands up. You crowbar your gaze away from Frank Dodson and you offer your hand to his wife. "Oh, I don't shake hands, handsome," she tells you. "I give hugs!"

And she does. You wrap your arms around this frail thing, this tiny thing, this body of bones and knobby joints and cool flesh. You are hugging Frank Dodson's wife. "It's so good to meet you," she says. "Marlene's told us so much about you." She pulls away from you, hugs her niece and sits back down at the table next to her husband.

Kids scream in the distance. Other kids splash in the pool. One yells, "Marco!" Another yells, "Polo!" A group of adults playing cards at a folding table beside you laugh. Two golden retrievers run together through the backyard. The white carboard sign staple-gunned to a wooden stake out in the front yard near the roadside that declares this is the place for the SMITH FAMILY REUNION! flaps with the breeze. The faint smell of cow and horse shit fills the country air.

"How long you two been dating?" Frank Dodson asks his niece.

"Almost eight months," Marlene tells him.

"Well, that's good."

Frank Dodson says it's good that you're dating his niece. Frank Dodson smiles at you again.

Flash one back to him. Smile. Now.

There you go.

"He treat you good, honey?" Aunt Laura asks Marlene.

"Of course, he does! He's a good man."

"He looks it!"

Your eyes sway back to the circles of slate.

There's no recognition. At all. He does not remember you, or throwing you to the ground, or driving you out to the country, or . . .

She grabs your hand. "It was good seeing you," Marlene tells them. "We'll be back in a little bit. I want to say hi to a few other people." She leads you away from the table.

You walk the way guys walk when they're side by side with their girlfriend, in a series of odd halting shuffles, not matching up at all with her gait. "Look!" she says. "There's my Aunt Tillie over there by the bounce house. I haven't seen her since the last reunion." Your legs move on their own. Robotic. Mechanical. You look back at the table. Aunt Laura and Uncle Frank wave at you. You see your free hand rise and wave. You turn back. You look ahead. "I can't wait for you to meet her."

But you're seeing something else.

Hamburgers.

That's all it was. That's it. You stopped for a couple of burgers at a shitty restaurant.

You'd just gotten off work from Kroger. It was—what?—ten, eleven o'clock. You hadn't eaten all day, because you weren't even supposed to work that day. Someone was out sick on the afternoon shift and John, the manager, called you up and asked if you wanted to get a few hours of overtime on your paycheck. When you're eighteen, it's less than a month after you've graduated high school, and you're saving up to get a new car to replace the rusty-ass Chevy Celebrity shit-bucket with the hole in the muffler, any extra cash was welcome. Besides, if Dad found out you turned down overtime . . .? Shit, the only family trips you would've been invited to join from that day forward would've been guilt trips. Overtime's better than no time, he used to say, and he said it all the time.

Especially when he was offered an extra shift at the Ford plant over Christmas or Thanksgiving.

Your shift ended, the store closed for the night, you started to head home, then your gut started grinding on itself. You made a beeline to Telly's Burger Shack, pulled in, parked, and saw a couple of teenagers talking shit in the lot. One, a tall blond guy wearing a varsity jacket from Catholic Central (the only other high school in town; the high school your parents couldn't afford to send you to), was getting in the face of a guy with long black hair hanging down to his ass. You heard, "fuck you" and "bitch" tossed back and forth more than a few times. Then the fists started flying. But you ignored it. Not your business. Another nugget of wisdom from Dad: If it's not your problem, it's not *your* problem. Besides, you saw crap like that every other day in the parking lot at Kroger. You kept walking.

You remember the inside of Telly's being nice and cool. The humidity was thick that night and it stuck to you like a damp blanket. You ordered a few burgers, a small fries, and a Pepsi. You heard someone in the back of the kitchen tell someone else to call the cops because of the "dickheads in the parking lot." You stood at the counter, ignoring the voice of whomever it was on the phone requesting that the cops "come quick," and forced yourself to read through the menu on the wall above the register probably half a dozen times (these were the days before cellphones). Finally, your food arrived. Fast food, right? Hardly fast, barely food.

You took your tray to a table in the corner, and you dug in. You were the only customer in there that night. Minutes later, you finished the first burger, made it half-way through the fries, and started to chomp into the second when the flash of red and blue lights snagged your attention. You looked up and saw a patrol car from the sheriff's department pull into the lot. You returned your attention back to the feast and tore through the rest of the hamburger and crammed the last couple of fries in your face, swallowed that large Pepsi in only a few sips, and took your tray to the trashcan. You went to the bathroom, pissed, washed your hands, checked yourself in the mirror, adjusted your hair, checked your chin and forehead for zits, walked out, went out to the parking lot, kept your head down, your eyes focused on asphalt beneath you, the cracks, the random squashed cigarette butts and mashed wads of bubble gum, walked to your car, ignoring the sounds, the chatter, the flashing lights, because, again, it wasn't your probl—

"Hey!"

You lifted your eyes from the parking lot and looked into his face, into his slate-colored eyes, into a face made reddish-purple from the swirling kaleidoscope of lights. "I told you to go over there with the rest of them!" You looked to where he was pointing. Most of the teenagers were sitting on the curb. The blond guy in the varsity jacket and the guy with the hair down to his ass were spread eagle on the ground.

"I'm not with them," you said.

He lunges at you, grabs you on the bicep. "Get over there!"

You pulled away. Not intentionally. No, you swear, it was just a reaction, a reflex, that's all. "I'm not with th—" You didn't even have a chance to get the last word out before you too went to the asphalt.

"Get on the fucking ground!"

A hand slammed into the back of your neck, another on your shoulder, and somehow that thing called gravity became a suggestion. Upright, then down. Blam! Hot pain coursed throughout your torso, your gut. If felt like you'd been hit by a truck going ninety. You couldn't breathe. You tried to suck in air, but it didn't come, like trying to sip a drink through a broken straw. You remember your arms being pulled behind your back, the cold metal on the wrists, the sound of the clamp, the tightness, your fingers tingling, going numb. "Up!" the man with the slate eyes demanded, hoisting you by your arm, and goddamn if your shoulder didn't feel as if it was going to dislocate right out of the socket. "When I tell you to get on the curb with your friends, I mean it!" he screamed in your face.

Then: "Fuck you!" That too was unintentional. Yes, even after all this time, you swear it was. You didn't plan it. You damn sure wouldn't have allowed yourself to say it had you thought about it, but you didn't think, it just came out of you like sweat, like tears. Like blood.

Someone laughed. One of the kids on the curb. A quick, firecracker of a laugh.

Again, the hand went to the back of your neck, the palm like a hot coal, the fingers like a vice. He moved you toward his car, opened the door, and shoved you inside. The door slammed shut.

The next ten minutes were spent in the back of a dark patrol car with only the sounds of your breathing, something borderline to hyperventilation, and muffled shouts from the asshole who stuck you back there to keep you company. You looked over the front seat, saw the asshole pointing at the kids, talking all kinds of shit that you couldn't make out except for the random "responsibility," and "respect." You leaned your head back and closed your eyes. You tried to ignore the pain in your chest.

Tried.

The sound of the door opening. You open your eyes. Not your door. The front door. The slate-eyed asshole got into the driver's seat.

You looked through the windshield. The varsity jacket and the long-hair were off the ground. The kids on the curb stood, mingled, looked at the car, at you.

The car was put into drive.

"Where're you . . .?"

"Shut up."

He pulled out of the parking lot and went south on Telegraph Road.

"Where are you taking me? I didn't do anything! I don't even know those people!"

The only answer was a small laugh.

"I wasn't with them!"

Save for the sound of the tires on the road and the soft noise of passing cars, silence.

He turned right on M-50 and headed east. You never noticed how dark that stretch of road was until that night. Hardly any streetlights, or houses after a while. Eventually, a mile down from the Telegraph intersection, there was only a house every so often. Sure, it's been built up since then with the BP station, the Merchant's Bank branch, the mini mall, but back then it was just a curtain of country darkness, something that separated the urban side of town from the rural.

Minutes passed, miles passed, the darkness always there, wrapped around you like a vulture's wing. It felt as if maggots were crawling in the spoiled melon of your gut.

The car made a right. You saw the sign. Dead End. The sound of gravel striking the side of the car and the undercarriage sounded like hard rain.

The car stopped. Bathed in the headlights was a wall of cornstalks.

He put the car in park, opened the door, and got out.

No, you told yourself. Don't cry. No. Don't. Bite down. Clench your teeth. Do not beg. Do not say anything. Whatever he asks, no matter what it is, don't say a fucking word. Even if he tells you to apologize, even if he says, "I'll give you one more chance . . ." Don't. Stay quiet.

Your door opened. "Step out."

Maggots. Vultures. Dead.

You turned, put one foot on the ground, then the other, and stood.

You looked at his slate eyes in the darkness. From the open car door and light shining inside it, you see the left half of his body, and his name tag. Deputy Dodson.

That's when the overhand right landed on your jaw. You didn't feel the pain. You remember that distinctly. There was no pain, but the force of it sent you flying into the side of the car.

The second punch, though . . . When it landed right there on the side of your cheek, it ignited a flame right behind your eyes that spread throughout your entire skull like a brush fire. You told yourself you weren't going to cry, but you could not help the tears rising in front of your eyes, spilling over, streaming down your face. And then the knee to the ribs. Yes, you felt the pain there, but you were too boggled to care, to scream, to cry out, to beg, to plead, to spit, to gnash, to threaten, to lie down and take it. Your ass introduced itself to the ground. Your knuckles and the tips of your hands, still cuffed, still behind your back, still bound, brushed against gravel. You blinked rapidly, the dim light from the inside of the car looked like a strobe. The tears kept coming and the fire was still there.

"Up," he said again, and, again, lifted you by your arm and, again, you thought your shoulder would dislocate. But he was gentler that time, wasn't he? Maybe?

He moved behind you and in that moment you saw at least a dozen visions of what was coming next. The brunt of his flashlight coming down onto the back of your head. The barrel of his gun shoved into the base of your skull and the trigger being pulled. A baton to the back of your knees, or kidneys, or dead center in your spine. Grabbing the back of your hair and shoving your head into the side of his car.

But you didn't expect the feeling of the cuffs being removed from your wrists, the feeling of freedom near your hands, and the feeling, literally, returning to your fingers, and him saying, "I'm releasing you." And added, "Pull any of that shit on me ever again, and I'll bury you out here."

You watched him get into his car and back down the gravel road until his rear tires met pavement. The car turned and headed west.

And you walked in that same direction, in that same darkness toward your car, pausing every so often to hold your side and choke back tears and vomit. An hour, maybe two hours later, you don't know, you made it back to the Chevy and drove home.

Both Mom and Dad were asleep when you got in, thankfully. You remember tiptoeing through the house, avoiding those familiar spots on the living room floor and on the stairs that would draw out creaks and groans, to the bathroom just to look at yourself in the mirror. You turned on the light and saw no bruises, no welts on your face, but you lifted your shirt and saw a black-purple patch right there on your ribs. At least you could hide that. If there were marks on your face, it'd draw questions. And you imagined them.

Dad: "What's that . . .? Who punched you . . .? Who . . .? Ah . . . Well, what did you do . . .? Bullshit, you must've said something . . . And how many times have I told you that smart mouth of yours would get your ass in a sling one day . . .? Yeah . . . Well, what can you do about it . . .? Look, it's how it is. I've told you time and again, the good ol' boys in this town don't give a squirt of piss for people like us, Esteban . . . I was like you at your age, had that same mouth, and, yeah, it happened to me, too. A bully with a badge kicked the shit out of me just because . . . Didn't like the way I looked, smelled, whatever . . . It happened to your grandfather, too, when he moved here. He probably got it worse than both of us . . . It happens. It's going to happen again. Maybe not to you, but to someone else. That's why I'm always telling you, make yourself invisible, mi hijo. And you know what my old man told me, right? 'Keep your head down, your nose clean, and your hands busy.'"

You shut the light off and went to bed. Sleep, however, didn't come along.

A decade. Weeks bled into months into years. Jobs came and went. Friends came and went. Girlfriends came and went. Then, four years ago you started in the mortgage industry, became a loan officer, moved to Ann Arbor, met Marlene at the corporate office, asked her out to dinner at Knight's Steakhouse, the small talk, the talk of likes and dislikes, and her asking where you're from originally, and you saying Monroe, and hearing her say she had family that used to live there. And that was all that was said about her family, until she invited you to go with her to the reunion in Blissfield, a small place, a village about forty-five minutes south of Ann Arbor you'd only heard about but never visited.

And here, now, walking hand in hand, like a kid being taken into a department store to shop for school clothes, her telling you about Aunt Tillie, and how Cousin James did this, and how her Uncle Fred, the guy who owns the farmhouse and this big-ass property just retired from GM, and how Cousin Danielle is studying to be a nurse at the University of Michig—

"Where's the restroom?" you ask.

"Oh. Uh, go through that door"—she points across the yard at a door on the side of the gray house—"and it's down the hall, all the way at the end."

You take your hand from hers and jog over to the house, past the voices, the people, the smell of barbeque, the dogs barking and running, and "Marco!" and "Polo!" You go into the house, down the hallway, the bathroom, shut the door, lock the door, and sit on the edge of the bathtub. The room is huge. His and hers sinks, a linen closet, a bathtub and a shower. About as big as your living room. It's . . .

Your hands. Shaking.

Did she notice?

If she did, she would've said something.

Right?

You take a breath.

Why won't your heart slow down? It was . . . Come on, for Christ's sake, it was years ago.

But it . . .

Stop.

You stand up. You walk to the sink, the one on the far right. You turn on the faucet and run your hands beneath the cold water and splash some on your face and forehead.

It was long ago. A lifetime ago. Right? And you haven't even thought about this shit for . . . How long? See, you don't even know. So, how much does this matter, really?

You turn off the faucet and dry your hands on the gray towel hanging on the gray towel holder on the wall.

You look at yourself in the mirror. You look like you do every minute of every day. Less hair, like your father. Thicker mustache like him. But no signs that anything's wrong. And why would anything be wrong? It was long ago. It's in the past. And even if it had just happened, even if those punches came only moments ago, and that walk in the darkness came to an end just a second prior, why would anything be wrong? That's normal. That's life. That's how the world is. Crying about that, tearing up, gritting your teeth, clenching your jaw, losing sleep, having nightmares, feeling those maggots crawl every time you see a cop, and even just thinking about it is all, every bit, every solitary bit, goddamn useless. It makes as much sense to dwell on it as it does to get mad at the clouds for giving rain. You do that, you're just wasting time and energy and life. Like running a marathon on a treadmill.

Her relatives. Her blood.

Hers.

But it's not like she knew anything about what happened that nigh—

A knock on the door.

"Just a second!"

A moment. A breath. Another. You smooth the front of your shirt. You turn. You walk. You open the door.

Slate eyes.

"Oh sorry," he says. "Didn't mean to rush you."

You feel like . . .

"No, no," you tell him. "It's okay. Totally fine. I was . . . just heading out."

He smiles and moves to the side like a doorman, like a butler, so you can leave. But you don't. You don't.

Why?

Sweat rises to the surface of your forehead. Your body feels feverish. The sound of your heartbeat grows louder than the voice of your dead father.

"Marlene said you're a cop?"

She never . . . What are you doing? Why are you talking to him? What are y—

"Yeah," he says. "Well, used to be. Twenty-five years in the Sheriff's Department."

Jesuschristwhatthefuckare "Used to be?" youdoingyouidiotshutup!

"Yeah. Early retirement, five years back."

Stopstopstopstopstop "Oh?" stopstopstopstopstop!

"Yeah . . . Hey do you mind?" He's gesturing into the bathroom, and you know he wants inside, obviously, and you can see him shuffling foot to foot, and he's wanting to end this conversation and get past you, but suddenly the chatter in your head, the chaos, the objections are overtaken by your heartbeat and sweat and fire and blood, and there's a clearness, and it's like sunshine peeking out from dark clouds after a night filled with wind and rain and sleet and terrors, and you're calm, at ease, stable like a thousand-year oak, and you stand here, planted, rooted, and there's a part of you, a small part of you, a large part of you, a dark part of you that's telling you to stand here for as long as it takes, as long as it fucking takes, until your legs give out, until the house burns down around you and falls into ash and ruin, and if he ever tries to push past you, you hold your hand up and you shove him back and make him stand in the hall and piss his pants, like a child, like a baby, and you don't ever let him get past you, and you swear you're never going to . . .

"Stephen?"

Was it him or your father?

You swallow.

"Sorry," you say.

You walk past him. Straight ahead. You don't look back. You pay him no mind. He's as important as the towel, the towel holder, the wall. Maybe that thing you're feeling on the back of your head, on the nape of your neck, is just your imagination. Maybe it's a breeze. Maybe a fly is buzzing around you.

Or maybe it's him staring at you, into you. Maybe now he recognizes you. Maybe he's been putting up a front, like you, since he met you. Maybe he remembers.

And if so . . .?

Before you walk out the front door, you hear the door down the hall close behind you and latch into place.

Outside. The sun is blinding. You shut your eyes.

"Marco!"

"Polo!"

You hear Marlene call your name from somewhere on the other side of your eyelids.

"Stephen! Come meet Aunt Tillie!"

Yelling in the darkness. Sounds of children from somewhere out there.

"Marco!"

"Polo!"

A gust of wind.

"Stephen!"

"Marco!"

10

"Riot policemen tend not to have to shout."

Not Their Type

Oluseyi Onabanjo

F riday at last.

I took my final call standing up and updated the fault log while stooped over the keyboard, car keys close at hand. The office had long emptied. It had taken several attempts before the remote software upgrade took, but the customer's server was finally up and running.

I didn't mind working late. In fact, I was beyond grateful that only a year after moving to Lagos, against all odds, I was fulfilling my village teacher's prediction that I would "become somebody." I rejected again with a slight shudder the flip side of his prophecy—that I would be the first indigenous principal of my hometown school.

Another letter had been brought to the offices from the village that morning. It sat, travel-stained and swollen with unread demands. I scooped it up and shoved it into my trouser pocket.

●

The night shift operator responded with a nod, which liberated a fresh slick of drool as I waved goodbye. I shook my head and slammed the door, hoping that would keep him awake for a while, then I hurtled down the steps to the parking levels and my pride and joy; a "versatile, fuel-efficient, runabout."

This bit of marketing propaganda probably worked in 1976. However, a decade and a half of exposure to Lagos' corrosive sea air and several previous owners had changed her. Now, she'd been reduced to four new-ish tires, a paint scheme that could best be described as *postmodern eczema*, and not much else. But I didn't care. She got me from home to work and back again with relative efficiency via my usual haunts. And most importantly, she was mine.

If I'm being honest, I'd admit that her charms were enhanced by one more thing; ownership of a vehicle put me far ahead of all those that had preceded me in the trek from our village to Lagos. Over the past decade or so, the most successful of these fine folk only had the disputed ownership of a battered Vespa to show for their time in the city. But I had a car. I called her Olubankẹ and ignored the office jokes about needing more than God to help me take care of her. The joke was on them, though. She was taking care of me, and she would do so until I could one day afford to trade her for a newer secondhand car.

But to get to Olubankẹ now, I had to navigate the building management guys.

As expected, there were a couple of them hovering around Olubankẹ, their smiles quivering in anticipation. They all seemed to share a single greasy pair of overalls, didn't have a matching pair of rubber flip-flops between them, and they never missed a chance to shake you down. I unfolded a few low-denomination notes from my left shirt pocket and handed them to the younger of the two. He snatched the money from me and vanished down the closest set of stairs, ignoring my shouts that the funds were for the both of them.

The other chap, probably relatively senior because he was today's wearer of the shiny overalls, looked at my empty hands. I shrugged at him. He responded with an unpleasant look and a hiss before shuffling off.

I slid behind the wheel and noted the discarded envelopes in the passenger footwell. Crumpled, dirty, my name and work address printed in bold type and even bolder typos, each recalled the envelope I'd shoved into my pocket earlier.

Shortly after taking possession of Olubankẹ, I made the strategic error of driving her to the one church in Lagos frequented by indigenes of my village. I was proud and wanted to show my new status off to old schoolmates and seniors, the parish priest, our resident palm wine tapper, and a host of others. News of my vehicular advancement got home before the end of the service. As a result, I have since received a weekly missive from the village letter-writer. The messages started out requesting, even plaintive but had lately shifted to a more commanding tone.

I was to present the car at my parent's compound immediately. There, prayers would be prayed, blessings would be blessed, songs would be sung, and drinks would be drunk (at my expense, of course). Only then would me and my car be "safe from all dangers seen or unseen" and "forever protected from the hunger of the road."

I pulled the letter from my pocket and filed it with the others. My written responses, outlining in vague detail the bureaucracy that was delaying my *inter-state driving permit*—paperwork that I implied was necessary for me to undertake the drive home—were a work of art. I justified my display of filial disobedience with the mental assertion that Olubankẹ probably wouldn't survive the trip home.

Seated behind the steering wheel, I thought of that first cold beer and my journey towards it. Our offices are located deep in the city's armpit, and on most weekdays, the traffic constitutes a test of heat, humidity, stopping, starting, hooting, honking, and plenty of vernacular hand gestures.

And that's before you've exited the ramp from the parking floors.

❋

By the time I'd merged with the traffic, I was possessed by one of the many personalities needed to survive in this schizophrenic city: I'd become a City Driver.

A City Driver measures the distance between his front bumper and the vehicle ahead in thicknesses of cigarette paper. A City Driver looks straight ahead, particularly when a random hawker bellows his sales pitch at your window (*This "medicine" will help you charm any woman, sah. Donkeys will envy your penis, sah. You will win the lottery, sah. Please, can you give me small money? I have not eaten today, sah?*). A City Driver ignores the gobs of vexed spittle that frustrated hawkers may leave on Olubankẹ's closed windows.

A City Driver takes advantage of any chance to beat the traffic.

As Olubankẹ and I grumbled past the brutalist building that housed the Ministry of Power, I found myself paused next to the group of traffic policemen lounging at the entrance. Seemingly tasked only with sweating through their uniforms, they all began to earn their unpaid salaries at once. Walkie-talkie radios glued to their ears, they ran around, waved arms, shouted, found more arms to wave, and shouted some more. But the traffic police were soon displaced by another bunch of policemen. Marked by how they fanned out in a fixed formation ahead of a motorcade, I knew these policemen were from the dreaded anti-riot wing.

Riot policemen tend not to have to shout.

Their sunglasses were reflective, uniforms spotless, crisply pressed khaki trousers tucked into combat boots, their gleaming automatic weapons pointed downward. They took over the space in front of the Ministry, with the tallest two jogging ahead—the vanguard.

The cars glided out of the building's gate, expensive, German, dark-colored, with even darker windows. An open-backed Land Rover led the motorcade, and another one brought up the rear. There were enough flashing lights and blaring sirens to make the street vendors, hawkers, and other pedestrians briefly look up in unison, their expressions blank.

The rearguard Land Rover slowed and picked up leftover riot policemen just before the motorcade took off, and the traffic parted as if they were leprous.

In the moments before the sidelined traffic policemen recovered their pride and positions, I saw a chance. The motorcade was disappearing at speed, and the traffic had not yet re-asserted itself.

I accelerated after them, searching for their slipstream. A City Driver once again.

I felt a car close behind me; the driver doubtless irritated I had reacted first. I could only glance at my rear-view mirror at the speed I was driving, which revealed the driver's snarl; even his headlights were hidden. There was angry hooting, accompanied by plenty of hand gestures. I knew a few of those myself, and I was glad for the opportunity to show them off. After a few minutes of this, I was close to my destination, and so I let my high-speed escort go and peeled away to join a short line of traffic. Devoid of hawkers, this stretch of road was all that was keeping me from my preferred Friday spot, a bar on prime waterfront property, within sniffing distance of the ocean.

I could almost taste that first beer.

✸

I pulled into a spot in the bar's car park, underneath a dogonyaro tree, great for shade and even better for discouraging birds and their droppings. Prime parking: another gift of good fortune after successfully piggy-backing a government motorcade and thus earning City Driver god-hood status.

I'm not sure when the good feeling went away, but it was at about the time I noted that the gateman was missing, as was the chap who usually sat close by, selling cigarettes, sweets, and snuff. I watched some customers exit the bar, walk in my general direction, then turn on their heels and head back inside. In haste.

I heard the screeching sound before I smelled rubber. The rear-view mirror, empty a moment ago, was now filled with the dark grille of a Land Rover. I looked over my right shoulder and saw a familiar open-backed model, disgorging one of the tall mobile policemen, part of that earlier vanguard.

I think my heart stopped. My brain definitely slowed as I tried to process my predicament. I wanted to bolt, but I couldn't. I heard a grunt so close by it felt like it was in the back seat. I looked to my left in time to see reflective sunglasses and a swinging gun butt.

Olubankẹ's window shattered, and then hands were on me, pulling me out.

I am tall, but they were both taller.

I grew up in the village and thought I was tough, but they chewed me up like sugarcane.

I am quick and almost slipped past them, but one of them cocked his gun, and I froze.

Afterward, I calculated that they only beat me for about five minutes. It felt like days.

They didn't speak, but I soon lost hearing in my left ear. I remember my eyes closed, and things got dark. I remember my lip split, and things got wet and salty. I remember I raised my right arm, and the bones cracked loud and warm. The pain crept up to the back of my throat, and sat there, tasting of blood.

My worst memory is of one of them grabbing me by the throat and lifting me until I was on tiptoe. He rubbed himself against me, and, through his khakis, I could feel he was engorged. With the one almost swollen-shut eye, I saw his own behind sunglasses: heavy-lidded and bright, perched above a lazy smile. His teeth were surprisingly white, and his breath smelt fresh, like the sea.

I don't remember the release, only the warmth as my bladder emptied.

Walkie-talkie gibberish buzzed all around me, and I only realized I was on the ground when I felt the vibrations of a heavy vehicle. Doors clanged open, and the air was filled with multiple hoarse, pleading voices. I was thrown into the metal box of the vehicle, warmed by other bodies, and made slick by their blood. I jammed myself into a corner, nursed my forearm, and leaned against another body.

The body was cold.

Another squint revealed faint light broken up by bars set high, and I realized I was in a Black Maria. I'd heard tales of the Black Marias. They were not good stories.

The rumors said that our nation's riot-policemen are mercenaries recruited from neighboring countries. They've been accused of, among other things, rounding up alleged prostitutes and taking turns with them in the back of their trucks as they drove through the night. Of disappearing dissidents. Of killing those who offer them the slightest displeasure.

I'd always shrugged at these stories, blaming the women for their choices, the dissidents for their smart mouths, and the others for their stupidity.

Now, I prayed for female forgiveness and to gods old and new, promising each that I would push Olubankẹ every kilometer of the way to our village if need be. That I would teach in the village school forever and free of charge if they would help. If they could get me out of this.

The Black Maria jerked forward, and bones grated in my arm. The noise was horrendous as we moaned, screamed, and cursed.

Time passed. How much I do not know, but eventually, the vehicle stopped, and our hoarse voices fell quiet.

Soft-footed steps approached the back.

I struggled to see beyond the opening door. I knew I would do anything to stay alive. I felt only pain and desperation. The shame would come later.

There were more riot-policemen, chattering excitedly as they dragged most of the women out, one after the other. My functioning arm being on the opposite side to my good ear made it difficult to block out the screams.

Eventually, they came back and started pulling the men out.

By this time, the whimpering inside the Black Maria drowned out any noises from the outside.

Sunrise was threatening when they came back to drag me out, together with the last two or three men. The others were lined up against the vehicle's side, many kneeling, some struggling to stand, all cowed and silent. We were united by fear and the acrid smell of fresh urine that clung to our bloody bodies.

A few yards away, there was an unmoving mass, ominous in its silence. We all edged away from it as if its current state was contagious.

We offered anything and everything while the policemen spoke in a familiar but incomprehensible language. Shepherded further away from the Black Maria, we clung together like orphans and watched as they pushed the others, barely protesting, back into the vehicle.

My eyes watered, stung by a salt-water spray.

I discovered that I was shoeless when my feet sank into cool, shifting sand.

I heard the engine start.

When my heart stopped pounding, the vehicle's noise had faded, and I could smell the ocean.

One of the other survivors sank to his knees, "Thank you, Chissos, thank you."

I croaked, "Why?"

His response, in broken English, made me go hot all over and then cold. "I speak their language small. Them talk say, as we done piss our body, we no be their type."

"'He's a dick. He was resisting. You saw it, you were there.'
'He wasn't responding the way you wanted him to.'
'He was resisting.'
'We'll see what the tape shows. None of this had to happen.'"

THE STOP

JEFFREY C. EATON

"**Y**ou're with me on this, right?"

"With you on what?"

"The stop. Everything."

"I was with you. The video will show that."

"I know you were there. Shit! But you're with me on this thing, right? The guy was a total asshole."

"Somebody was an asshole."

"What the hell is that supposed to mean? He was resisting arrest. You were there, you saw it."

"I saw the whole thing."

"Then you're with me on what happened? You'll back me up? You backed me up. You were there."

"I was there, alright. I can't deny that."

"C'mon, Tom, don't be stupid about this. Just back me up is all I'm asking."

"Stupid? I'm stupid? And you were so smart out there on the highway? This isn't going away, Mike. The guy's a cop, for Christ's sake! You knew that. None of this had to happen."

"He's a dick. He was resisting. You saw it, you were there."

"He wasn't responding the way you wanted him to."

"He was resisting."

"We'll see what the tape shows. None of this had to happen."

"Yeah, it did. We stop speeders, that's what we do. You do understand that much, don't you, Tom? We're State Troopers. Not some dipshit municipal cops."

"I know the job. It's not because I don't know the job that we're in this situation."

"What situation? I did what I had to do. You were there. You were with me the whole time. What's your problem anyway?"

"The question is, what's your problem, Mike."

"All the guy had to do was show me his identification. That's all. Cop or not, he owes me compliance, just like anybody else. Not when it suits him. When I tell him!"

"Collis tells me you two aren't on the same page with this thing."

"It's not the way I would have done things, Lieutenant."

"Collis says the guy wasn't cooperative."

"He was slow. He didn't give Collis the respect he wanted."

"Was Trooper Collis wrong to pull the detective over?"

"The guy was speeding. It was obviously an unmarked police car he was driving, especially once he got pulled over and turned on his flashers and wigwags."

"And he was speeding, right?"

"He was speeding."

"So Trooper Collis was right to pull him over."

"Is that what all this is about, Lieutenant? Really?"

"What do you think this is about, Trooper Nolan?"

"I'm not sure, sir. Attitude, I guess."

"The detective's attitude."

"And Collis's."

"You think Trooper Collis's attitude was bad that day? The man has an exemplary record. I don't know of any time when his attitude has gotten in the way of his work. At this very moment, everything's in place for him to receive a promotion."

"So I hear."

"And *I* hear these days that you and Trooper Collis are not close."

"You could say that."

"And that you've asked to be reassigned from the inspection detail you and he have been on together for . . . let's see . . . the past four months?"

"I want to get back out on patrol."

"That's it? Nothing more to it than that?"

"I like working on my own."

"And there's no personal animosity between you and Trooper Collis?"

"Like you said, Lieutenant, we're not close."

"And that's why you're not supporting him on the matter of this stop?"

"How am I not supporting him, Lieutenant? You've seen the video. I'm right there with him the whole way. And my incident report is in line with his. What haven't I done?"

"You've done your duty. It's just that Mike isn't sure that you're with him."

"I don't think what he did was right, if that's what you're asking, Lieutenant, but I backed him up at the stop, and I'm in it with him. I think the whole thing was unnecessary. And there was no reason to hit the guy."

"He wasn't resisting arrest? Mike is quite definite that he was."

"That's what Collis says."

"And that's why Trooper Collis hit the detective."

"That's what Collis says."

"Why else would he hit him?"

"Maybe because he wanted to."

* * *

"Is this never going to end?"

"It's going on four years now."

"So, what is it this time, Tom?"

"It's a civil suit. The guy's looking for damages. You know, he lost his job. I don't know what else."

"But you said he wasn't badly injured."

"No, but he's messed up. At least he's making it look that way. He was doing all this heavy breathing when we were in court. Acting real nervous, jittery. Who knows? Probably going to say he can't have sex with his wife because Collis hit him over the head."

"This whole thing hasn't been so great for us either, Tom. Who can I sue?"

"Me, I guess."

"I'm sorry, honey. I'm not helping matters. But this shouldn't be happening to you. You didn't do anything to that guy. Why can't they just leave you out of it, cut you free from this whole thing and let Collis defend himself?"

"Never happen. The State Police would never hear of it. They figure doing that would send a message to the jury. The plaintiff's lawyer wanted to separate me from the case right from the beginning, and the State's attorney wouldn't let it happen. I'm just going to have to go through it."

"But you didn't do anything wrong. You shouldn't have to go through it."

●

"Thank you for coming in, Trooper Nolan."

"No problem."

"I'm James Sudol, and I've been retained by the State Police to represent you and Sergeant Collis in the civil suit filed against you by David Warren. I know that you've been through the facts of the case many times, but I need to hear your recollection of the events of July 10, 2006. It's especially important, given your—what should we say—estrangement from Sergeant Collis, that we make sure there are no discrepancies in your accounts, and if there are that we do everything we can to harmonize them. But before we do this, I'd appreciate it if you would tell me a little bit about the falling out between you and Sergeant Collis. Detective Warren's attorney will want to do everything she can to exploit this as something that happened as a consequence of the traffic stop and arrest of her client. I need to know if you will corroborate Michael's version of the stop."

"It's on the tape. Everything that happened is on the tape."

"Yes, of course, but Warren's lawyer is going to want to know if you have any reservations about Sergeant Collis' approach to his work and to this stop in particular on the day in question. It's fair to say that you are displeased with the way Sergeant Collis went about the stop, I mean, just between the two of us."

"Collis was heavy-handed. Warren was a jerk—I'm not denying that—but Collis was heavy-handed."

"What do you mean by 'heavy-handed'?"

"The guy, Warren, pissed him off. Collis decided he was going to show him who was top dog."

"As you know, this case is about whether Sargent Collis used excessive force in subduing David Warren. Is 'heavy-handed' the same thing as excessive force?"

"There's no way the jury's not going to see excessive force on that tape, no matter what I think. None of this ever should have happened."

"But it did, as is true of so much that occurs in police work."

"Everything probably would have been okay if Warren had shown Collis a little consideration, you know, a wave or a smile or hold up a badge, something to say he appreciates Collis's authority and the authority of the State Police. But he didn't do that, and Collis didn't like it that he didn't do that."

"And it was downhill from there."

"You've seen the tape."

"I have, Tom—may I call you Tom?—I've seen the tape numerous times, but what concerns me right now is your feelings about Sergeant Michael Collis, and given your feelings, what impression the jury takes away from your testimony."

"I think he was wrong. But I backed him that day, and I backed him in my report and in every previous trial. I'll back him in this case. I don't have to like him for that, but I'll do it."

"I appreciate all your support, and I know Michael does, too. I know he regrets offending you."

"You mean for calling me 'bunny' because I have a cleft lip? That's the kind of guy Collis is. And what he's sorry about is that I heard him do it, and even that wouldn't bother him much if he didn't need my testimony now. I know Collis. He's a guy who always needs a victim. I've dealt with people like him all my life."

"I'm sorry things went down this way, Tom. But at least let me say on behalf of the State Police that I appreciate your loyalty."

"Spare me, okay? With all due respect, the State Police are only interested in cutting their losses. For God's sake, they promoted Collis! After this happened! After they saw the tape! And I've heard he's up for another promotion if he gets through this okay. Collis is their guy."

"Michael has a distinguished record of service on the force."

"Collis has the right friends."

✹

"They're appealing the verdict. A smaller award, they'd probably have let it go."

"How much they give him?"

"Two hundred fifty thousand compensatory damages and three mil punitive."

"Holy shit! I thought you said he wasn't hurt that bad."

"The jury didn't like what it saw on the tape."

"Where's that money coming from? Is Collis liable?"

"No. It's the Turnpike Authority that has to pay. I told you, didn't I, that at the last minute they separated me from the case? Hey, c'mon, Richie, knock one out of the park, buddy!"

"The kid's got a beautiful swing, Tom."

"He loves to play, that's for sure."

"Like his old man."

"There was a time, Steve. I'm just glad now when I can get out here to watch the kids play. If my hours at work were different, I'd apply to coach. Maybe when I retire."

"That's a long way off."

"A little over seven years. Believe me, I'm counting the days."

"I remember when you liked the job, Tom."

"You see too much. It gets old. Yes, Richie, way to go, kid!"

"That was a nice hard shot."

"And a good catch by the kid in left field. You don't mind an out like that, y'know. They're playing the game."

"Unless the powerful are
capable of learning to
respect the dignity of
their victims, impassable
barriers will remain, and
the world will be
doomed to violence,
cruelty, and bitter
suffering."

-Noam Chomsky

12

"Steph still looks like a star, but one that's imploded, collapsing in on itself until nothing remains but a lingering ache in the darkness where you feel a shine had once been."

17 Year Cicadas

James D.F. Hannah

The Camry tires crunch over dried cicada husks as Tess pulls up the dirt road. It's the summer of the cicadas' 17-year cycle, and the fuckers are legion, purring a droning churr that makes the mountains sing. Tess read that it's a mating call, the cicada equivalent of hanging out a car window hollering at another cicada coming down the sidewalk, except there are millions of them, pleading for the chance to do their cicada business and then vanish for another 17 years.

Tess knows guys like that.

The noise is almost enough to drown out the Dixie Chicks playing on the cassette deck, but she turns the volume down anyway

Nearly one in the morning, Steph's house dark. Weird showing up this late. No matter that Steph called her. No matter how many times Steph has called before. Tess parks behind Mitch's unmarked state police cruiser. The driver-side door's open, dome light on. She kicks the door shut.

The front door frame is splintered, but Tess knocks anyway. No answer. Hits the button for the doorbell. Even against the cicada army calling for love and attention, the bell is loud, and it practically feels obscene considering the hour.

There's a scratching just inside, then the door swings open, and through overlapping layers of silhouette and shadow Tess makes out Steph's form.

When they were seventeen, Stephanie Wilson was the most vibrant person Tess had ever known. She was the personification of stars they'd studied in science, the ones that burned brighter and hotter than others. Mr. Tyler, their science teacher, said those stars, their life was finite, and they couldn't shine that way forever.

Not Steph, though. Her glow was huge. Captain of the cheerleading squad. Homecoming queen. Class vice president. Class salutatorian. Every photo of Steph then is a glimpse of a butterfly slowly stretching out her wings.

Compare to Steph now: Shoulders slumped, right arm in a cast, shapeless flannel pajamas hanging off her thin frame. It's July, 80 degrees in the middle of the night and somehow, she's cold.

Steph still looks like a star, but one that's imploded, collapsing in on itself until nothing remains but a lingering ache in the darkness where you feel a shine had once been.

Tess tries to close the door behind her, but it doesn't catch in the latch, flies back and the knob hits her in the ass.

"He broke the door down," Steph says, voice hardly above a whisper. Gestures to a kitchen chair. "You gotta use that."

Tess jams the door shut with the chair, then takes Steph by the hand through the house. She ignores the damage in her peripheral vision. An overturned coffee table. Fist-sized holes in the drywall. Smashed picture frames. Shards of broken glasses and plates across the floor like debris after a war.

She notices the wedding photo. Steph and Mitch on the happiest day of their lives. She's resplendent in white, he's stone-faced in his formal state police uniform.

The photo's stabbed to the wall with a kitchen knife, the blade shoved through Steph's face.

Steph shields her eyes with the arm in the cast when Tess turns on the kitchen light. There's fresh blood on the cast, splattered across the pajamas, and Tess sucks air through her teeth at the sight.

The kitchen table is also on its side, floating in a sea of more shattered dinnerware. Tess kicks pieces aside with the toe of her white hospital shoe. She's still in her pink scrubs, just off a late shift. She'd only stepped through her apartment door when Steph called.

Tess checks Steph over. There's a purple half-moon underneath Steph's right eye. Cuts across her face. Finger-shaped bruises thread around her throat. Her left eye is a glop of red pushing into a sea of white.

The broken arm worries Tess. Getting Steph to have it examined after Mitch broke it had been a fight. Tess had finally called a doctor two counties away who'd set the fracture and put on a cast and didn't ask questions.

Tess throws stitches into the cut above Steph's left eyebrow and cleans the others. Steph never makes a peep, even as pink peroxide bubbles fizz like soda over her skin. When she's done, Tess makes coffee. Not like they'll be sleeping tonight.

Two cups survived somehow, and she fills them both, hands one to Steph.

Steph stares into the top of the mug as tendrils of steam rise. Tess turns on the radio next to the toaster oven. The AM station out in Hendrix, and an old Vicki Lawrence song, tinny and scratchy. She couldn't care less about the music, so long as it's a noise other than the cicadas.

Steph brings her own cup to her lips and sips tentatively. "When'd the cicadas come around last time?" she says.

Tess closes her eyes and leans back against the kitchen counter.

"Must have been the summer after we graduated high school," she says.

A hum from Steph. "The summer I met Mitch."

⬤

They're at the local pool the same day as Mitch Cooper, stretched out on towels, tanning, and pretending they don't notice him as he climbs the high dive and executes a back dive that barely causes a ripple. His lithe torso glistens like diamonds in sunlight as he comes out of the water and in their direction.

"Don't I remember you girls from somewhere?" he says to them.

Neither believes Mitch remembers them. They'd been freshmen when Mitch was a senior, tiny guppies in the high school pond, too small for a big fish to notice.

They, of course, remember Mitch. Girls always remember Mitch Cooper. Three-year All-State baseball star, a full ride to a Division I-AA school, racking up numbers getting attention from scouts. In this little do-nothing town, Mitch Cooper is a god. He comes home for the summer, works with Little League camps. Ten-year-olds asking for his autograph, wanting to touch The Baseball Bat. That's right, *the* Bat.

The bat is his good luck charm, the only one he's used since his first at-bat his high school sophomore year—when he drove in two runs off a home run – and he never even considered another. Even calls it "Wonderboy," after the one Redford uses in *The Natural*. He tells people he saw that movie nine times in the theater, in the *only* theater in town.

People love it when they hear that. They eat that shit up.

That day at the pool, it's clear Mitch is more into Steph than Tess, becoming crystal clear when Mitch asks for Steph's number. A few dates in and they're the talk of the county, the baseball star and the homecoming queen, the match made in small-town heaven.

After college Mitch lands on a double-A farm team and chases that dream like a grounder through the infield while Steph goes to college and gets a degree in education. She dismisses her goal of becoming an attorney because Mitch convinces her teaching will be better since she'll have summers off to watch him play ball.

But Mitch's small-town ambition can't exceed the competing talent pool, and when he realizes he's never going to be Roy Hobbs, he joins the state police academy. It's a perfect fit for him; a badge and a uniform mean he still gets to be a hero.

Mitch rises through the state police ranks, and his baseball player physique softens. He's less like a figure ripped off the top of a trophy and more like other men in the community: doughy and round, with a simmering anger behind the eyes. Why isn't he Roy Hobbs, Mitch thinks? Did those Bon Jovi songs promise him more than the world could deliver?

He makes sure Steph keeps her own figure. Weekly weigh-ins are noted on a chart on the wall. He notices her portion sizes while he gets second helpings. She maintains a diet of cigarettes and Altoids. She stops smoking when they try to get pregnant, then starts back after the miscarriages. Eventually, the doctor recommends they stop trying.

That's when Mitch begins to hit Steph. It's usually after a night of drinking and he decides something's wrong: she didn't keep dinner warm; he doesn't like how she's wearing her hair; she doesn't feel like a half-hard, half-hearted, drunken fuck.

One night, Mitch discharges his service weapon into the TV. Steph calls Tess. Tess calls 911.

Tess and the state police arrive at the same time. Mitch is passed out on the couch, twisted at impossible angles. The TV tube is spiderwebbed out from the bullet hole in its center. Steph's face is swollen like special effects makeup, like she'd been caught mid-transformation into something from "Chiller Theater," mutated by 1950s radiation.

The trooper's a kid just out the academy, greener than a freshly mowed lawn. He won't look at Steph, like meeting her eye to eye may turn him to stone. They stand in the front yard, and he shakes his head and talks to a space right above her left shoulder.

"Are you sure you want to file a report?" he says. He kicks a stone that isn't there. "Husbands and wives all got problems, ma'am. Think of his career."

Tess whips into the trooper's face. "Fuck his career. You see what he did to his wife, and you're worried about his retirement?"

The baby trooper's face hardens. "I'm gonna need you to back up, ma'am," he says in a tone implying she should respect the uniform—never mind it still has creases from coming out of the bag.

He asks Steph if they can talk privately—somewhere "we won't get disturbed"—and shoots a glance at Tess. At the end of the driveway, they're out of earshot, two shapes in the dark. He's kept the cruiser's flashers off the entire time, so the neighbors probably don't even know the state police are there.

Tess can see the baby trooper trying to seem authoritative. Probably saying how he understands the situation, but Steph loves her husband, right? She must know the stress he's under. The baby trooper'll talk to the post commander, and that'll set Mitch straight. This won't happen again.

But Tess knows it will. Guys like Mitch don't change. They're resistant to tectonic shifts and evolution. They're like sharks and giant turtles, plowing through history and saying the world should adapt to them, not the other way around.

Mitch does apologize, Steph says. Tears in his eyes, his voice a big wet gasp of sorrow, his giant bullet-shaped head flushing full of blood. It's the job, he says. He's on a new assignment to a drug task force and the pressure's so much. So fucking much.

Steph believes him, because that's who she is. She trusts people. It's the first-grade teacher part of her brain that convinces all the other parts that Mitch won't do again.

The next time it happens—or at least the next time Tess knows about—it's at the new house outside of town. A sprawling farmhouse away from the state road, at least a mile from the nearest neighbor. Bought because Mitch wants separation from the world when he's not working. It seems like a lot of house on the combined salaries of a cop and a teacher, Tess thinks.

When the state police major arrives, he's in an unmarked car, and no lights on this time either. Dressed in his long-sleeved grays with the tie tucked into the shirt, and he looks like a painting of someone who got famous for killing Indians.

Mitch is sleeping it off upstairs as Tess fumes and Steph makes coffee and the major explains to her how important Mitch is to the marijuana eradication unit. What a key member in the War on Drugs that Lieutenant Mitch Cooper is. Oh, and two sugars in the coffee, please?

Nothing changes.

Nothing ever does, Tess thinks.

Mitch's unit handles drug raids that go down like a movie: battering rams at the front door, helmets and body armor and semi-automatic weapons. The newspaper even does a story on Mitch, their local hero. The photo is him with bundles of seized pot, holding his baseball bat in both hands. He rides with it in his car. Still his good luck charm.

Headline's just the word "Wonderboy."

Steph still loves the attention her husband gets. Tess tunes it out whenever she tells stories about Mitch's job, no matter the excitement in her voice. Tess doesn't really care, but Steph is her best friend, so she listens.

But when Steph mentions that Mitch brought home two grand from a raid, that does get her interest.

"Like, as a bonus?" Tess says.

"Of course not. No, he found it, so he kept it."

The raid had been on a grow house, where the owners also happened to have roughly $100K scattered throughout the place. Stashed in air ducts. Hidden in couch cushions. Behind ceiling tiles.

"Mitch was doing a sweep when he found it in a cubby hole in the floor, underneath a rug," Steph says. "He says we should use it to go on a cruise."

"But it's not your money," Tess says.

"From drug dealers. It doesn't count," Steph says. "Besides, who'll notice?"

No one, it seems. Because stoner drug dealers aren't accountants, and they don't have a fucking clue how much money they have. Plus, they're criminals, after all, peddling poison to innocent children—thank you, six o'clock news—and Mitch and the rest of the drug task force are practically the Knights of the Goddamn Round Table. When Mitch and Steph go on the cruise, it's a reward for his hard work in saving the world from . . . weed.

Steph tells Tess this isn't the first time, either. Drug raid cops discover plenty of loose cash, and it often comes home with them.

And buys homes for them, Tess thinks.

In photos from the trip, Mitch and Steph gradually get tan and drink from hollowed pineapples and he wears loud Hawaiian shirts, and she wears sarongs. They look like an ad for first-world imperialism.

Three months later, Mitch breaks Steph's arm.

Steph tells Tess to not bother calling the police. What good does it do?

They drive back from seeing Tess's doctor friend with a fresh cast on Steph's arm and Garth Brooks on the radio. Midnight miles pass with nothing but the car's headlights hinting at what's ahead. Even the moon's hiding, behind clouds in a sky so dark, the world seems like a void in someone's indifferent imagination.

"He's still taking money from the drug raids." Steph says. She holds the arm in the cast close to her chest. Trying to protect it. Or maybe use it as a shield. "The money's dirty anyway, right? And these guys are breaking the law. It's okay."

Working night shifts at the hospital, Tess sees ODs all the time. Used to be coke or heroin, but now it's all prescription drugs—people getting fucked up via the medicine cabinet. Everyone waking up in the middle of someone else's American Dream and finding out it's just that, and they're left with night sweats and five-figure debt and waiting for a rich man's success to trickle down the way it was promised, but here, swallow this handful of pills to shave the hurt away until then.

She thinks it's bizarre that cops bust people selling weed, but no one does shit about pharmacies pumping out opioid prescriptions like they're Tic Tacs. They ignore what they really are: heroin in a convenient pill form, and that's the thing people are actually dying from.

Pot dealers, though, Tess is good with. Anti-drug signage in the hospital calls pot "a gateway drug." Yeah, it's a gateway to Blockbuster and Cheetos. She's got her own guy, hooks her up to smoke. She gets drug tested for work but a friend in pediatrics keeps her in clean piss. So bizarre she'd lose her job, probably end up in jail, if she tested positive for smoking pot when all she did was get stoned and watch a *Friday the 13th*.

Drug laws are fucked.

A few weeks later, Tess is coming off a twelve-hour shift, walking to her car and singing a Martina McBride song when she hears her name. Sees Mitch leaning against his personal vehicle, a Chevy Silverado, this massive fucking steel-and-chrome embodiment of what must be Mitch's . . . shortcomings. Plus, there's his big ass Colt .357 clipped to his belt for the whole world to see.

Tess wonders if Mitch has ever actually seen his penis, or he simply assumes it's there.

She brings cigarettes and a Zippo out of her purse. She sparks the lighter to life, touches the flame to the end of a Virginia Slim.

Mitch flattens his lips in disapproval.

"Those'll kill you," he says.

"So will life if you give it enough time." She gestures toward him with the glowing cherry of the cigarette. "What do you want?"

He makes a show of stretching out his shoulders, twisting his head around, working to make himself seem fierce.

"It'd be a good idea if you stayed away from Steph," he says. "We've got a lot going on, and you muddy the waters. She'd do better if you let her do her own thinking."

Tess sighs a cloud of smoke. "Is that her thinking, or your thinking you want to be her thinking? Because I doubt you know there's a difference."

Mitch steps closer toward her. Tess doesn't move.

"I'm not asking this; I'm telling you to go the fuck away. Don't come around. You do, well . . ." He let his voice drop, like a body tossed off a cliff. "Bad shit happens plenty to women in these parts."

"That sounds like a threat, Mitch."

"Just a fact of life. You read the paper, watch the news. The world's a terrible place, and I've got my own to protect. Can't say anyone'll be there to protect you."

Tess doesn't doubt Mitch can make any number of horrible things happen and no one would ever know. If the police will ignore what a cop does to his wife, why would they care what he does to someone else?

"She's an adult," Tess says. "Makes her own decisions. Decides what friends to see. How tight you plan to hold that leash?"

Mitch hooks his thumbs into his belt loops. "Tight enough."

Tess knocks ash to the ground. "And what happens if someone finds out about the money you're stealing during those drug raids?"

Mitch freezes, and that's when the facade nearly cracks. But it doesn't, and he catches himself as a smile creeps up onto his lips.

"So you know." Shrugs. "You think that matters? I'll show you how much it matters." He pinches a space between his thumb and forefinger about an atom wide and holds it in front of Tess's face. "Here's how much. Because you're nothing but a fucking know-it-all bitch, and I'm a goddamn hero around here." He spits on the ground. "You're nobody."

Mitch climbs into the pickup and roars the diesel engine to life. Lowers the power window and stares at Tess with all the contempt he can muster. "Go do something with your life, and stay out of mine and Steph's."

Tess watches as the truck roars away with the rumbling growl of a jet fighter zipping off a battleship and vanishes out of the parking lot.

Tess doesn't hear from Steph for a few days. She checks admittance records at the hospital, knowing that Steph would never come local. She calls hospitals out of town, out of the county, and she's relieved when she doesn't find her. It doesn't touch the worry etched along the pit of her stomach, knowing anything could happen at that house out in the country.

When Steph does call, Tess knows why, and it's the most fucked-up relief she can imagine.

⚛

Tess's coffee has turned cold in the cup, and she doesn't feel like more. She sets it aside and says, "Show me."

Mitch is splayed out across the bed like an oversized starfish, wearing nothing but his own blood and boxer shorts. His face is smashed like Play-Doh pounded by a sledgehammer. Nose flattened, cheeks concave, mouth open in a gasp with jagged or empty spots where teeth should be.

The Louisville Slugger lies on the floor beside the bed. There's a glint of something embedded into the wood.

A tooth.

Steph squats beside the bed and runs her fingers along his arm. Blood pools and cakes in the crook of his elbow.

"He was drunk, and I wouldn't let him in," she says. "He knocked the door open, and he said he knew you knew about the money. He said he'd make sure you never told anyone, and he'd make sure I wouldn't tell anyone else."

She draws her fingers back, the tips covered with blood as thick as syrup.

"When he was done, he came in here, fell asleep. I waited. I waited until I knew he wasn't getting up, and then I got the baseball bat out of his car—that goddamned baseball bat he's so fucking proud of—and I made sure he couldn't get up."

Tess's hand drops onto Steph's shoulder. Steph looks up.

"What are we going to do?"

Tess knows people. People happy to help get rid of someone like Mitch. People with saws and shovels and lime and empty land.

She squeezes Steph's shoulder. Outside, the cicadas' buzz makes Tess think of the hum of a power line, the whine right before it pops.

13

"Graff life was cool, but things began to change when Mayor Koch declared 'war' on the artists and threatened to release killer wolves in the subway yard, basically giving po-po permission to bruise a few boys to get the word out."

GRAFF ART CRIME

MICHAEL A. GONZALES

The sounds of police sirens make me weak.

The sounds of police sirens make me weep.

Weak, weeping and thinking back to that muggy August night in 1986, when the police murdered my boyfriend Melvin Reid: we were both twenty-four years young, but old enough to be in real love and living our artsy life in New York City.

A half-hour before the brutal blows rained down from the blue boys, me and Mel were at our favorite dive bar, Lenore's, throwing back brown liquor while playing pool as soul songs roared from the jukebox. While the Isley Brothers fought the power, I sunk the eight ball in the corner pocket.

Our homegirl Audrey Wrigley bartended at Lenore's on 2nd Avenue, a nothing-fancy-or-frozen joint where beer-logo mirrors hung on the wall alongside paintings from the local artists. Most Friday nights, I'd meet Melvin when he got out of his film class on 7th Street near 3rd Avenue, and we'd walk down to grab a drink.

"Hey Shelly," he said through pretty teeth and plump lips on this particular Friday. My government name was Michelle, but few folks called me that. Clad in well-worn Doc Martens, black jeans, and a Thin Lizzy tour t-shirt, he looked so handsome. He smiled and kissed me tenderly on the cheek. "I missed you, *baby*."

"Ahhhh, isn't that sweet. I missed you too, baby." Mel laughed as he put his left arm around me. He had long dreadlocks, smooth brown skin and, in his right hand, carried a Pearl Paint shopping bag stuffed with art supplies.

A visual artist since his Harlem boyhood days tracing Jack Kirby comics and tagging "MEL 151" on subway station walls, he'd crossed over to canvases and hardly ever looked back. Dudes like Lee, Dondi, and Fab 5 Freddy were clocking mad dollars from these rich white folks who were just beginning to invest in what those guys had been giving away to the public for years.

Our Brooklyn apartment was full of Mel's impressionistic paintings of those Harlem streets where he'd spent his youth: going to Catholic school, playing pinball at Jesus Candy Store, riding his five-speed on Riverside Drive, buying comic books from the well-stocked newsstand on Broadway and 157th Street, chilling with his friends on the corner.

"Still, every now and then, I gotta tag a wall, a train or something," Mel explained over coffee on our first date. "That rush from the streets can't be replaced. Of course, cash from the paintings is great, but that street rush is heaven." Graff life was cool, but things began to change when Mayor Koch declared "war" on the artists and threatened to release killer wolves in the subway yard, basically giving po-po permission to bruise a few boys to get the word out.

Repped by the East Village gallery Bliss, everything was everything, though Mel sometimes complained about "stoopid" clients and their special requests. "This one old biddy is trying to get me to do a pink painting for her bathroom. Do I look like a dude that does pink paintings for bathrooms?" Lately, though, he'd become interested in moviemaking and was taking a beginner's course at the Anthology Film Archives twice a week.

It was after we watched a double feature of *Smithereens* and *Stranger than Paradise* at St. Marks Cinema that he was encouraged to enroll. "It's so weird with these newjack filmmakers," Mel said when we exited the theater and walked towards the 14th Street subway station where we took the #4 train to Brooklyn. "They so cool and hip, but you would think that we didn't exist."

"We?"

"Yeah, you know, us Black folks. These cooler-than-thou white people are more elitist than they think. They're just as square as their parents when it comes to race. Shit, I've been to CBGB's, I used to be a busboy at the Mudd Club, and I go to Danceteria. They still act like we're not part of the scene too."

"If you feel that strongly about it, maybe you should take some classes and make your own films. Tell your own stories."

"Seriously?"

"Why not," I replied as we walked down the stairs towards our train. "We already know from your paintings you've got an eye, now all you need is a camera."

Over the noise of the steel wheels on the tracks, we talked about the lack of Blacks in New York City narratives unless it was Mugger #2 in a *Death Wish* flick or an episode of *Kojak*. Thirty minutes later, we were pulling into the Utica Avenue station.

I might've planted the film school idea, but it took a few months for Melvin to actually register. Finally, he signed up in the spring, excited from day one with the prospect of making a movie. He started carrying a notebook, jotting down random ideas that he planned on turning into a screenplay. However, before he could make his feature film debut, he first had to make a short film for class, which led to a VHS renting frenzy as he filtered through influences.

He kicked around a few ideas, but at the last minute decided to freestyle with the camera as though he was Cassavetes. He was going to hang out with a few of his musician friends on St. Marks Place: Vernon Reid, Jared Nicolson, Jean-Paul Bourelly, and Bruce Mack. The plan was just to bring the 8mm camera to lunch at Dojo's and start filming their bugged-out conversations.

At the bar, Audrey always welcomed us with open arms and heavy pours. We chatted with her for a while, played pool and downed a few shots, but, with his first shoot happening the following day, Mel wanted to leave early. "I'm not trying to be all hung over tomorrow," he said. "I need to be fresh." We left the bar early and relatively sober.

Whereas most dudes would've been nervous the night before shooting footage for their first film, Melvin was giddy and acting silly. He held my hand as we skipped towards the subway station. Before walking down the stairs, he sat on the bench in a nearby playground and tightened the laces on his boots. I sat beside him, and he moved closer. Out of nowhere, he kissed me on the cheek.

"What's that for?" I asked.

"Just 'cause. You know, for the way you encourage me and all that."

"All that, huh?"

"Tomorrow I'm starting production on my first short. Who knows what this could lead to? Maybe I'll do a few videos, get my shit on MTV and Video Music Box."

I laughed. "You really just want to be on Video Music Box."

"True, but who am I to deny the masses my brilliance? I think Frantz Fanon said that."

"More like Fred Flintstone." I had two tokens in my pocket and handed one to Melvin seconds before we raced down the stairs.

The 2nd Avenue station has for years been one of the bleakest in the city, full of sleeping drunks, crazy homeless people, and more than a few rats. There was also plenty of stairs, but rarely any cops. After we went through the turnstile, there were five steps to the next landing. That's where Melvin said, "Let me show you how much I love you."

Old tagger habits never go away, I suppose, but I was surprised when Melvin reached into that Pearl's shopping bag and pulled out two Pilot jumbo markers. One was black, used to outline the image. The other was red, which he used to go over the piece. After placing the shopping bag against the wall, Mel drew a beautiful heart with arrows and crowns. Inside the valentine, next to black and red fireworks he wrote, "MEL 151 & SHELLY 4EVER." For a few seconds, my heart fluttered, but it quickly crumpled when I heard the raised voice behind me.

"Alright, Picasso, drop the markers and kneel on the ground," the steely cop voice barked behind us. Shocked, Mel and I spun around. Both cops stared at Mel as though he was Outlaw Number One. The one closest to him already had his piece pulled while the rookie called for back-up.

"Officer," Mel said. That was the last word I heard him say clearly before the rookie slapped him across the knee with a night stick. Mel screamed, dropped the markers, and fell to the dirty ground. Everything after that moment was a blur. Mel tried to stand, and again he was hit.

"So, you wanna write on walls, nigga?" one of them screamed. They swung; Mel groaned. Behind me I heard more cops running down the steps. "What are you doing?" I screamed. One burly white boy pushed me to the ground as those cops swarmed around Mel like ants on a discarded piece of bread. It was a blur of swinging arms, kicking feet, and Mel howling like a whipped dog, his pained voice echoing through the station.

For a moment, I was conflicted: should I stay or go? For a moment, mine and Mel's pained eyes connected, and I saw blood streaming from his nose, his straight white teeth crimson-stained. "Run," he muttered. "Run...run." I dashed up the stairs and east on Houston Street until I was back at Lenore's.

Crying like a crazy person, I rushed through the door and started banging my fists on the bar. From the rear of the bar, Audrey glanced upwards and rushed over. "What the fuck?" she screamed as I collapsed in the booth close to the door. "Where's Melvin? What happened to Melvin?"

"They're killing him," I screamed. "The police, they're killing him."

"What the fuck happened?"

For the longest time I sat there, crying, wailing, and screaming. Finally, I stammered out some words as Audrey poured me a shot of Jack Daniels and lit me a cigarette. Looking out the window, I saw an ambulance racing up Houston. Across the street from the bar, I saw the burnt-out shell of an abandoned car. Death was in the air.

"We have to go back," I mumbled. Audrey's busboy agreed to take care of the bar and we walked to the subway station. There were about fifty squad cars parked up and down the street, the blue and red lights flashing on the sidewalk that was now crowded with curious people. The EMS workers came up the stairs carrying a body that they quickly hustled into the ambulance. "They done fucked that boy up," a junkie standing behind me said. "They didn't have to do him like that."

I went with Audrey to her place on Avenue C. We called the 9th precinct and local hospitals until someone told me Mel was taken to Bellevue.

"Let me get a few things before we leave," Audrey said, deciding to take her camera, a 35-millimeter Nikon. We took a taxi there, speeding up 1st Avenue until we reached 27th Street.

I was shocked that there were so many people out front. "She must be the girlfriend," someone shouted as I pushed by reporters and television news crews. The plan was to meet Mel's family in the lobby, but as soon as I walked into the building, I was surrounded by police who informed me that I was being arrested for fleeing the scene of a crime.

"You have the right to remain silent," the cop said, reading me my rights. Silent, I thought, I had no intention of staying silent. There were too many eyes in the hospital for them to brutalize me, but they were still rough as they pushed me against the wall and handcuffed me.

From the corner of my eye, I caught the pale face of a smirking cop, the same guy who first struck Mel. With a toothpick in his mouth, the pig was taking much pleasure in my arrest. When the arresting officers marched me outside, the smirking cop was right behind me.

"You saw nothing. You hear me, bitch? Nothing." His breath was hot in my ear and felt kind of nasty. I was a native New Yorker, made to feel as though I was in a so-called Third World country, a place where human rights didn't matter, and the regime could kill you at any time without rhyme or reason.

The same freedoms that America defended in countries on the other side of the world didn't apply to those of us whose ancestors had been dragged here in chains. Five hundred years later the new overseers were policemen, and most were just as brutal as their great-great granddaddies were on the plantations.

At the police station they marched me upstairs and shut me in a small room with a table and chair. Those cops never charged me, but they interviewed me for hours hoping I would change my story of how their colleagues beat my man like a runaway slave. They tried to call me a liar, a whore, a drug addict, but I never changed my story.

Two hours into my interrogation, they were thrown for a loop when my father showed-up at the station house with Warren Michaels, one of the best civil rights lawyers in the city. Just because I was a struggling artist, didn't mean my parents were broke too.

A blind man could've seen the city's desperation as they tried to make this case about "just another dead nigger" who would still be breathing if it wasn't for drugs, drinks, and bad behavior. They told their story to *The Daily News*, *The Post*, and *The Times*, depicting Mel as though his beating was deserved, pretending that he brought it on himself, because of intoxication and ignorance.

With all the chaos going on at the hospital, no one paid attention to Audrey or her camera. Even I had forgotten until the following day when she showed me the upsetting pictures she took in Mel's hospital room. "I'm taking these to the *Village Voice* later today," she explained. "I talked to the photo editor this morning. I think they might want to use some older pictures I have of you guys. Is that cool with you?"

"Yes," I mumbled. "Yes. Anything that might let them see he was a real person and not some scary black King Kong the papers are acting like he was."

Days later, Audrey's brutal portrait of Mel was published on the *Village Voice* cover, a single black and white shot of him comatose in his hospital bed: eyes black and swollen, tubes running out of his nose, bruises around his neck and bandages wrapped around his head. It was the kind of photo that made people cringe, made them uncomfortable, and made them think about their own children on the streets of the city after dark. I was transported in time to when I was a little girl going through Grandma's *Jet* magazines, and by chance saw a picture of Emmett Till's brutally beaten face. I often tell people, "That was the moment I lost my innocence—the day I realized what could happen to someone with whom I shared a complexion."

For the next sixteen days, Melvin was in a coma, kept alive with the life support. The cops continued to deny that they had beaten him, telling the press and the public tall tales about how he tried to escape and fell down the stairs. Although he was in a coma, they handcuffed him to the hospital bed.

Mel's family, my dad, and I camped out in the waiting room a few doors down. When the memories and tears became too much, I took the elevator to the first floor where, outside the revolving doors, there was a protest march that included people of all races, classes and religious persuasions who were tired of hearing these stories of yet another beat-down black man, another half-dead brother-man, suffering because of the boys in blue.

"No justice, Just Us! No justice, just us!"

Standing next to the door was that cop again, who I found out from the *Village Voice* story was named Patrick Waters, a nice Irish boy from Brooklyn. Though I refused to look at him, I felt his eyes staring hard, trying to figure me out and perhaps uncover my weaknesses. Cops held all the power, but most of them thought they were smarter than they actually were.

Finally, when I couldn't take it any longer, I turned around and faced him. Waters stared, smiled, and winked—a gesture that almost made me start screaming. But, at that moment I heard someone call my name. "Oh, man, it's so good to see you," I said to Gerald Rodriguez, one of Mel's best friends. A fellow artist also down with Bliss Gallery, he and Mel had been together the first night we met. He gave me a loving hug and a kiss on the cheek.

"Where the hell you been?" I asked

"Don't get me started. I've been doing fundraising and stuff at the gallery. All the artists from Bliss have been working on stuff, trying to raise money for Mel's family. The gallery owner sent me over here with a check to give to you. Help you out with bills, groceries, you know, whatever you need."

"I don't know what to say. Please tell her I said thank you."

"You want to go get a coffee or something?"

"Sure. There's a place around the corner."

Minutes later we were sitting in a booth ordering coffee and Danish. Out of nowhere, Gerald laughed. "What's so funny?"

"Nothing. I just thought about the crazy story Melvin told me once about getting stopped by some cops on 57th Street when he was seventeen. They pushed him against the wall, patted him down and told him they stopped him because somebody Black had stolen a car. Melvin told 'em, 'If I stole a car, wouldn't I be driving down the street instead of walking?'"

We both laughed. It felt good, though minutes later I was crying again, wiping my dry eyes with rough napkins.

●

Seventeen days later, Mel was dead. In the middle of the night, he faded away. His death was covered on every morning show, every radio program, and the headlines on every newspaper were huge. In the hospital waiting room, many tears were shed, screams were released, tempers raised, but the riots Gerald predicted never happened.

That night, many of Mel's friends and family met up at Lenore's where we shared memories of the man they knew: the slick dude on the basketball court, the shy guy with women, the music and film fan, the intense artist who loved New York City more than it loved him back. His beautiful mother Margret talked about taking him to the Metropolitan and Guggenheim Museums when he was a boy. "He looked at the Van Goghs for hours," she said sadly. "There was something about those pictures that he connected with, a strange force that he connected with."

Of course, the cops and the media hung the word "graffiti" around his neck as though it was another noose. They spit out the word "graffiti" like it was a curse, as though anyone in that world of spray paint and markers deserved to be exterminated like roaches.

At the bar, Audrey and I had hung Mel's paintings on the wall before the reception. Most of his work was a celebration of his early life. In those vivid pictures, kids gathered in candy stores, older Black women sat talking on stoops, stylish players puffed reefer on Riverside Drive benches, pretty teen girls danced outside a record shop, and hip-hop DJs spun in the park.

My favorite was an intense self-portrait of Mel with a hint of a smile, eyes intense, serious as hell, staring at the world defiantly. He posed himself in front of the uptown building where he was raised, a red-bricked pre-war with a black fire escape scaling down the side. Lost in his haunting gaze, I felt his presence and knew that through that picture, he would live forever.

Outside, somewhere in the distance, a police car siren screamed.

"The reality is that the police exist primarily as a system for managing and even producing inequality ..."

-Alex S. Vitale

14

"'Too many boys get halfway through the *Rocky Road to Dublin* and then turn into fucking Eddie Van fucking Halen.'"

THE BALLAD OF 223

PRESTON LANG

T he cop had never seen a lute before.

"What the hell is this?"

"It's a little—guitar."

Alan didn't like the way Officer Richter handled the instrument, gripping it loosely by the neck like a two-liter bottle of Coke.

"This is not a guitar," he said. "I know what a guitar is."

"It's a lute."

"If it's a lute, don't call it a guitar. I know what a guitar is."

Richter was state police, a sturdy man in his forties who knew what a guitar was. He tucked the lute under his left arm while he brushed something off his pants with his right. Alan's sole means of support was wedged into a cop's armpit, getting wet on a drizzly morning.

"Where you going?"

Alan was on his way to Hopkins Glen. One of the biggest ren fairs of the season was starting Friday. He was ahead of schedule. All he had to do was hitch 90 miles, then find a floor to crash on. A little rain and this big, mulish man were wrecking all his plans.

"It's illegal to walk on the side of the highway. You know that?"

"I'm sorry."

"You have any dope on you?"

"No."

"Let me have the backpack."

Alan didn't love this, but it wouldn't sink him. Inside was a tee shirt, socks, jeans, tights, tunic, and pointy shoes. No drugs. Alan didn't use in season—not historically accurate. He wasn't sure why he kept to this rule, considering all the other ways he was anachronistic. You made your real money at ren fairs playing pop tunes like they were written in 1499—*Enter Sandman, Hot for Teacher*. Alan had a high willowy voice and the mien of a humble bard. He was a servant, not a rockstar, and he was ready for anything. If someone wanted Paula Abdul or "that song from that rib commercial" he played it. Alan had made plenty of florins with the theme to *Duck Tales*.

Richter sniffed the bag—it smelled like sweat and feet, not weed. He put his hand inside and rooted around but didn't take anything out. Another cop called from the car.

"What's going on?"

"Get in the car," Richter said to Alan.

Were they really taking him in? They really wanted to drive around with a grimy picker who hadn't showered in a week? Richter shoved him in the back uncuffed, then walked around to drive while his partner, Murphy according to his name tag, did a crossword on the dash. No one spoke as they drove, and the station was empty when they arrived. The two cops were equal in rank, but Murphy was younger, and he seemed to find his partner almost comically stupid.

"You got a drug charge or what?" he asked Richter.

Richter, realizing he didn't, emptied Alan's bag out on the floor. He was not pleased with pointy shoes.

"What's this for?"

"I perform at fairs."

Alan thought they'd already covered this.

"Dancing around in tights and slippers?"

"I play the lute. I sing songs from the late Middle Ages and Renaissance."

"Everybody dressed up like a faggot back then?"

Alan had no response to this. Murphy gave him a commiserating look—*What a moron my partner is.*

"What do you want to do, Richter?" Murphy said. "You think he's the king-pin? A few more questions you'll break him? Brokaw will be talking about it on the news tonight."

Richter looked hard at Alan.

"Officer Murphy is going to call DC and have them fax your record to us." Richter said *fax* like this was a new thing for him. "If there's something to find, we'll find it."

"Oh, Christ," Murphy said.

Richter kept his eyes on Alan and continued.

"You need to tell me now if you've got any priors, outstanding warrants."

"I was arrested for vagrancy in Virginia one time—last summer. Charges were dropped."

"That it?"

Was it? Alan got stopped a lot, cuffed a few times, but none of that would be in some DC database—if that was even real.

"Machine's out of paper," Murphy said as he left the room.

"Yeah, we're not sending," Richter said to Murphy's back.

Alan lived much of his life in the 1400s, but this didn't sound right. A machine out of paper would be a problem either way. He hesitated but then had to ask—the sooner everything came through, the sooner he'd be back on the road.

"I'm sorry, officer. Is there paper in the fax machine?"

"We're waiting for a fax to come *in*." Richter spoke as if Alan was a slow child.

"Right. But if there's no paper in the machine—"

"We're *receiving* a fax."

"Sure, but—"

"You really don't get it?"

"I guess I don't."

"So just shut the fuck up."

They waited for ten minutes. Alan looked out the window at the parking lot. It was raining harder now. The fax machine made a noise, but nothing came out. Richter fussed with it. He was pushing buttons when Murphy came back in the room with a stack of fax paper. He pulled out the tray and loaded the machine.

"Richter, you're a God damned retard," he said.

"Okay, look—"

"You really think we get the actual sheet of paper they send us from DC? That's what you were waiting for?"

Murphy nodded to Alan.

"Even this Greensleeves motherfucker here knew better." Murphy gave Alan another glance like they were in it together. "He really thinks a piece of paper travels through the ether, from DC into our machine. That's really what he thinks."

Richter didn't respond. Instead, he kicked around Alan's clothes a little more. When he got tired of that, he opened the lute case and plucked the strings. Then he pulled them off one by one. To Alan this was like having the hair yanked out of his head. Hurt like hell, but no permanent damage. At a fair, someone could always hook you up. It didn't have to be perfect. Alan had improvised before—violin strings, electrical wire. You were playing outdoors to people who were drunk on ale from plastic tankards, throwing little wooden ducats at you when you took their requests. Alan was trying to stay positive—tomorrow all that would be his.

When Richter reached inside the lute, he didn't find anything. It looked like he was going to put it on the desk, but then he lifted it violently over his head with one hand.

"No."

Alan stood up and reached for his instrument. Richter dropped the lute and hit Alan full in the face. He'd taken shots to the head before—from period string players and improvisational sonneteers. But this was a bull-strong rural cop. Alan had a moment, still on his feet, seeing the lights. It seemed like a long time. He saw Dr. Chan who'd taught him to play the lute and got him his current axe from a dead colleague. Then he saw the fairgoers throwing those giant turkey legs that they'd buy but get tired of halfway through. Then Richter hit him again and ended the concert.

Alan was in the hospital for three days before arraignment. His public defender was a very tired woman from legal aid who advised him to make a deal—fifteen years. It took him a few minutes to figure out why he was in so much trouble.

"You'll be out in eight," she said. "That's not bad considering you fired a gun at a police officer."

"I fired a gun?"

"You'll have a bed. Three meals a day."

She saw him as a vagrant with pointy shoes in a bag, not a poet of the highway who had a gig to make.

"At the trial—I can explain."

The lawyer was fundamentally deflated by this—*please, don't make this hard.* She laid it all out again, and it still made no sense.

"Your prints are on the weapon. There's a bullet in the fax machine. Three witnesses have sworn to what you did."

He imagined a trial—he'd profess his innocence while his lawyer rolled her eyes and shook her head.

"Where's my lute?" he asked her.

"Your what?"

⬤

Once a week he'd get 90 minutes in the music room. They had two bad guitars and a banjo with three strings. He looked forward to this all week. The rest of his life was hell. Endless tedium jolted by violence. And then, for no apparent reason, the music sessions were cancelled, and Alan tried to find a reasonable method of suicide.

Instead of hanging himself, he took the strips of an old shirt and tied them taut at the end of his bed to approximate the tuning of a lute. Of course, it wasn't perfect. And his cellmate punched him in the gut and wrecked the strings the first night they went up. But Alan put it back together. There were a few weeks of fighting over this, but finally the big man stopped caring. Anything he did to Alan now was unrelated to whether or not there was a make-believe lute in the cell.

The guards were also antagonistic at first, but they quickly shrugged it off, and Alan was moderately happy in the hours when he could sit alone and play.

And then came Catherine Delong from Minson College, providing monthly musical enrichment. She talked about the healing power of sound. The guitars and banjos had disappeared from the music room, so Delong played woodwind instruments while a few prisoners banged out percussion accompaniment. One time, Delong brought in an old French reed and had them clap out 5/4 while she did fancy glissandos and tricky high-note passages up top. She was excellent, and Alan liked to hear her play. She told them how excited she was about a spring concert of ancient monastic music at Minson. Just a small chamber group—Delong on winds, percussionist, harp, and a guest performer on something called viol de gras. Alan told her he knew how to play one, and she nodded—cons lied to her all the time. He was lying to her now.

"Bring it next time," he said. "I'll play it for you."

Alan had never made a call from prison before, but the next Tuesday, he phoned collect to Dr. Chan at Eastman School of Music. He'd taken lessons with her for a few months when he was sixteen. Chan told him to come to Eastman after he graduated high school—just said it like it was the most natural thing in the world. *Of course, you'll get in.* But Alan never graduated high school, and then he needed to move. Life had never run smooth. He wasn't even sure Chan would remember him, but the good doctor accepted the charges.

"I don't understand, dear. Why are you in prison?"

"Don't worry about it, Doc. Can you tell me how a viol de gras is tuned?"

Chan didn't know off the top of her head, but she found the book she needed quickly, which provided a description of the instrument and its tuning, along with sheet music for one of the few surviving pieces written specifically for the viol de gras.

"Sing it to me, please," Alan said.

Dr. Chan had a weak, raspy voice, but as with most great musicians, there was something compelling in the way she sang. Phrasing and punch and sheer musicality counted for a lot, but when she got to a fast, high part, she stopped.

"Let me get the axe," she said.

Dr. Chan put down the phone. Half a minute later she came back on Cordoba C5 and played until someone ended the call and shoved Alan away from the phone.

Alan tuned the strings of his bed to those of the viol de gras, and he practiced as best as he could. The next month, Delong didn't bring a viol de gras, but she had a program for the spring concert—three months away. The guest string player was named Oscar Cervi. Alan asked again after the viol de gras.

In March, Delong finally brought a viol with a plastic body and nylon strings. She wasn't going to bring the genuine article into prison, but she handed this imitation to Alan. It was a bit of an adjustment from what he was used to, but he played *Al Sien Escient* damn near perfect.

When she took back the instrument, she held it a little more carefully.

"Where did you learn to—do that?"

He shrugged.

"My grandmother was an old French woman."

As the day of the concert came nearer, Alan had trouble getting on the phone. Twice he managed to call, but Dr. Chan was out. Eight days before showtime, he finally got through. Chan wanted to talk about the viol de gras. She'd gotten interested and done some research, but Alan knew he had to lay things out quickly.

"Doc, I need one favor. There's a guy named Oscar Cervi—"

"Yes, I've heard some of his—"

"If you can invite him to Eastman to do a recital or masterclass next weekend, I'll really appreciate it."

"Why?"

"It would help me—a lot. And tell him you'd like to discuss a faculty position for him."

"I don't have that kind of power."

"I know. When he shows up, tell him you made a mistake or something, but it would be really good for me if he's at Eastman next weekend."

"Even just from a technical standpoint, he's not that accomplished—"

"I know, I know. Can you please just ask him?"

Did Dr. Chan understand the urgency? Would she remember the name and the date? Always absent-minded, she was getting older, and it was very short notice. When the line cut off, Alan wasn't sure of anything.

The next Tuesday Delong came in as scheduled. When Alan asked how things were going for the spring concert, her jaw tightened.

"We had a cancellation."

She was not happy at all with Oscar Cervi. A gig booked months in advance, and he dumps it for a better offer—*Eastman*. She cursed the school—a fancy name, unearned prestige.

"We have to rearrange everything. It'll be fine, but—"

"Get me out for the day, I could play it."

He said it lightly, but he saw it register.

"Do they let you out? I mean—can you request that?"

"My power is pretty limited in here."

But Delong was very good at getting what she wanted. He heard nothing for the next three days. The day before the concert he was brought to see the warden just before dinner.

"You're leaving at 5 PM tomorrow for Minson College. You don't take one step without the OK from Officer Gattis or Officer Turner. You understand me?"

"Yes, sir."

Gattis was big and a little lazy. Alan didn't know Turner, but he was the junior partner on the mission. This was offsite overtime, a gift for two men who were tight with the warden.

Alan was shackled hand and foot for the fifty-minute drive to Minson. Then Gattis freed his hands and sat in on rehearsal in the small, windowless practice room. Delong offered Alan a dark blazer and tie. Gattis let him put on the blazer, but he hesitated a bit before letting Delong make a single Windsor around her own neck before draping it on Alan and pulling it tight.

Alan went through the whole set list with the rest of the group: a stout woman on harp, and a longhaired dude on percussion. The first tune they did really sang. Alan plucked thick staccato cords and left the melody to the ladies. Some monk in Languedoc 600 years ago had worked it out, and now it was here with them in a stuffy little room that to Alan was starting to smell like freedom. They did the other three numbers, and it all sounded good. The big woman on harp had a few minor suggestions, but they were all happy and relieved that Alan was legit. Maybe they were even a little excited at the novelty and danger a man in orange pants and shackles lent to a night of ancient music.

The small auditorium could hold about 500 people. It was less than a quarter filled with undergrads clogged near the back. Alan was guessing they were required by class to attend. But the bored kids perked up a little at the site of his leg irons, and a few glanced at the bulls by the doors.

The first tune was the easiest, and it all went as written. The lady on the ancient harp nodded at Alan—he'd taken her notes. The dude on percussion gave him a comradely clap on the shoulder. Alan messed up the fingering on the second song, but he recovered reasonably well, and no one noticed other than the harpist.

For the third song, Alan just plucked a single ostinato line underneath some wild horn passages from Delong. Terrific stuff. Clearly the wine flowed pretty freely at some of the French abbeys back in the day. But not everyone was a fan. Alan could see Gattis shifting uneasily from foot to foot. Turner had actually taken a seat on the arm of a chair near the side exit. Just before the finale, he sat down properly, fading fast.

The last piece was fifteen minutes long, and there's only so much 14th century chamber music a corrections officer can take. Turner's eyes shut and his head nodded back. During a four-bar rest, Alan put the viol down carefully and made a leap off the side of the stage.

It's not easy to run in leg irons, but it was only a five-step shuffle to the exit.

"Move, move!" Gattis called from the back of the auditorium.

But Alan had his hand on the doorknob before Turner was awake and out of his seat. The exit led to a short hallway filled with stacked chairs and music stands. Alan shoved them in front of the door and hobbled off. The hall led to another building. One flight down then out a rear entrance. From there he was at the top of a hill that spilled across a grass field. He tripped once and rolled a bit but never stopped as he dashed for the road, a one-lane path where he stood in the middle of the lane and waved down the first car to come along. It was a red Honda with Phish stickers on the front, and it stopped half a foot from contact.

"What the hell, man?" the kid yelled.

"Please, you got to help me," Alan said. "My friend just called—told me he'd taken all of it."

"All of what?"

"The acid. Now he's talking about jumping off the roof. He's not a guy who can trip alone. You know what I mean?"

The girl in the passenger seat was nodding, the boy was still clutching the wheel.

"He's talking about erasing himself. Please, I'm worried. We have to hurry."

"Where is he?" the girl asked.

Alan gave an address he'd memorized months earlier when he'd gotten a glimpse of a map of the area. As they drove, he worked his tie into the left cuff and flossed it back and forth—this was the only useful thing his cell mate had taught him.

"What are you doing to your shoes?" the girl asked.

Alan was still young enough to be a college student, but with the light on his face, it was clear he wasn't an undergrad. Still, they kept driving. Half a mile from the address, he told them to stop the car.

"What's going on?"

"I lied to you before."

They didn't speak, and Alan held up the metal.

"You can keep the leg irons if you want."

He saw them tense up in front. After being a universal target for nearly a year, it was odd and a little exhilarating to be feared and obeyed.

"Why do you have those?" the girl asked.

"I'm a fugitive. They made up some charges and put me away. You think that's right?"

"No," the boy said.

"So I'm going to ask you to keep all this to yourselves."

"Yeah. No, yeah—we won't tell anyone."

"You guys are the best."

Alan hopped out of the car and ran—fast and easy now—into the woods.

*

After that, a lot went right for Alan. The kids never talked, the dogs never picked up his scent, and he slid past the roadblocks in the back of a flatbed, under piles of plastic-wrapped deer meat. Freezing, starving, and penniless, he knew it was blind luck that led him all the way to Queens where he managed to rent a basement apartment for 50 dollars cash per week. He bought a mandolin and tuned a cheap radio to 87.95 on the FM dial that broadcast Celtic music and news 24/7 from a small tower eight blocks away.

In two months, Alan felt ready enough. He developed the slight brogue of the Irishman who's overstayed his visa by a few years. And while his Borstal boyhood was false, his chops on the mandolin were real. He hit a few of the open jams at Irish bars in town, and it didn't take long for him to pick up regular gigs—pubs, weddings, festivals. No one thought it was strange that he insisted on taking his pay in cash, and musicians appreciated his skill and restraint.

"Too many boys get halfway through the *Rocky Road to Dublin* and then turn into fucking Eddie Van fucking Halen."

On no occasion did Alan turn into Eddie Van Halen. He plucked out the cords, sang harmonies, showed up on time and sober, grew a thick beard. He didn't talk much or reveal anything about himself, but this was respected. When he evaded inquiries, there was always someone to pipe up for him.

"Leave him be. If the man blew up a Tesco in Liverpool, that's his business."

One time a fiddler asked if they'd met at Mountjoy. Alan just shook his head.

"Well, you done your time somewhere."

It was probably pretty obvious. Alan didn't like to sit with his back exposed to the room, and he'd cross the street to avoid walking past a cop car. But the quiet man who gives you rock-solid rhythm on mandolin doesn't get booted from the trad music community for a criminal past.

The hunt for the fugitive lute player grew passive. The picture Alan once saw in a post office looked nothing like him. All the same, he could never climb too high up the ladder. He did a few live radio shows with The Mangertons, but when they wanted him to appear on PBS, he had to say no. A year later The Blind Time wanted him to tour—Canada, UK, Ireland. That would've slid him into the kind of respectable sideman status that was probably his destiny from birth. But he had to turn them down. Instead, he scraped together a local living of small gigs, dance classes, lessons for kids whose parents insisted on "all this Lucky Charms bullshit."

Years passed. Alan had many acquaintances but no close friends, and he never dated anyone longer than a few weeks. When Dr. Chan died, he bought a bus ticket to Rochester so he could hear *Bouree in E Minor* while they lowered the great woman into the earth. But he didn't go. The next year, Chan was replaced on faculty by Oscar Cervi.

⬤

It was a beautiful ceremony. A big glass house with a yard in front and the Long Island Sound in back. A June evening so thick with romance that it was hard to imagine that anyone could go home alone. They all clapped along as the bridesmaids performed a stepdance to *Silver Spear*. Lovely young women in green with perfect confidence and a deeply flawed sense of rhythm.

On a break, Alan made himself a plate and went out to eat on top of the dune, away from the crowd. Ten minutes in, he saw a man approach from the house. There was no escape as the father of the bride sat down in the sand next to Alan.

"Hey there, Mandolin," the father said. "I just wanted to thank you for everything."

"You have a lovely family."

"A lovely family, yes." the father copied Alan's quiet brogue. "Look at this house. The property. Thank you so much."

"You have a lovely home, sir."

"And I'm thanking you for it."

"I don't understand."

And then Alan recognized the man. Officer Murphy hadn't aged well. He was the sort of Irishman who went suddenly ancient at 55. His skin hung loose and leathery off his face.

"You know what I made riding the fucking highways in that stupid hat? Pad all the overtime you want, you're still making less than a kindergarten teacher. Is that right?"

Alan didn't answer.

"You remember Richter. That fucking idiot. Turns his back and you grabbed his gun. I had to pop you one in the face—knocked you cold. They told it to the news like you were a beast, not a skinny Greensleeves motherfucker in pointy shoes—but I never let Richter forget. Still, if you'd known what you were doing, you could've killed us both instead of shooting the damn fax machine."

Murphy smiled. This was all true to him. And a lot of it was true—the pointy shoes, the bullet in the fax machine, slow-witted Richter. Even the phrase *Greensleeves motherfucker* was exactly what Murphy had called him so many years earlier.

"The story got attention, I got introduced to this man from Auburn Hills. He thought I had the right look, the right instincts. Next thing I know, I'm a *private security consultant*." He waved back at the house. "It was a good time to get in the business."

"I think you have me mistaken with someone else."

"I don't forget a face. I forget names. I can look it up, though. What was it '96, '97?"

Faintly, Alan could hear the fiddler tuning from inside the house.

"I think they need me," Alan said. "It was nice having a chat with you, sir."

As Alan walked back in the house, he felt it all coming together in the Dorian mode, a ballad, a chronicle of the misdeeds he'd suffered and the deception and cheap brutality of the men who ruled him. He'd heard of this kind of inspiration—songs coming to you whole in a dream, written in water on a clear pond.

Alan took the mandolin out of its case. Low E was flat. He tuned it past the mark then pulled it back. Perfect. But Alan didn't play. He put the instrument back in its case and went out the front door, across the yard to a dirt road. Away from the water and the million-dollar homes and the lovely people enjoying the generosity of Officer Murphy. On the highway, axe slung across his back, he walked on the shoulder of the road.

" 'You're full of it. It's
not against the law
to run.'

'Yes it is. Especially
for us.' "

-Kenneth Eade

15

"This investigation has concluded that PO Delacorte acted within department policy."

THE REPORT

ANDREW CASE

September 28, 2020
Incident Report 2019-IAD-22
Reporting Officer: Allison Edderson, Scottsdale PD Internal Affairs Department

Introduction

The following represents the final report of the investigation into an officer-involved shooting that took place on Saturday, June 22, 2019, at 3:35 p.m. at 12657 North 81st Street in Scottsdale, Arizona. The report is based upon review of record evidence and interviews with the following individuals: Stewart Jensen, PO Anthony Delacorte, Communications Officer Claudia Estrella, PO Dan Halversham, PO Bryan Reyes, and Lieutenant Elysse Scott. Summaries of those interviews are appended to this incident report.

Facts

On Saturday, June 22, 2019, at approximately 1:59 p.m., Scottsdale 911 received a telephone call from the residents of 12655 North 81st Street reporting an attempted home invasion. The 911 operator properly obtained a description of the suspect, later identified as Stewart Jensen, who, at the time, resided next door at 12657 North 81st Street. During the call, which was recorded, Mr. Jensen can be heard stating "it's hot out," and "we just wanted to use the pool," and "you didn't have to be an asshole about it." The telephone call lasted approximately four minutes and thirty-two seconds. At the conclusion of the call, the 911 operator asked the caller whether he wanted Scottsdale Police Department units to respond. The caller answered in the affirmative.

At 2:05 p.m., a call was put out for a potential home invasion in progress at 12655 North 81st Street. The radio run shows that PO Bryan Reyes and PO Dan Halversham, on patrol in the West Sector at the time, were the nearest units to the location. They responded to the call at 2:08 p.m. and stated they were en route to the location. At 2:14 p.m., PO Reyes and PO Halversham radioed to confirm that they had arrived at the location. They interviewed the caller and inspected the property.

The caller stated that the neighbor had tried to enter the backyard of 12655 North 81st Street and had attempted to unlock the gate to the backyard pool. Upon being confronted, the neighbor had tried to enter the house. After the resident called the police, the neighbor had turned and left. PO Reyes and PO Halversham determined that there was no current evidence that anyone was attempting to enter the home or trespassing the property. The neighbor was no longer on the scene.

The original caller then stated that without police intervention, he feared that the neighbor would again attempt to enter his property.

PO Reyes and PO Halversham, at the original caller's request, therefore approached the next-door home at 12657 North 81st Street and rang the doorbell. From behind the door, they heard an adult male state, in an agitated voice, "Go away! I don't want anything!" After ringing again, they heard the voice state, "I have my daughter in here! Go away!"

At the mention of a daughter by a person who, based upon his vocal tone, appeared to be in distress, PO Reyes and PO Halversham grew concerned. They rang the doorbell again, but there was no answer. PO Halversham stated in his subsequent interview that he heard crying inside the house and, based on his training and experience, determined that the crying was coming from an infant in distress. They rang the doorbell again, and this time they once again heard the voice inside state, "Go away!"

Concerned for the safety of the child, PO Halversham and PO Reyes called for tactical assistance and a hostage negotiating officer at 2:26 p.m.. Over the course of the next twenty-eight minutes, sixteen uniformed officers, including PO Anthony Delacorte and Communications Officer Claudia Estrella, who has received specialized training in hostage negotiations, arrived on the scene. Under the direction of Lt. Elysse Scott, the officers established a secure perimeter. Communications Officer Reyes then established contact by determining the telephone number inside the house and calling it from a secure SPD line.

Officer Estrella made contact with the individual inside the house. The individual confirmed that he had approached his neighbor's house, but stated that he "only wanted to use the pool," and had "asked if he could take his daughter for a swim." He stated further that it was hot and that "my air conditioning is not working." The recorded outdoor temperature at the time of the call was 119 degrees. Based on visual observation of the house, PO Reyes determined that the evaporative cooling system appeared functional and noted that the individual in the house had therefore made a false statement to a law enforcement officer.

At 3:08 p.m. Officer Estrella heard the sound of crying over the secure line and asked the individual whether the child was in distress. The individual stated that "she is just hot," and then alternately stated that "she needs to have her diaper changed." Based upon these contradictory statements, which were relayed to the team, Lt. Scott determined that an extraction was necessary to prevent potential harm to the child.

At 3:16 p.m., Officer Estrella once again called the house. Once again, the resident responded. At this point Officer Estrella stated that the team would perform an extraction and that the resident should stand away from the front door to avoid injury when the team broke it down. The resident stated that "you don't need to come in," and that "everything is fine, she just needed a diaper."

At 3:22 p.m., a woman, later identified as Rebecca Jensen, arrived on the scene. She identified herself as a recent resident of the house, the ex-wife of the current resident, and the mother of the child. She asked Lt. Scott why the officers had surrounded the building. Lt. Scott stated that the officers were in place to protect the safety of Mr. Jensen and the child because Mr. Jensen's contradictory statements suggested that the child was in danger, and his misleading statement regarding the air conditioning.

Ms. Jensen stated that she was the child's mother, and asked if she could enter the house and speak to Mr. Jensen. Lt. Scott determined that allowing Ms. Jensen to enter the home would be detrimental to the safety of the child, Mr. Jensen, and herself, and denied her permission to enter.

At 3:29 p.m., Mr. Jensen called back Officer Estrella on the secure line. Mr. Jensen asked the officers to leave. Officer Estrella stated to Mr. Jensen that they were not going to leave and asked him to exit the house. He stated, "how do I know you aren't going to shoot me if I leave the house?" Officer Estrella stated, "We aren't going to shoot you if you leave the house." Mr. Jensen responded, "I'm going to carry the girl. You won't shoot me if I'm holding the girl." Officer Estrella did not relay this portion of the message to any member of the on-site team.

At 3:32 p.m., Mr. Jensen opened the front door of the house and stepped outside. He was holding his two-year-old daughter, identified herein as FJ, in his arms. Once he exited the front door, he hoisted FJ over his head, extending his arms fully above his head with the girl face-down in his hands. As later recounted by PO Reyes, he looked up, apparently meeting the girl's eyes.

According to each person interviewed, the girl appeared to be listless in Mr. Jensen's arms. PO Halversham stated that she was "not really moving," and PO Reyes stated that she "may have been asleep." PO Delacorte stated that he thought the girl had been injured, and stated that she appeared "limp." No other officer corroborated PO Delacorte's description that the girl appeared to have been injured.

At this point, the officers present formed a semi-circle at a perimeter of approximately thirty feet from Mr. Jensen's house. He walked towards the officers for a period of forty-six seconds, then turned and started walking back towards the house.

Officer Delacorte stated that after Mr. Jensen turned around, he pulled back his arms as though preparing to throw the girl to the ground. No other officer corroborated this statement, though PO Reyes and PO Halversham both stated that they believed that Mr. Jensen was returning to the house to harm the girl. PO Delacorte ordered Mr. Jensen to freeze. Mr. Jensen continued to walk back towards the house. PO Delacorte at this point took out his weapon, aimed it at Mr. Jensen, and ordered him to "put down that girl."

Mr. Jensen continued to walk towards the house. In an effort to protect the girl from potential harm that Mr. Jensen might inflict on her, and concerned that the officers would lose contact with the girl if Mr. Jensen made it back into the house, PO Delacorte fired at Mr. Jensen. The shot missed Mr. Jensen, but struck the girl in the upper jaw. Mr. Jensen screamed and dropped FJ at this point. The single shot was fired at 3:35 p.m..

Communications Officer Estrella called for EMT at 3:36 p.m.. Officer Halversham restrained Ms. Jensen while PO Delacorte arrested Mr. Jensen. The paramedics arrived at 3:42 p.m. and took FJ to Scottsdale Memorial Hospital, where she was declared dead at 4:06 p.m.. PO Delacorte detained Mr. Jensen, who was arrested for trespassing and endangering the welfare of a minor. Mr. Jensen is currently in the Maricopa County Jail awaiting trial on those charges. Ms. Jensen was brought to the hospital to attend to her daughter and thereafter released from custody.

Analysis

Actions of PO Halversham and PO Reyes

PO Halversham and PO Reyes followed department policy prior to the attempted extraction. They responded in a timely and professional manner to the call and obtained a complete statement from the complainant. Despite the fact that they did not observe a crime in progress, they took action recommended by the complainant to prevent future criminal conduct in accordance with the Scottsdale Police Department Patrol Guide and the Arizona Victims' Bill of Rights. Once they were confronted by a belligerent and uncooperative subject, they properly radioed for additional members of the service to ensure that the scene was safe and secure. Had they attempted to enter the house by force at an earlier point, they would have risked harming themselves, Mr. Jensen, or FJ. This officer concludes that, up to the point at which an extraction was ordered, PO Halversham and PO Reyes acted within department policy and entirely properly.

Actions of PO Estrella

PO Estrella properly established contact with the uncooperative suspect, allowing the SPD team access to Mr. Jensen. She maintained this contact over the course of an hour, relaying key information to the team, including information regarding Mr. Jensen's agitated mental state and the apparent distress of FJ. This information allowed the secure team to evaluate the relative risks of performing an extraction or waiting for Mr. Jensen to leave the house.

Further, PO Estrella demonstrated exceptional skill in convincing Mr. Jensen to leave the house voluntarily. PO Estrella's actions avoided the potential risks associated with an extraction, and allowed the secure team to hold their positions rather than enter the house, where they could have been subject to a surprise attack by Mr. Jensen.

PO Estrella failed to notify the surrounding team of Mr. Jensen's final communication before leaving the house, namely that he had an unreasonable and paranoid fear that he would be shot by the officers, and that he was holding FJ above his head in an effort to ensure that the officers would not open fire. It is impossible to determine whether this information, had it been conveyed, would have altered the outcome of the incident. Nevertheless, this investigation has determined that the statement was "material" within the meaning of the Scottsdale Patrol Guide

Regulation Number 118-9, which requires communications officers to "relay all material information to the ranking officer on the scene," in this case, Lt. Scott.

Therefore, this investigation concludes that PO Estrella violated PG 118-9, and recommends as discipline that she be made to forfeit five vacation days, to be assessed as one reduced vacation day during each of the next five years of service.

Actions of Lieutenant Scott

Lieutenant Scott properly secured the scene and engaged Ms. Jensen, when she arrived, without allowing her to enter the house, which could have posed a danger to Ms. Jensen, Mr. Jensen, or FJ. Lt. Scott's orders were straightforward and clear. She evaluated the information that was passed on by PO Estrella and properly concluded that the danger to FJ was sufficiently imminent that an extraction was necessary.

After PO Delacorte fired, Lt. Scott properly took control of the scene, directing PO Estrella to contact emergency services and detaining Ms. Jensen for her own safety and the officers' safety. She accompanied Ms. Jensen to the hospital and consoled her over the loss of FJ. It is the official opinion of the Scottsdale Police Department Legal Bureau that Lt. Scott's actions contributed to Ms. Jensen's decision not to file a cause of action against the Scottsdale Police Department. For her actions, the Scottsdale Police Department has decided to promote Lt. Scott to Captain and assign her to be the commanding officer of the North Sector Precinct.

Actions of PO Delacorte

This investigation has concluded that PO Delacorte acted within department policy. The Scottsdale Police Department Patrol Guide Regulation 60-1 states that deadly force may only be used when "an officer reasonably believes that an individual is in imminent danger of suffering death or grievous bodily harm, and reasonably believes that deadly force can stop that threat." During his interview, PO Delacorte stated that he believed that Mr. Jensen had pulled back FJ over his head and was about to throw her to the ground, which would constitute an imminent danger of grievous bodily harm. Although no other officer corroborated this account, none definitively stated that Mr. Jensen did not pull back the child as though to throw her to the ground.

Further, PO Delacorte did not know (because PO Estrella had not informed the extraction team) that Mr. Jensen had stated that he was holding FJ over his head to ensure that he would not be shot, or that Mr. Jensen had an unreasonable and paranoid suspicion that officers would use deadly force against him. Therefore, it was reasonable for PO Delacorte to conclude that Mr. Jensen's behavior was extremely unusual and demonstrated reckless disregard for the welfare of FJ.

While it is a tragic accident that PO Delacorte missed his intended target and instead hit and killed FJ, PO Delacorte acted all times within department policy and in the interests of protecting FJ from Mr. Jensen. To ensure that PO Delacorte provide the best possible protection to the people of Scottsdale going forward, it is recommended that he undergo an additional forty hours of firearms training, to be administered as ten additional hours over each of the next four years, to improve his accuracy.

This concludes the report of the Scottsdale Police Department Internal Affairs Bureau on the above-referenced matter.

16

"The pipeline from failing schools to dollar-an-hour labor in private prisons subsidized with your tax dollars is a feature, not a bug."

DEFENSE FOR THE PROSECUTION

ZAKARIAH JOHNSON

If you're sloppy, as a district attorney like myself, framing prisoners can be legally risky. But it's never politically risky. Getting accused (but not convicted!) can actually boost your poll numbers, provided of course the "thugs" you're getting off the street have sufficient priors and represent the right ethnic and socio-economic groups.

Oh, you've heard about the FBI investigation? They got nothing. The word of a disgruntled employee I fired years ago won't count for diddly. But they have their role to play—mostly in creating publicity that reminds my constituents I don't work for the hated gub'ment, I work for them, and that I'll do "whatever it takes" to keep them safe. Don't act so shocked. Yes, #BlackLivesMatter and all that, so don't bother turning my name into a hashtag for your latest armchair activism project (the ACLU and Southern Poverty Law Center already tried—it didn't trend for an hour, nobody cares!) The pipeline from failing schools to dollar-an-hour labor in private prisons subsidized by your tax dollars is a feature, not a bug. And the cops tasked with fielding your "customer complaints"? They're merely IT support on wheels, untrained techies dealing with irate rubes who keep buying the same products from the same two companies—Republican or Democrat? Apple or Microsoft?—despite decades of declining quality and indifference to customer service. The real engineers, the system designers, they never field customer calls. Hell, most of those original coders are dead—hail Steve Jobs and Chief Justice Marshall!

The real system lives behind a screen we all agree to pretend is real, so when a cop hauls in a man for walking down a public sidewalk he damn well should have known wasn't really public, and maybe he ends up killing him, it's treated like an anomaly instead of what it is: an essential feature at the heart of our most familiar machinery.

What's to be done? Well, nothing. Many of us make a good living at it. As a DA in one jurisdiction and a judge in a second, I see through the flaws in the system, but I know my offices serve the same role as an ER: "Pass 'em through!" I occasionally do my good deed, dropping charges or granting leniency for some good-looking kid with a promising future (particularly when his parents are campaign donors or on the right boards). Mostly, I just stick to the consultant's credo: "If you're not part of the solution, there's money to be made prolonging the problem." Lots of money.

So bite me. My daughter's already partner-track at a well-known law firm, my grandson's in a private preschool, and my wife does more charity work than you ever did (she founded "Friends of Pine Creek," so there.)

Besides, not one cop on our city force has ever been convicted of a crime, but their expert testimony has helped put away plenty of hard cases.

What's that, you say? My office is the one that's supposed to prosecute police misconduct, but I also rely on good relationships with the cops for getting the testimony that keeps our convictions rates so high? Well, what did I say about it being a feature, not a bug?

Did you go to public school, or did you get a real education? Never mind, standards are slipping everywhere. Ever heard of an "ouroboros"? No doubt you haven't, so let's forego the classical references and call it "that snake eating its own tail." Some Viking crap, maybe Persian. Supposedly it represents eternity, but to me it looks more like entropy: Eventually the snake will consume itself, but if it ever stops eating, it'll starve. Welcome to the real world, children: Entropy *vincit omnia*. Capitalism, colonialism, five-year plans, the Great Leap forward—every system contains the seeds of its own destruction. Whatever. My mortgage is paid, my wine cellar's full, and my re-election's assured for both my jobs. At least, it was before James grew a conscience.

Good old James. Bit of a throw pillow that one, but once he had promise. It's one reason I put him on the Mercer death penalty case. That, and because I hate those. Not the death penalty—I'm indifferent to sentencing, and there's little correlation between sentencing and crime rates anyway: If you're undisciplined enough to kill someone in hot blood in front of a barroom full of witnesses, you're not mentally equipped to weigh the difference between 10 and 20, life without parole, or the hot seat. (Most people who commit violent crime are mental defectives, and their lawyers know it. Ask one over a drink sometime.) No, my objection to the death penalty is that it's pointless and expensive. You can blow a year's budget on a single prosecution, and it turns into an automatic appeal anyway. It's a great bargaining chip, don't get me wrong, but put a woman away for 30 years in the state pen fielding calls for the state department of tourism ("Aurora Falls? Oh, yes, it's just beautiful! I can recommend some nearby B&Bs . . ..") and the public has been well-served.

Cop killers though, that's touchy. The murder of a cop exposes our façade of civilization as a Potemkin village. Cops are burly, tough, and well-armed; alert, paid to bear our paranoia for us so we can sleep at night (though I find a gated community and a reputable alarm company help, too). If a cop can be killed, who among us is safe? The community demands an example be made. After any arrest for cop-killing, the trial and sentencing are strictly pro forma. And a death penalty prosecution becomes a political necessity.

James should have known all that. He knew Officer Mercer was on the "no-call list" I keep (or rather, kept) in the bottom drawer of my desk. No title, no names, just their initials to remind us which officers' credibility under oath had been called into question too many times, have drinking or domestic battery problems, or, most often, too many excessive force complaints from the community. It's not my fault, not the chief's or the sheriff's either, that we can't get rid of these losers. The union always goes to bat for their guys, no matter how incompetent or vicious they are, and the state legislature's tied our hands when it comes to firing government staff. I could tell you stories, but I recognize it's a high-stress job, sometimes people crack. Sometimes they come to us cracked already. For the really bad eggs, we lay out the case to the union rep, then get together and lean on the guy to resign—"Hit the road, Jack, and we'll lose your personnel file as a bonus." We'll even guarantee a letter of recommendation for their next police job down the road (preferably out of state), but only if they go.

That still leaves the other side of the problem—the "victim" (so-called)—to deal with, but as has been noted before, the weakest link in any civil rights case is always the plaintiff. "Yes, sir," "No, sir," "Here's my ID, sir," can save you so much hassle—even your life—but these people never learn. Nine times in ten they've got priors or bench warrants, weed or whatever in their bloodstream, delinquent child support payments, something that's enough to turn a jury against them and they know it. So, they drop the suit in exchange for lesser or dropped charges, and then we try to clean house in private. If the complainant doesn't play, they go to jail. Tell the judge and jury an unemployed parolee with alcohol on his breath took a swing at an officer and he doesn't have a prayer. Tell them that he KILLED a cop, and the jury might even bum rush him with pitchforks.

So, Officer Mercer was dead. He hadn't called in before making the stop. We'd have had no suspects at all if the killer had done a runner. But, no, the stupid punk had to call it in himself; climbed right into the cruiser and radioed the dispatcher for an ambulance:

"Hello?"

"Who is this?"

"Hey! Thank God! I need an ambulance. This cop's on the ground twitching, well, he was twitching. He's down. You got to send help!"

"Who is this?"

"Raymond Frommer. He stopped me and . . . oh, shit. Just send help, OK?"

"Location?"

We listened to the recording in my office. James, myself, Chief Rosie, and Mayor Pat.

"You talked to Mercer's widow?" I asked the chief, but Pat answered:

"I called her. She'll be at the press conference today. I expect you to announce you'll be seeking the death penalty."

"You don't find that premature?" James asked.

"Premature?" Mayor Pat was nearly hysterical. "The community's screaming for vengeance, Jim. Are you on board or not?"

Notice Pat didn't say "crying" over Mercer's death. It's just screaming these days.

Truth is, it was two months before the primary election, with Pat being squeezed by challengers from both the left and the right, which meant announcing a death penalty prosecution was required to boost the mayor's "law and order" bona fides (Pro tip: You want to pull a capital crime? Be sure you do it AFTER an election, not before. You'll get a better deal).

"It's not premature at all, Mayor," I said, reassuring Pat we were on board. "We'll be right beside you at the presser." The chief nodded her assent.

"What about the Brady list?" James said.

"What's that?" snapped the mayor.

"It's unrelated," I said.

"Mike—" James said.

"Stow it, Jimmy. We'll make it work, Pat." Pat was savvy enough not to ask a follow-up about the "list."

James was smart, but never savvy. I made sure he was right beside me in front of the TV cameras when I announced we'd be seeking the death penalty. Secretly, I hoped the accused kid would find a lawyer who'd demand the trial be moved far, far away, so as not to prejudice local juries against his client. Hell, I planned to suggest it. As for the "list," every prosecutor has one, though they go by many names, "Laurie List," "Shit List," but usually "Brady List," after Brady v. Maryland. It boils down to a list of cops with such problematic histories that you will never, ever put them on the stand because their mere presence in a court room virtually guarantees an acquittal for the defendant. Had Officer Mercer been on the list? Does the Pope shit in the woods?

After the presser, I retired to my office to rub my temples and assuage my headache with a medicinal bourbon. Liquor poured, there was a knock at the door.

James popped his head in. "You free, Mike?"

"Yeah. Grab a glass. You know where the ice is."

He got a couple cubes from the mini to drop into the single finger he poured himself and sat on the edge of the low seat across the desk from me. He leaned forward, face blanched, holding his sweating glass on his knee in both hands without drinking it.

"Mike, what are we going to do?"

"About what?"

"About what? About the Brady list. About Mercer's history. He'd given his notice already. How do we explain that?"

"It's a classic: officer killed, two days before retirement."

"It's no joke."

"I know. But if it comes to it, Rosie's the one who kept him on the streets. Any screw-up he pulled is on her. Why do you think she was so quiet in the meeting?"

"But it's our list. We should never have let him give two weeks' notice. What if the other victim comes forward?"

About a month earlier, Patrolman Mercer had committed his final violation on our dime, or so we'd hoped, stomping some junkie drifter toothless under an overpass in full view of his dash cam (moron). Chief Rosie McCracken, James, and I had met with Mercer and the union rep in that same office and watched the replay, then unanimously leaned on him to resign (Jury awards to victims hit local treasuries hard, which means less money for raises, so the union was fully on board with us this time). Mercer agreed to go. Foolishly, the chief let him stay on two more weeks for form's sake. But James's attitude was my immediate worry:

"*Other* victim?" I shouted. "Some junkie? The *only* victim here is a dead cop, James. Or don't you see it that way? Besides, that junkie got two hundred dollars and a bus ticket when he got out of the ER. With any luck, he converted the cash straight into fentanyl, and he's no one's problem but Saint Peter's. Don't worry about it. Let's focus on the present, which is prosecuting this case." I opened my top drawer, pulled out two Advil, and washed them down with Jim Beam. Yeah, I know what it says on the label.

"Mike," James said. "The kid that killed Mercer could have run. Mercer hadn't even radioed in the stop."

"The kid didn't know that."

"No, but he called the ambulance. Have you read his statement? Mercer was pummeling him for nothing."

"You can't kill a cop!"

"He says he picked up a rock and lashed out without thinking. I think Mercer might have been trying to kill him. There was no reason to even pull him over. At best this is a manslaughter case—*erk!*"

I yanked Jim into the edge of the desk by his tie and pimp slapped the little bitch three or four times across the face. Fortunately, his untouched drink went over his pants, not my Turkish throw rug.

"Jimmy, you will not blow this case. You will not mess this up." I shoved him back into his chair. "In fact, you're going to be lead prosecutor. Win or lose, it's your career you're defending now."

❋

It was a week later I discovered the Brady list lying face up instead of face down in my bottom desk drawer. It hadn't flipped itself, and not many people could sashay into my office without arousing suspicion.

"Janet?" I said into the intercom. "Could you step in here?"

"What's up, Mike?"

"Did James come by while I was out?"

"Right after you went to lunch. He dropped off that memo you wanted—right there, the yellow paper in the in-box."

"Oh, great." I said, reaching for the slip of whatever b.s. James had used as a pretext for entry. "If it'd been a snake—"

”—it'd a bit-cha!“ she smiled, dismissing herself.

"Yeah," I said to the empty room. "If he'd been a snake . . ."

Discovery was a week away. In brief, that's where the prosecution and defense pretend to trade all the information they'll be bringing to court—witness lists, DNA tests, and so forth (again, Brady v. Maryland set the precedent). If James had swiped the list and copied it (as I assumed), it was a given he planned to share it with the public defender, even if it torpedoed his own case, and career.

His sudden burst of conscience was so ridiculous—we don't deal with people, we deal with stats: crimes committed, arrests made, conviction percentages. And thinking the choice of whom to prosecute is actually ours is a fantasy. "People" get hurt, whichever side of the line they fall on, but ultimately, we draw the line where the community tells us to. I deal with corrupt cops the way I do because voters elect politicians, who've given power to the unions to challenge any firing, power to disgruntled employees to sue, to turn an employer's—even a government agency's—right to fire somebody into an expensive, drawn-out struggle that can bankrupt your whole city if a jury sees a hint of discrimination. The public also controls the tax rates that affect funds available for police training and salaries, the same public that decides to pay for private schools for their own kids, but defund the public ones that produce hordes of drooling miscreants that crawl like zombies over their perfect lawns and peep in their windows after dark without Joe and Jill Taxpayer ever seeing their role in cause and effect. The public designed this garbage scow to float as close to the waterline as possible without sinking and then hired people like me and Rosie to man the bilge pumps to keep it afloat while they enjoy a drink on the upper deck. If the boat flounders, they won't blame themselves or changes in the weather—#BLM, etc.—and they sure as hell won't blame the system that normally benefits them. No, when protesters congregate on street corners with their Molotovs, towing pearly-toothed FBI agents in camera-ready suits in their wake, when peaceful chants turn into rioting and property values plummet because no one in the country wants to live in the new Ferguson, when these things happen, does the public suddenly develop introspection and blame themselves for trading Justice for low taxes, for planting the very weeds that choked their garden? No. They blame me.

You know that as well as I do.

So bite me again.

I had a week to teach James the basics of the seamanship we practice here or jettison him as ballast.

I called him Friday after lunch. "James, ready to go over discovery?"

"Oh, you want to review that today?"

"Hey, it's our first death penalty case in a decade. It's your case, but it's my department. I'm exercising my privileges of oversight. Besides, I'm curious."

"OK. You want to come by now?"

"I'm in court this afternoon. We'll do it after hours."

"Six?"

"Make it six-thirty, in the main conference room. See you then. Bring everything."

He came, bringing everything and then some on a trolley filled with accordion-binders. I let him drone on about his strategy as I flipped through the files, looking for evidence that he'd pinched the list. I finally found it, initials retyped in a different order, mixed in on a page with a bunch of other personnel info. I might have missed what it was if I hadn't been looking for it, but he'd have been a fool to leave it out on me entirely.

"Oh, good," I said. "You're giving them the Brady list."

"Uh, yeah. I figured if they found out elsewhere that we'd hidden it—"

"No, no. Quite right. But you never asked me for it. Janet wouldn't have known what it was to give it to you. Did you have it memorized?"

"I, uh, kept dual records. You never know."

"Sure. This is all on your laptop?"

He nodded.

"Any other copies you've made yet for the defense? Thumb drives, something on your phone?"

"No, nowhere."

"You haven't communicated this to the defense yet?" I was keeping a jocular tone, but he stopped answering and looked up in fear.

"Mike . . . I . . ."

"Shh. Hush now. You broke into my desk, James. These initials here, 'WR'? There's no cop in the city or county with those initials. Ditto with this one, 'QB.' You stole my fantasy football sheet. That's the only 'Brady list' in the building, dumbass."

"No! That's not true! We've gone over it—"

"Over what? I've no idea what you're talking about. Neither will Pat or Rosie. All I know is I have an incompetent member of my staff who's compounded his uselessness with breaking into my desk."

"Mike . . . Mercer was dirty! We can't railroad this kid!"

I pulled his laptop and the stuffed folders of discovery materials toward myself, sat back in the chair, and thumbed through a stack. "Looks like you've done a good review, James. Plenty of priors, an ex-girlfriend he abused. This will come in handy for whoever takes over from you."

"What . . . what do you mean?"

"Clean out your desk, James. You're fired."

❋

That was five years ago. After Pat got reelected, we let the kid who'd killed Mercer plead guilty to second-degree murder. When he went to the state pen as a labeled cop killer, the prison guards turned their watchful eyes elsewhere until he was killed in the showers halfway through year three. It had been Chief Rosie's idea to salt the list of problem officers with false initials to suggest a fantasy football league. I hadn't mentioned it to James, but I doubt he's ever watched a game anyway. Pansy. He packed up his precious conscience and went to Nepal for six months after his wife left him, then came back and joined the ACLU. I have to assume he put them up to the current lawsuit from the kid's parents for civil rights violations and such. The Justice Department is looking into the city's practices for possible prosecutions, but I'm not worried. At best, we'll get put on notice to straighten up, maybe even score a federal grant to help with our training budget. Works for me. Any physical list is a thing of the past now anyway.

So, what now? Do you think I became a murderer when some gangbanger knifed that kid behind bars? Don't be stupid. I might have felt a twinge or two of guilt over it, but no regrets. As I said, somebody always dies; it's not individual lives, but balance that we protect and maintain. When I saw the riots erupting in Missouri and Baltimore, the marches in Chicago and Oakland, the prosecutors and cops and small-time politicians losing their jobs for doing precisely what the public had been happy to pay them to do with a wink and nod for years, for decades, hell—*for centuries*—I knew I'd done the right thing, done what I'd been hired to do.

And you? Don't feign such indignance. James was the city's real enemy, not me. Me? I work for you, boss. I've been doing your bidding all along.

"Now, what we've been doing is looking at the data and we know that police somehow manage to de-escalate, disarm and not kill white people every day. So what's going to happen is we're going to have equal rights and justice in our own country or we will restructure their function and ours."

-Jesse Williams

"Could my abusive cop be so insecure?

"Of course he could, as I always remind new investigators. Bad cops aren't complete psychopaths."

JEROME

JEFF SOLOWAY

I never ask about Jerome's face. His right cheek hosts a constellation of chrome studs that glitter in the light like the facets of a disco ball. Passersby tend to glance and re-glance at him. Having one facial piercing is dashing, and two is edgy, but three is already bordering on disturbing, and more than that is downright scary. Jerome had about a dozen. He was also six-foot-four, Black, and, for at least the last two years, homeless. I sometimes wondered what possessed him to acquire all those piercings and where he found the money.

We sat outside on the empty concrete flowerpots installed to protect our office building from terrorist trucks. Today the disco-ball half of his face was swollen and a swath of it obscured by a gauze bandage, which was already looking a little crusty. He pointed to it. "I got a constitutional right to make a complaint!"

He looked insulted, which was a relief. It's when he's all worked up that I have to worry. Jerome tends to get emotional about his complaints. "That's why I'm here," I said.

I work for the Civilian Complaint Review Board, the agency that investigates complaints against the police department. As any police-reform activist will remind you, the people who suffer most from police misconduct are the poorest and least connected, those society finds it easiest to ignore (until, that is, they misbehave). Our problem at the CCRB is that such people, having relatively little free time and lots of preoccupations, tend to file the weakest complaints, if they manage to file them at all.

Jerome was an exception.

He was what we called a frequent filer. He seemed to enjoy the sense of purpose that filing a police complaint gave him. And he was good at it. Admittedly, his speculation as to police motives tended to be ill-informed and even paranoid, which would have doomed his complaints in the old days, but in this modern era of body-worn cameras and ubiquitous cellphone and surveillance video, his claims could be thoroughly checked. Surprisingly often they were right on target. If he could have got his act together enough to show up for a lawyer's appointment, he might have won a life-changing settlement from the city, but showing up on schedule was not one of Jerome's specialties.

Passersby leaving our building for lunch were giving us double-takes and either slowing to examine us more closely or, more often, hurrying on, as if afraid that he would leap up and demand money. Jerome's presence gave off a kind of chill that he was entirely unconscious of. When he smiled, the chill lifted, but he couldn't smile every second of the day.

"Why won't they let me inside?" he asked, a little plaintively. Security had refused to send him up to our offices, or even to let him wait in the lobby.

"Because last time you screamed at the receptionist." It was impossible to convey to him just how terrifying it was to be bellowed at by an enormous scruffy man with a face like a cyborg. He knew he was harmless. Even when he lost his cool, he never so much as touched another person. Every cop who had claimed otherwise had been shown conclusively to be mistaken or lying.

"I never scream at you," he said.

"On the phone you do."

"Only before I know it's *you*. I like you. You always come out to talk to me."

"I like you too." In the past, flattering Jerome had proved helpful in getting the story out of him quickly. Also, when he wasn't screaming at me, I really did like him.

Jerome grinned. In investigating his complaints, I'd come to learn that most cops who got to know him liked him, too; unfortunately, he moved around the city so much that he was constantly bumping up against new cops, and his volatility and his face tended to combine to make a poor first impression.

He signed our waiver with a careful flourish. I asked him to describe his incident. As he spoke, I nodded and smiled, partly to encourage him and partly to reassure passersby that our encounter was consensual.

"Okay," he said. "So it's the 23rd St. bus shelter, south side, by Second Avenue. Near your place, yeah?"

"Right across the street." We had discussed this in the past. There was a methadone clinic on 24th and 2nd where Jerome sometimes went when he was, as he put it, "working on myself."

I heard the jingle of a door opening, and looked up to see two cops sweeping out of a nearby deli. They came strolling our way. Since Jerome was opposite me, they would be able to see only my face, not his, unless they glanced down at him as they passed by. One of them pointed up at a crane extending precariously over the steel skeleton of a half-completed building. *Keep watching it*, I thought. If a cop stared at him, Jerome always noticed.

The movement of Jerome's face as he talked was a kaleidoscopic symphony in the spring sunlight. I forced myself to gaze into it and not at the cops, but I could see their legs and their blocky shoes in my side-vision.

Jerome went on: "I'm there with my friend George waiting on a bus in a *fully seated* position,"—as opposed to lying down on the bus-shelter bench, which was a violation—"when this cop shakes me awake and tells me to get the eff out, only he don't say eff." Jerome nodded at my recorder to explain his modesty. "*That's illegal touching*, I tell him. You know what he does?" Jerome's voice was already rising.

The cops passed by without stopping. Jerome was too absorbed in his story to notice them. I released a breath I hadn't known I was holding. "What, Jerome?"

"I'll tell you what!"

From behind, I heard two words: "Hold up."

I glance behind me. The cops were staring at us from 20 feet away. The sun was above them, which meant, from their perspective, it was lighting us up beautifully. Jerome's face must have been resplendent.

I heard a yip and turned back again. Jerome was leaping up from his planter and flinging his arms in the air. "He spins me around the bench and sucker-punches me, that punk-ass piece a—"

And now I heard pounding footsteps. "Jerome, breathe!"

Jerome nodded heavily and repeatedly. "I am calm."

"I know you are. Take a seat."

The footsteps slowed and stopped, but I didn't dare look away from Jerome. He lowered himself stiffly to the planter, like a much older man. "Count for me," he said. He was staring down at his ragged Timberlands (where did he get them? Where did he get anything?), and not, thank God, up at the cops.

I counted to seven as he breathed in; then to four as he held the breath; then to eight as he released it. Some counselor at Bellevue had taught him the technique. I sometimes used it myself.

I could hear the cops' breaths in the long pauses. When Jerome was done, I looked up at their faces. One cop wore sunglasses and was completely and infuriatingly inscrutable; the other's eyes were wide with puzzlement.

"We're all right," I said.

Now Jerome saw them too. This was the moment when intentions were mis-judged, and nerves overloaded.

"It's no crime to nod off at a bus stop," Jerome said, loudly but in measured tones, his face aimed somewhere between mine and theirs. "It was nice and sunny."

I smiled in genuine relief and lifted my hand to the officers: *Everything under control, thanks for your concern.* I could see my own fingers trembling, their tips glowing orange in the sunlight.

The cop with the sunglasses retreated half a step. Then I heard both cops move away.

"Ripped my cheek right open," Jerome added. "Want to see?"

Jerome reached for the bandage.

"Wait."

"What?"

Had the cops' footsteps halted? Were they turning to listen? "Let's just sit for a second," I said. "I need to be emotionally prepared."

No, I could hear them moving away.

"Okay, ready," I said.

"You're such a baby." He laughed at me, crinkling his bandage. He gingerly peeled back the tape at one end, and then, even more carefully, the bandage itself.

What was revealed was a jagged gash between two of his studs, stitched up but oozing. I snapped a few pictures. "Are you changing that bandage?"

"Just yesterday I changed it."

"Who stitched it up?"

"Doc at Bellevue." Jerome went to explain that, after the cops had slugged him, his friend woke up yelling. The cops then shifted their focus to jumping his friend, and Jerome was able to hustle away down the street. Bellevue was just up First Avenue, on 28th St.

"Everybody's looking at me," Jerome said. "Staring. Like I'm a bum. And I wasn't doing nothing wrong! Just having a nap."

"Did you get a name or badge number?"

"How could I? I *just woke up*."

"What did the cop look like?"

"White dude. Bald."

That was half the force. This was hardly Jerome's best work.

"And he didn't arrest you?" That meant there would be no paperwork—no way to get the officer's name.

"No."

"Okay."

"Don't say okay."

"I didn't mean it like that."

"I got a scar forever. Because of him. Lucky if that's all I got. My face—it's delicate. Might get infected." That was the first reference he had ever made to his face's unusual nature. "I got to keep going to Bellevue for bandages. And I ain't always got time. So, you gonna get this guy?"

I shut off the recorder. "We have to find him first," I said.

I turned to see that the two cops were still standing at the street corner, deli-bags dangling from their hands. They were delaying lunch to watch over us. To protect me.

❋

2

The next day, I flashed my badge at the manager of my local Duane Reade. Jerome's bus stop was just outside the store's entrance and, I suspected, prominent in its security footage.

The manager played the video for me. As it turned out, Jerome's story was absolutely accurate. The video showed a bald white cop shaking him awake at a bus shelter. Jerome, startled, flailed his arms, and accidentally smacked the cop in the nose; in response, the cop bashed Jerome in the face with his radio. Meanwhile, a Black female cop was scuffling with Jerome's friend. She must have called out, because the bald cop sprinted to assist her. Jerome was able to scramble to his feet and escape down the street.

The badge numbers on the video were unreadably blurry. That afternoon, I requested duty logs from the local precinct, but none of them mentioned the incident. I also requested the ID photos of all the precinct's uniformed officers. Several were of bald or shaven-headed cops, but none could be definitely matched to the grainy bullet-head on the video.

Whoever that cop was, he had almost killed Jerome for the crime of dozing off at a bus stop. This man was hotheaded and violent, like all too many men in New York City; but as a cop, he also possessed a taser, nightstick, badge, and gun, along with the authority to use them at any time.

The only person who could possibly bring this guy to justice was me. As I told Jerome, I first had to find him. Luckily, I knew just where to start looking.

⬤

3

I live with my father in a city-subsidized complex built in the 1970s. Apartments here are big and cheap, which is why we all hold on to them so tenaciously, and also why our residents in general are getting so old. People only leave when they die. This also explains why I still live with my father.

He was a leftwing radical in his youth, though he's now retired from activism and, indeed, all other forms of physical and intellectual activity, except reading, kvetching, and freelance copyediting (which is really just a combination of the first two). But when I told him I was planning to attend the local community policing meet-and-greet, he surprised me by responding, "Maybe I'll come too," and heaving himself up from his chair.

To get to our complex's community room, you have to venture out to our central plaza and re-enter through an outside door in the H building. A uniformed NYPD officer was stationed at that entrance. He was wearing his patrol cap, so I couldn't judge his baldness.

Jerome's incident had occurred just across the street. The cops attending this meeting would be our precinct's neighborhood beat cops. One of them was likely the cop who had attacked Jerome. I just had to figure out which one.

Every seat in the community room was taken, so we had to perch on a radiator cover in the back. Four cops, three men (one a white-shirted lieutenant) and one woman, stood in a row at the front of the room. The lieutenant explained the NYPD's latest community policing initiative. He ended his talk with arms extended in load-me-up position, as if to say, "here we are—start bellyaching." His three companions looked less enthusiastic.

The cop on the video was obviously not a white-shirt, so that ruled out the lieutenant, and he was not a woman, so that ruled out the one female on stage. That female was, however, Black, and her flat, straightened, cherry-red hair resembled that of the partner in the video. Of the other two officers, both male, one had a dark buzzcut; the other, a sergeant, was entirely bald, probably shaved. My best suspect.

The lieutenant introduced his subordinates on stage. They all looked now not just unenthusiastic but mortified. The sergeant couldn't decide whether to lock his hands behind his back, at-ease style, or hold them stiffly against his sides, so he alternated between the two, which made him look as if he were repeatedly being handcuffed.

Could my abusive cop be so insecure?

Of course he could, as I always remind new investigators. Bad cops aren't complete psychopaths. Under normal circumstances, they're as even-keeled as any of us. Like most abusive people, including spouses and parents, they're driven to rage only occasionally, by an overflow of emotion, whether fury, humiliation, or terror.

"Their job is to get to know you!" the lieutenant declared. "Go to them with any concerns, any at all."

The word "concerns" set people in the audience to shuffling. Some grumbled out loud to their neighbors; others fidgeted in their seats; a few tossed their heads like horses.

Mrs. Beverley from the D building immediately stood up, leaning hard on her cane with both hands. The general rumble quickly subsided. Everyone knew Mrs. Beverley, and everyone figured this would be good. She was a tiny Black woman, maybe the oldest person in our complex, but she was still able to stand up and excoriate our board of directors at every public meeting.

"We live," she said, "in a state of fear. Junkies lying on the sidewalk. Drunks dressed like Santa. Hoarders parking their shopping carts in the plaza. Thieves. Rapists. Teenagers. Who will stop them? We depend on you." Since her hands were occupied with the cane, she pointed at the cops by leaning toward them, like a hunting dog.

Every one of the four nodded, even the sergeant, who was also trying to catch a glance at his phone.

"How about the homeless?" called a voice from across the room. "They're everywhere. They open the door to the CVS and want to get paid. Who asked them? And what about laws against panhandling? Or loitering? I'm talking about some filthy guy, on drugs, demanding a dollar. What are you going to do about it?"

Several people applauded.

The lieutenant explained that there were rules they had to follow. Some were NYPD rules, some were local laws, some were Constitutional. "A guy's got a right to sit on the street and open the door," he said. "These are human beings with complicated lives. A lot of them take meds. Or should take meds."

His subordinates all nodded vigorously as they gazed out over the room. It wasn't the first time I've admired cops, but it was the first time I've admired them right there in my apartment complex.

"Plus," the lieutenant added, conceding something to the mood of the room, "we've got authorities above us calling the shots."

A man stood up near the entrance: "So what *can* you do!" It was Jason Healey, who lived just down the hall from my father and me. At times of great excitement, such as a package-delivery screw-up or alleged newspaper theft, his pale face would grow fiery red to the roots of his white hair. It was red now. Being just under 60, he was the youngest audience member to speak so far. "I mean about the homeless!"

The lieutenant said, without expression, "We can dismantle permanent encampments."

"You mean Stuyvesant Cove," Jason Healey said. "By the river. *That's* where they live."

I wondered if that's where Jerome lived.

"That's right," said the lieutenant. "Regarding that encampment, we expect to be able to move quickly."

The room, so long prepared to vent dissatisfaction, was unimpressed. Mrs. Beverley, who had somehow remained standing throughout the discussion, spoke again: "I have lived too long to finish my life in fear."

The room exploded in applause. Before it died down, my father began to lean forward. I saw that he was raising his hand.

My surprise almost immediately gave way to dread. My father was a recluse and a homebody, but when he did speak, he was always driven by a single passion: to set people straight.

"Dad, not now," I whispered.

But the lieutenant was already pointing at him.

My father stood. He had been living in the building for 30 years, since before I was born, but rarely spoke to people, even when he was holding a door open for them. A few audience members nodded approvingly at him, simply because, like them, he looked angry.

"This city," he began, and his voice was suddenly deeper than I'd ever heard it, even sonorous, "is *drowning* in fear."

"Damn right," someone called.

There was no stopping him now. His eyes swept the audience from side to side, like a searchlight over a stormy sea. He ignored the cops.

"We walk our kids to school till they're 13," my father said. "We shop in daylight only. We avoid eye contact with strangers. We make our security guards check ID in the plaza playground, to keep out riffraff kids from other neighborhoods. We never leave the house without a cellphone, so we can call 911 at any time. We refuse to give money to panhandlers. We're all afraid."

He paused, giving space for nods and *Uh-huhs* and other versions of the secular amen. And then he went on:

"And what for? Year after year, the city is safer. The streets are safer. We're all safer."

The encouraging nods and *hms* broke off. Even the shuffling ceased. The speech had veered off course. Of all the audience, only I had any idea where it was going.

"That's right. Look at the stats! Crime's never been lower in 50 years. Murders are down, robberies, rapes, even car crashes. But listen to us and you'd never know it. We're terrified. We're seeing disaster that's not there. And why is that?"

He paused, not quite long enough for anyone to jump in with objections.

"Because we're all old coots, that's why! Just listen to yourselves. You're afraid of some junkie stumbling on the sidewalk. He can barely find his own fingers, let alone your pocket. He needs the methadone clinic, a room to sleep in, and a bath. And what does he get instead? The cops called on him! By one of you!" He scowled at the audience, then turned to the lieutenant. "What if some homeless guy—some law-abiding, peaceful homeless guy, just minding his business—tells you he's cold and tired and needs to get inside? What do you do then?"

The lieutenant's face had been stone throughout the speeches, but now it softened slightly. "We say . . ." Here the lieutenant lifted an eyebrow, and it was as if he and my father were instinctively collaborating. "'Hop in. We'll give you a lift to the shelter.'" He eyes settled back gently over the crowd, but with an unmistakable air of challenge.

"Good!" My father pretended this was exactly the answer he had expected. "See? You cops aren't so bad. Probably because you're not so old. You still shoot too many people. Nobody's perfect."

The lieutenant kept his face impassive; the other three allowed themselves various twitches.

"The real fascists," my father concluded, "are all around us."

He grinned at the crowd, welcoming their attack, but the glares he received were full of scorn rather than hate. To these people my father was hardly a threat, just a fool.

I was about to applaud—someone had to—when I heard a rap on the plate glass behind my ear. I turned and got an eyeful of a grinning, glittering face outside. It was Jerome. He was in the plaza. He stepped back and laughed, then pointed, presumably to the community-room entrance. *No*, I mouthed, causing a fog-flower to bloom on the glass. I wagged my finger, by which I meant, *wait for me across the plaza*. I suppose what I really meant was, *wait for me across the plaza where no one else can see you*. This was my fault. I had set this up in advance. I had told Jerome to meet me here, on this night, so that he could potentially identify his assailant.

Now, however, seemed like a very bad time to introduce to this flustered and paranoid crowd a man whose face set off metal detectors. Luckily the fluorescent lights inside were so bright that no one but me could see past the window's reflection to the twilit outside world.

I turned back to my neighbors. They were still glaring at my father, and now also at me. More of them at me. My father, being old and crotchety, looked like everyone else. I on the other hand was young and therefore obviously naïve, careless, and stupid. I had probably put my father up to this outburst. I probably also supported the misguided mayor and ineffectual police commissioner in their efforts to coddle the city's degenerates.

"Let's go home," my father said. "'Night, Officer!"

I always warn new investigators never to address a sergeant, still less a lieutenant, as "Officer." But all four cops either nodded respectfully, or, in the case of the female officer, waved. They knew an ally when they saw one. The rest of the audience took a breath and prepared to launch a new barrage of gripes.

And then I heard a howl from just outside the community room: "I got to get in!"

People twisted their bodies or necks to look.

I shot to my feet, and saw, over the heads of neighbors, Jerome fidgeting just outside the vestibule of the community room. The cop stationed there was blocking his way. His response was delivered at twice Jerome's volume: "Back *right* off, buddy!"

I began to sidle toward the vestibule. The room was packed tighter than when I'd arrived, with more latecomers having resorted, like me, to sitting on the radiator in the back. People were now rising to get a better view. Many had canes or were leaning hard on seatbacks, and I had to be careful not to push or even nudge them. I managed to catch a glimpse of Jerome's face as he craned his neck to see over the cop's shoulder into the room.

When Jerome spotted me, he hopped and waved and grinned so hard it made his studs jut out. I almost laughed. He looked like a birthday kid wearing too much glitter.

But shouting rose up all around me. As I had feared, the audience saw his facial ornaments much differently, as a kind of post-apocalyptic armor designed not just to protect the warrior but to terrify his enemies.

Someone screamed "MI-5!" presumably meaning "MS-13," and someone else: "They're in the building!"

Now everyone who was able, including a number who likely hadn't known they were able, stood up. Jason Healey was grabbing vacated chairs and sliding them toward the vestibule, apparently to build a kind of barricade. The resulting clamor excited the crowd further.

The guard-duty cop blocking Jerome looked uncertainly across the crowd to the lieutenant.

Mrs. Beverley's voice rose above the tumult: "What are you doing?" Somehow—I would never know how—she had managed to climb up on a chair. She had one hand on someone's shoulder and the other clamped on someone's head. Her stringy arm muscles were tight with the strain, but her voice was clear. "Get that man out of here!"

All around me, people shouted their own versions of this terrified and outraged command. I picked my way faster and more recklessly past the bodies around me.

I wasn't fast enough. When next I could see Jerome, the cop had slung his arm around Jerome's throat. Jerome was still staring in my direction, but his eyes were bulging, his mouth gaping, his cheeks sucked in. The arm that had been waving at me was now flailing. I could hear nothing but shouting. People were lunging or staggering toward me, to escape the fight in the vestibule. I had to let them push past me. Then Jerome's head dropped from my view like a swimmer dragged underwater.

Finally, the bodies were past me. As I crashed through the gauntlet of overturned chairs, I just avoided body-checking the female officer, who must have rushed from the stage. "Get back!" she ordered. I thrust my CCRB badge at her.

Jerome was on his stomach in the vestibule. The guard cop had his knee pressed against Jerome's back. At least he had released his chokehold. He was now fumbling for his cuffs.

"Stay down, Jerome!" I called, and Jerome grimaced as he tried to turn his head my way. I swear I could hear, even over the screaming behind me, the scrape of his studs against the concrete. His bandage was half off and his cheek was bleeding.

"He's my guest!" I yelled at the kneeling cop, but he paid no attention. The female cop, however, was now beside me. She lifted a finger to show that she heard, then knelt beside her comrade, who was kneeling on my friend.

I could only see, and not hear, her murmuring, but I knew that the kneeling cop was learning where I worked.

"That's what we deal with!" someone was moaning behind me. "Every day!"

"Jake!" Jerome called out. His fingers, held at the small of his back, were shaking. Was he about to scream, lash out, run, kick? If he did, there was no way I could protect him.

"Breathe, Jerome!" I said.

"Tell them my cuffs are tight!" His face being mashed into the floor, he had to contort his mouth to speak. "I got big wrists."

The lieutenant finally marched up behind me. Again, I showed my badge. "What's he being arrested for? Trespassing? He came to meet me."

"This guy started a riot." The lieutenant gestured behind him, where the other two cops were holding back the crowd.

I looked out over the faces of my neighbors, expecting to see spite, fury, and satisfaction at Jerome's punishment. What I saw instead, on almost every face, was relief. They were gazing thankfully, even gratefully, at the cop tightening cuffs over Jerome's wrists. The police were only providing what my neighbors wanted—a show of authority to ease their panic.

The female officer helped Jerome sit up. She had likely saved him from a beating. One loop of her red hair had detached from the rest of the mass and now stood upright.

Jerome wiggled his shoulders to adjust the strain on his cuffed arms. He leaned forward and called, "Jake! That's the guy."

"Which guy?"

"The guy who busted me the other day. This guy right here!"

The guard officer was getting out his memo book. His cap was askew. He was bald. I looked at his badge number, which I had already taken down on the way in: 4351. Officer name Meltzer.

"You'll be hearing from me," I said to Meltzer, who continued to pay no attention. For now.

"You better lock him up!" someone behind me yelled.

I turned again, and saw Mrs. Beverley, escorted by two friends. She'd been granted a favored spot at the front edge of the crowd. "Now you see," she said triumphantly. "Now you see what we live with."

She was glaring not at Jerome but at the female cop. Their two faces were locked in a private struggle. Neither spoke.

18

"'I know what I signed up for,' he says. 'I'm here to protect and serve. I'm not worried about it, you know what I mean? With God and the law on my side, I don't have anything to worry about.'"

COURTESY. PROFESSIONALISM. RESPECT.

RICHIE NARVAEZ

Veronica sits and watches the kids. Jade chasing Christian around the picnic table. It would make a cute Insta but her phone's dead. She forgot to charge it overnight. The kids' mom—Veronica's sister, Nelly—is paying them no mind. She's just giggling at her new boyfriend, Nestor, who keeps jumping on a branch to show off how many pull-ups he can do.

Lucky that branch don't break, or he'd fall down and bust his ass, Veronica thinks.

Stuck here at her nephew's birthday party in the middle of the park, she's having the worst time of her life. Christian is a sweet kid, cute, going to be a heartbreaker one day. But Nelly feeds him too much sugar, so he's like a rocket all the time. And Jade's a little bitch. She always says, "I hate Titi Veronica, I hate Titi Veronica," so that spoiled brat can keep to herself.

If only Veronica'd had a good comeback when Mami asked her, "What else you got going on? You got big plans?"

She should've. Nineteen years old in New York City and all her friends away or busy. What kind of lonesome shit is that?

Damn. The sun's frying the table, the air is thick, and people just make it worse. The black family at the next picnic table have a giant umbrella, a big, goofy dog, and flames coming out of their grill. Just ten feet the other way are three white guys who made their own fire pit out of stray bricks. They're drinking six packs, chain smoking, although no one's supposed to smoke in the park.

Veronica sweats like she's in a sauna. *This place is overcrowded and boring and boring and hot.*

She looks at her moms piling food onto the dirty old grill, raw chicken next to the burgers and dogs. Veronica wouldn't be surprised if they all get food poisoning by the end of the day.

Mami's got her ridiculous Puerto Rican getup on. The Puerto Rican flag crocs, the too-tight Puerto Rican flag shorts, and the giant Puerto Rican flag t-shirt.

"Hey, my little eye-roller," her mother says to her. "What you rolling your eyes about now?"

"You, Mami. Oh my god, you look so ghetto with your outfit."

"It's June in New York. It's what every self-respecting Puerto Rican wears, mija. I got you a nice one."

"I can't. I just can't. That stupid parade was last month."

"Orgullo, baby. *Every* day is Puerto Rican Parade Day to me." Mami laughs her big, embarrassing laugh. Veronica is sure the people swimming down in Coney must have heard it.

"Mija," Mami says, "you don't understand what our people went through to wear this flag. For decades they wouldn't let us show it. Decades. You feel me?"

Veronica doesn't believe it. She's in her second year at BMCC, hasn't heard a thing about it. Back in the day Mami was a big protester, went to all the rallies, then she stopped going for no reason.

Veronica was never into that scene. None of all that marching and yelling and protesting makes a bit of difference to nobody. People got flags all over themselves, like it means anything. Fuck all that noise.

"Mami, I'm so bored!"

"Mija, help me with the decorations."

"Oh my god, Mami, the kids don't care about the decorations."

"I care about the decorations, okay?"

"Can I, like, go to the bathroom first?"

"Who's stopping you? Please don't take forever. And don't get lost."

"Get lost?" Veronica says, like she hasn't been going to this park for a million years.

✹

Veronica dawdles as long as she can in the women's bathroom, but there's a line out the door and only so long she can stand in front of the scratched metal mirror, with people constantly bumping into her. Besides, it stinks.

Once outside, she doesn't know what to do with herself. She is in no hurry to get back and just be bored all over again.

That's when she notices the ice cream stand and right next to it a *young* police officer getting handed a water. The officer takes out a dollar to pay for it, but the ice cream man waves it away.

The cop is tall. Wearing shorts. His calves are hairy. Muscles like rocks. She *knows* he's got tattoos under that dark blue shirt. Mmm, mmm, men in uniform—she could eat them all up all day long.

Veronica decides she's going to make something good out of this day. She walks straight up to him, reads his name tag. "Good morning . . . Officer Conlon. I mean, good afternoon, hah," she says. She giggles and covers her mouth.

"Good afternoon, miss," he says.

Hazel eyes! He cracks open the water, takes a long drink. Water spills down his bulging Adam's apple. Veronica dies and goes to heaven.

"It's so hot today," she says and immediately regrets it. *So stupid.*

"You could say that again."

His voice is deep. She loves deep voices. So many of the boys at school, so many of the boys she meets seem like they're still waiting for their testicles to drop.

"You know, I'm thinking about becoming a police officer myself."

"Are you?"

"But I get scared about it. Don't you ever get scared, you know, like, that your life's in danger?"

"I know what I signed up for," he says. "I'm here to protect and serve. I'm not worried about it, you know what I mean? With God and the law on my side, I don't have anything to worry about."

While he's talking, she spots his ring, knows it would be a dealbreaker for her friends. But it doesn't matter to her. It's not like she's saying she wants to keep him.

She asks him if he likes Puerto Rican girls.

His face lights up with the sweetest smile. Bright white teeth. Not a smoker. "I like all types of girls. So how old are you anyway?"

"Old enough," she says and tries to play if off by laughing. She decides she wants to come off more classy, so she says, "I'm in college. I graduate in two years."

"Good to know," the officer says. Then he looks around, like he's looking for something, for trouble, for criminals. "I guess I'll see you around."

Man's gotta go back to work, she thinks. She gives him a smile she hopes looks sophisticated and sexy. "Yeah, see you around, Officer Conlon."

"My name is Veronica, by the way," she says, walking away, feeling it's the cool way to exit.

"It's been very nice to meet you, Veronica," he says, and he bows his head, looking hard at her from under his thick eyebrows.

●

Veronica plops herself back at the picnic table. The kids are still running around. Nelly and Nestor are arguing.

"Ai, c'mon, why do you gotta be like that?"

"Like what?"

This is normal for them. It's the same exact relationship Nelly had with her baby daddy, except Nestor likes the Mets and not the Yankees.

"Mami," Nelly says, "we'll be right back. We need some privacy."

"We just about to eat."

"We'll take ten minutes. We just need some privacy to talk like adults."

"If you see a store, get more soda," Mami says. "Christian likes orange."

"I know what my own son likes."

A minute later, little Christian pushes his older sister into the dirt and screams at her.

This day at the park just keeps getting better.

An hour later, the sun is still hot, the black family is gone, an Ecuadorian family is setting up in their spot, and Nelly and Nestor are nowhere in sight. Mami doesn't want the meal to start until they get back. "I don't want them to feel bad that we started eating without them," she says.

The kids don't care because they're on their tablets now. Veronica really doesn't care either, not as long as there are cheese doodles. She digs, almost to the bottom of the bag, when she first realizes one of the three white men has come over to their table. The other two hang back by their fire pit. One looks asleep.

"Hey!" says the one who came over. He's wearing white shorts and a t-shirt, in a blue that's almost pretty, sleeveless so he can show off his wrinkly, old man muscles. He's got greasy gray hair, a red face. "Hey!" he yells at Mami.

"Excuse me," Mami says.

Christian and Jade look up from their tablets, start staring at the man.

"Why are you wearing that shirt?" the drunk says, although with the way he slurs it sounds like "shit." "If you're an American citizen, you should not be wearing that shirt in America. You ain't an American."

"I am American, one hundred percent total puro Americano, because I am Puerto Rican and Puerto Rico is part of the United States."

The man steps closer. "If you're an American, you wouldn't be wearing that."

Her mom puts her hand up, a sure sign she is losing patience. "You may not know this, sir, but Puerto Rico is part of the United States, and has been for a very long time, okay. Excuse me, we are not immigrants. We are Americans."

"You people come over here. You're in America. Be Americans!"

"Please, mister, could you please let us alone? We were doing perfectly fine before you came over."

"Are you an American citizen?" he says.

●

Police, Veronica thinks, *I should get the police.*

But the anger from the drunk man is like a glue. She's stuck to the picnic bench. But he's loud enough that he's getting attention.

There—a policeman walks toward them. *Yes!* It's the cute one Veronica saw by the ice cream stand. Officer Conlon. *Thank God. He'll make those people leave. Three on one don't matter. They're drunk and look at his calves.*

"There a problem here?" Officer Conlon says, but to Mami, not to the drunk man.

Veronica tries to catch his attention with her eyes, starts a smile. He glances at her for a second, but there is no recognition there.

"Yes, officer," Mami says. "This man is getting in my face for no reason."

"I'm going to need you to calm down, ma'am."

Mami looks surprised. "I am calm. What are you talking about, calm?"

"Please lower your voice when I am talking to you."

Mami shakes her head, which Veronica knows means she really wants to blow up. But she stays calm. "Officer, I'm renting this area. We're trying to have a little party for my grandson, who just turned four. And this man over here is harassing me about the shirt that I'm wearing."

"Your shirt? Why would he do that?"

Officer Conlon doesn't even look at the drunk or his buddies. He just stands right in front of Mami.

"I'm not gonna lie," Mami says, "I think he's had a little too much to drink, and he doesn't know what he's saying."

"Ma'am, everyone's here just trying to enjoy the day. I'm sure you've had a couple of beers yourself."

"Me? We didn't even bring beer. You can check the coolers."

"I'm sure you don't want me to do that. I'm sure everyone just wants to go back to enjoying the day." The officer turns around to finally look at the drunks. "Timmy," the officer says. "You just want to enjoy the day, right?"

The drunken man named Timmy nods like one of those dog toys in a car window.

The officer tells Mami, "Why don't you all stay to your side, and they will stay to their side. Does that sound fair?"

"He doesn't have the right to come here harassing me just because he's drunk."

"Ma'am, I asked you not to raise your voice." Officer Conlon is getting in Mami's face, raising his voice.

Veronica sees something she rarely see in her mother's eyes: fear. Mami takes a step back and bows her head.

"Listen," Officer Conlon says. "Everybody just enjoy their day at the park, okay?"

He waves at the drunks and walks away, looking for trouble, looking for crime. *What the fuck just happened?*

When Mami turns around, Veronica can see she has tears in her eyes. "I never would've thought I'd have to deal with that shit again," her mother says. "I never would've thought."

She sits down at the picnic table. Veronica climbs in next to her, rubs her back, puts her head on her mother's strong shoulder.

⬤

"Where's Nelly and Nestor, man?" Mami says a little while later. "What the hell is taking them so long? This is ridiculous, and the kids are starving. C'mon, we're gonna eat."

Veronica thinks this is great news. The sooner they eat, the sooner they can get out of there, away from the heat and the noise and the dirt and those men.

The kids are running around like hurricanes again, both pretending to be the goofy dog they saw earlier. Veronica gets them seated at the table, cleans their hands and faces with wipies.

The Ecuadorian family has set up a giant tent. The three drunk men are still there by the tree, smoking and drinking, but now they are quiet, in a huddle.

Mami faces her, shaking the buns out of the bag into a messy pile. Veronica helps, taking each bun and neatly opening and placing them on plates. That's when she notices the drunken man named Timmy staggering toward them, right behind Mami. His arm is raised, holding a brick he brings smashing down.

19

"'Maybe you need to step out of the car,' he says.

"Suddenly the odds of becoming a statistic have increased."

BY THE NUMBERS

MICHAEL DOWNING

I t was only one glass of wine. Not enough to cloud your judgement or impair thinking, especially since you only took occasional sips while mingling with the crowd at the fundraiser. It didn't take three years of law school to figure out that you couldn't drink more than that, especially if you were getting behind the wheel. There were too many stories—friends, and friends of friends, who had gotten a slight buzz, insisted they were fine to drive, never thinking anything would happen to them right up to the DUI checkpoint when everything changed.

That isn't going to happen to you.

You aren't going to be that kind of statistic.

You are a Black woman who lives in Atlanta. You know the way it is.

The last thing on your mind when you leave the Buckhead restaurant is having had one too many drinks to get behind the wheel. Your life is going too well to mess it up like that. One of the best things about summer nights in the South is that daylight lingers until almost nine o'clock. It's still early, not yet dark, and you roll down the windows with Marvin Gaye then The O'Jays loud on the stereo—old school like you used to listen to on car rides with your dad when you were younger. You're driving a year-old Lexus RC coupe in a white suburb, but you don't think too much about it as you light a Virginia Slims Light. You don't give the police cruiser you pass a second thought, even after it speeds up and begins following a few car lengths behind you. Even when you roll through the yellow light it's not a big deal because another car shoots through after you, quickly changing lanes and accelerating past your car. You see the flashing blue lights in your rearview mirror and slowly ease to the side of the road, even though nothing will come of it. You haven't done anything wrong.

The odds are in your favor.

⬤

Your older brothers—one who lives in New Jersey and the other in a trendy suburb outside Detroit—get stopped by the police all the time. Profiled by cops for broken taillights that weren't broken when they got behind the wheel. Improperly changing lanes or failing to use a turn signal. Going too fast even though they have learned to stay five miles an hour under the speed limit all the time. Passing through the wrong neighborhood—one where they aren't welcome. Being told they match a description of somebody who doesn't really look like them.

The bottom line is too often they are stopped for the crime of being Black.

⬤

You have learned to get your driver's license ready while keeping both hands visible so cops can see them. Other people's mistakes are a great teacher. Every person of color knows what to do. Instinctively you hit the video button on your phone to record the encounter—just in case. If you have learned anything from the deaths of George Floyd, Philando Castile, and Andrew Brown it is that "just in case" happens too often.

Most of the cops you've met fit the stereotype you grew up with—overweight, squeezed into a uniform two sizes too small. Hard-assed attitude. White. Moving slowly and calculating each step they take like the energy expended costs something more than they want to give up. This one was different. White like all the others—except for a few security guards on your college campus and the ones you see on the news after a Black or Hispanic person is the victim of an officer-related-shooting and the local police force brings out a cop of color for the optics—all the cops have been white. This one is tall and fit. Athletic and attractive with short blond hair. The slight beginnings of a smile on his face as he gets out of the car. If he had been wearing a suit at the fundraiser he might have passed for a young executive on the rise—one of those "30 in Their 30's" businessmen you read about in Atlanta Magazine.

In his dark blue uniform, though, there's no doubt he's a cop.

❋

You were pulled over once before. You hadn't been driving; just a backseat passenger in a car driven too fast through your college town by two friends during junior year. One was Black and the other white, and right away there was a difference in the way the cop spoke. If your white friend had been driving nothing would have happened. But in a small college town where minorities were a very small part of the demographic mix, a Black guy named Lamar behind the wheel attracted attention. It didn't matter that he was driving his father's Benz, or that he taught at your university and was well-known enough to occasionally show up on TV. The cop saw Black and didn't care about the name on the license. There was a side of the road interrogation where every answer was met with skepticism. When the cop finally sent you on your way with a ticket for careless driving, Lamar was shaken; your white friend acted like it was no big deal, but you knew that they were looking at the same coin from two different sides. It would always be that way. Not just in the small college town but everywhere.

❋

The cop approaches from the passenger's side of the car and you turn off the music. The sudden silence is deafening. There's no reason for him to shine the flashlight in your eyes but he does it anyway and the glare is blinding, forcing you to flinch and turn your head.

You are tentative but polite. "Officer?"

"Miss," he says, leaning down so you can see him. "Do you know why I stopped you?"

You shake your head.

"You ran a red light."

You shake your head again, a little more emphatically. "It was yellow. I saw it clearly."

The cop bends forward into the car and returns a stare that is neither angry nor compassionate. Emotionless. You can see the name stitched on his pocket says PARKER, as well as the gun on one side of his belt and the taser on the other. You avert your eyes and stare at the handcuffs in his pocket.

"It was red."

"I didn't speed up. Didn't race through, trying to beat the light before it changed."

"You didn't beat the light. It was red."

You have learned to be soft-spoken and deferential. A Black girl behind the wheel of an expensive car is still a Black girl behind the wheel, especially inside the Perimeter. "Officer Parker," you say. "What about the car behind me? If I ran it, why didn't you stop the car that followed me through the intersection?"

Parker ignores your question, asking for your license and registration. You lean across the seat and hand it through the open window. He steps back, examining it for what seems like an exceptionally long time.

"Desiree Taylor," he finally says. "That's a very pretty name. A pretty name for a pretty girl."

"Where are you going?" he adds as you blush. "You're a long way from home. This isn't your hood."

You frown. Hood? Like every person of color shares a gangster commonality? You grew up in a Philadelphia suburb where drive-bys and gang colors were parts of other neighborhoods.

His smile is disarming. You tell him that you are heading home to the address on the license. A high-rise apartment you can barely afford, even after splitting the costs with a roommate who is rarely there. Friends from college. Both of you putting in long hours at your jobs because somewhere down the road is that pot of gold at the end of the rainbow—the one with a high salary, benefits, an impressive job title on the business card, and status that lets you roll with other executives.

"Nice car."

"Thank you."

"Been drinking?"

"Just one glass of wine," you tell him.

"Nobody has just one glass of wine," he says.

You shrug.

"If I look inside your car, am I going to find something that shouldn't be there? Something illegal?"

You shake your head while mentioning something about probable cause.

"Are you a lawyer?" he asks, still smiling.

"No."

"Here's the thing," he says in a tone reminiscent of an adult talking to a child. "You clearly ran a red light. I can make a case that you were driving erratically as well. That's enough for me to think you might be impaired. That's all the probable cause I need to check you and check your vehicle."

His smile is still polite. "You see how this can go, right?"

You keep shaking your head. "But I'm not impaired. I only had one glass of wine. Barely even drank that."

You're holding the cigarette between your fingers and the smoke curls through the window, some of it drifting into the cop's face. His smile turns and his expression hardens.

"You want to put that out?" he asks.

"I shouldn't have to put out a cigarette in my own car," you say but you drop it into the half-empty Starbucks Expresso can in the cup holder. When you turn in the seat your knee hits the can and you quickly reach for it to keep it from falling to the floor. Officer Parker tenses and takes a step back, his hand moving quickly to his taser with his finger resting on the trigger.

"Maybe you need to step out of the car," he says.

Suddenly the odds of becoming a statistic have increased.

❂

Even though you pulled over, your Lexus partially blocks the right lane and traffic crawls past as you stand on the side of the road, turning away from other drivers' stares. Officer Parker has already called in your license, but it will come back clean—there are no violations or warrants in your past to worry about. You are more concerned about his eagerness to grab that taser on his belt loop and use it if you make another unexpected move. All this for running a yellow light. You think it's a bit excessive, but you're that Black woman in a white suburb, which always makes you suspect—they just have to find the crime you might fit.

You've been recording everything and Parker notices that when he comes back from checking your license.

"Get off your phone."

"I'm not on my phone," you say. "And I have the right to record this. It's my phone. My car. My property."

You point the phone at him as you speak but he grabs it. He clamps a hand on your wrist and holds tightly, squeezing as he keeps the phone just out of your reach and quickly stops the recording, deleting the video before you can stop him. Parker puts the phone on the roof of the car and pushes you against the car, running his hands under your blouse, cupping your breasts, and then moving his hands into your pockets and eventually down your legs. As he pats you down, he lets his fingers linger. You swallow the nausea and comply, not sure what he's looking for, hoping that silence will end this quickly.

"You're doing all this for running a yellow light?"

"It's just routine," he says, but nothing about it feels routine. It's a routine based on color, complexion, and gender, and not the intricacies of police procedure.

●

Another cop car shows up and two white officers get out, one a female cop and the other one older, with more tripes on his sleeve, who fits your familiar stereotype. The name on the female cop's pocket says FLYNN, and she stands with you while the other one joins Parker at your car. There are no stripes on her sleeve, and you guess that she's close to your age, with probably less pull in this kind of situation than you might have. A rookie along for the ride like in the Denzel movie "Training Day." You stand next to her, watching Parker talk with the other cop while nodding and gesturing in your direction.

"I think we need to get a supervisor here," you say, remembering something your brother once told you. When in doubt, ask for their boss.

"Just do what they say," the female cop tells you. "It's routine. Things like this happen."

"Nice car," she adds.

"Worked hard for it," you say.

"I bet," she replies without much conviction.

There's something in her voice that makes you want to apologize for owning a Lexus.

The RC coupe was your first extravagant purchase. The monthly payments take a huge chunk out of your take-home pay, but it is a first step in a gamble on yourself. A reward for four hard years of good grades and Honor's List at UGA that got you a full-time job at an entertainment company downtown and a career moving in an upward trajectory. You have earned this car and you shouldn't have to explain anything. You watch as they go through your car, opening the glove compartment, checking under the seats and flipping the visors up and down. The cop with the stripes opens your pocketbook and spills the contents on the seat for Parker to go through, poking through everything you have—lipstick, a small makeup kit, tampons, a cigarette case, breath mints, and your birth control pills.

It is like your whole life has been spilled on that seat for them to analyze. Any secrets you might have kept hidden are scattered across the passenger's side of the car.

After twenty minutes the other two cops leave without saying anything else. Parker turns and says, "We're going to let this go."

He starts back to his car when you realize he is still holding your license. When you tell him he pulls out his cell phone and takes a picture of it. He brings it back with that same smile, saying, "You should go home, Desiree."

You get back in your car, feeling the eyes of every car that passes.

It should end there. Maybe turn into something for others to laugh about but you will never find any humor in it. You're a statistic now. Part of a cautionary tale to talk about with friends over drinks at Friday night Happy Hour; white friends won't understand but Black friends will nod knowingly because they have heard this story too many times and maybe experienced it themselves.

Except this time, it doesn't end there, and it's not the end of the story.

You are sitting at home a few nights later when there is a knock on the door. Surprising because your high-rise has a 24-hour doorman who is supposed to announce visitors, and even though you've lived here for almost a year, you don't know too many neighbors who would stop by. There isn't that kind of familiarity. You open the door and the first thing you see is the uniform.

It takes a moment to put the face together with the uniform in your doorway.

"How'd you get in here?" you ask. "There's a doorman in the lobby."

Parker smiles as he pushes past you into the apartment, closing the door behind him. "Nobody sees anything but the uniform," he says. "Nobody asks questions."

"What's this about?" you ask. "Why are you here?"

"I thought we had a connection. The other night," he says, and you just shake your head at the depth of his misunderstanding.

You wonder how he knew where you lived but remember him snapping a picture of your license before returning it.

He moves through the apartment, taking in the view while looking around. It's not much. Not a lot of square footage for you and your roommate to share but the floor to ceiling windows in the living room give a magnificent view of downtown Atlanta, even though you're only ten floors up. The view is worth the rent you pay.

"Very nice," he says. "Guess you do quite well for yourself. A beautiful woman with a nice car. Nice apartment. You got it all."

"I have a roommate," you say but he cuts you off.

"She's working," he says.

"I'm a cop," he adds, which makes you wonder what else he knows.

He takes a step forward and you recoil a little at his touch. He touches your arm, sliding his hand down the front of your pants, his mouth hot and sticky on your neck as you try pulling away. He's forceful, not awkward as he presses against you, steering you hard against the wall—he doesn't notice or care that you're uncomfortable and resisting, telling him no. He keeps coming forward. Running his hand up your butt and lower back. This isn't the first time someone has tried something like this, going to a place you didn't want to go. You've had guys try things, touching you in the same way he gropes you. But they didn't have his kind of power.

"Stop it," you tell him.

You try fighting back but he overpowers you.

"Maybe you can start calling me David," he says before he rapes you.

⬤

You never wanted to be this kind of statistic. Never wanted to turn into "one of those women." Defending your credibility. Asking people to believe your story. You never wanted to have your name talked about in whispered conversations—the kind that stop when you walk into the room and people turn away. You didn't want any of that but suddenly a bad day has turned into a much worse week. You squeeze your eyes shut and pray it will end soon, all the time thinking that this is just some kind of bad dream you are stuck in, hoping that it will pass, but you know it is all real. Your chest squeezes tight.

There are words but all you hear is your pounding blood and a dull ache in your head that drowns out any other noises.

You don't remember much about it. It happened too quickly. Maybe you put up a fight and struggled to stay away from him, but the memory is a blur. Your thoughts are filled with pain and surprise. All you remember is that afterwards he said, "Maybe we can do this again."

❋

The last thing he says before walking out the door is "Don't tell anybody. Nobody's going to believe you anyway, and there's nobody you can call. I'll tell them it was consensual. Who are they going to believe?"

You lay in bed, squeeze your eyes shut and cry softly into your blanket.

❋

The text messages start a day later, coming from unfamiliar numbers at all times of the day and night.

DON'T TELL ANYONE.

You get a sickening feeling in your stomach when you realize that not only did Parker copy your address, but he has your phone number as well. For a moment you think it's evidence but then quickly realize that each message comes from a different number—most likely burner phones, like the kind bought from convenience stores. There's no way to prove it's him. Just ten numbers that could come from anyone.

❋

Parker seems to be everywhere. At first, you see him walking down the street near your office—he's out of uniform and doesn't appear to notice you. It could be coincidence because you don't think he knows where you work. And if you didn't know who he is you might not have given him another look, but the sight of him makes your heart race and not in a good way.

Then he's in the same Publix, passing a few aisles away, never looking at you but always there.

You change your route when you drive to work—you stay home more and don't go out with friends or your roommate on the nights she's not working.

"What's wrong with you?" she asks.

"Just not feeling well," you say.

"You haven't been feeling well for weeks," she says. "Maybe you need to see a doctor?"

You don't answer and the conversation fades away. You have run out of words. There's nothing to say and nothing to tell her. All you want to do is curl up on the sofa and scream into a pillow. Tears drip down your face and you don't wipe them away.

Twice, you spot a police cruiser behind you in light traffic, but the car always turns off at an intersection before you hit your exit. You can't tell if it's Parker behind the wheel, but it doesn't matter. The sight of any police car makes you shake.

Then for a few days, you don't see him at all, and you think you're safe. That the nightmare is finished, and you can move on. You can start concentrating on putting it all behind you. Somehow. You engage in meetings at work and don't seem consumed or distracted when people talk to you. Go outside again, even if only for a short walk around the corner. Maybe take the first few steps towards reclaiming your life.

⬤

He comes back a few nights later and rapes you again.

This time he lets himself in by picking your lock.

"There's nothing you can do to stop me," he tells you. "I can make up a story and everybody will believe it."

"Besides," he adds, "you want this as much as I do."

When he leaves you summon all your courage and pick up the phone without thinking too long, and without taking too much time to talk yourself out of it, dial 911 to report the rape. You tell the dispatcher that it was a cop who raped you.

Two uniforms show up within an hour, this time getting buzzed in and announced by the front desk. It takes them forever to make their way from the lobby—you've taken the elevator hundreds of times and it's never taken this long to reach your apartment, but finally there's a knock on your door. Both are white—an older cop with sergeant's stripes on his sleeve and the other much younger, looking like he's fresh out of the Police Academy, the same as the female cop that night you got pulled over. "Training Day" all over again.

You let them in but as you close the door two more white cops push forward into your apartment.

"What's this all about?" the sergeant asks.

The four of them stand shoulder to shoulder in the living room and you feel a tightness in your stomach. It is more than you can handle. You feel intimidated and overwhelmed, and although you tell them that, no one makes a move to leave.

You wonder why they haven't sent a female detective who might be better suited to talk about this.

"I got raped," you tell them. "By a cop."

"One of ours?' the young cop blurts out, getting a sidelong glare from the sergeant. He fades back a step and does not say another word. The others stay silent as well. Nobody looks you in the eyes.

"I'm not going to let him get away with it," you tell them.

You think that this is where the story finally ends. That there will be interviews, reports, and a long road ahead, including a trial and testimony, but you are determined that Parker is not going to get away with it. You're going to become all the things you don't want to be—a statistic and a story other people will talk about, but you don't care. The only way to put this behind you is to end it.

❋

Instead, it's just the beginning.

They spend time looking around the apartment, commenting on how nice the view is the same way Parker did and point out the few nice things you've managed to acquire—asking questions like they doubt everything you tell them. The interview is brief and abrupt. They stand in your living room full of attitude, sharing glances that pass between them as you tell what happened. Nobody writes any notes, which you think is strange, especially since a crime has been committed. They mention that there's no sign of a struggle. Question how much of a fight you put up. Act like this has all been imagined. You're asked repeatedly how long the two of you have been dating, and when you try explaining what happened, it's apparent they have already made up their minds.

"Maybe you need to send your supervisor," you say. "Somebody else."

You are told, "We'll take care of this."

❋

You're not satisfied so you go to the hospital to report it. The doctors examine you and do what they typically do when a patient reports a sexual assault—they call the police. You sit in the emergency room for hours, waiting for a cop to come to investigate or send a forensic nurse to conduct a rape kit but no one shows. While you wait for a cop who won't come you glance at the doctor's report and see the words "sexual assault and rectal bleeding" and throw up.

When you finally get home, you call the sergeant for an update, hoping to find out that Parker's been arrested. Suspended. Disciplined. That someone is taking you seriously. It takes forever before he picks up the phone and when he does there is no warmth or compassion in his voice—at least none of the feeling you might expect from someone who is dealing with a sexual assault victim.

"Talked to Officer Parker," he says. "Told me what happened."

"What do you mean? What happened?'

There's a long silence. "Not the first time a one-night stand didn't go the way you planned."

●

You knew a girl in college who had been raped. A cheerleader. Bright and energetic, the life of every party until she wound up at a frat party and had too much to drink in a room full of boys who didn't take NO for an answer. When she came back to class there was a hollow look in her eyes, and she could never meet your stare. Someone who was completely broken. Conversations with her were limited to a few words, and she dropped out before the end of the semester. You remember thinking back then that she should have been stronger and found a way to work through it. Support groups. Counselors. People who would understand. Ways to recover. Except now you realize how terribly wrong you were. You can't summon the courage to do anything, and you start taking time off from work until your boss finally calls to ask if everything is okay. In less than one month you have missed more days than you worked. You lie and tell him it's some kind of flu, and in the COVID environment he tells you it's okay to work from home. It's still impossible to do any kind of work. You miss deadlines, fall behind on projects, and blow off conference calls. Because you cannot concentrate. You keep seeing Parker's face and hearing his voice. You can feel the way his fingers grab at you and the way he forces himself into you. You can't get him out of your thoughts.

He has permeated every part of your life even when he's not there, and there's nothing you can do about it.

●

The texts keep coming. Most times you don't even read them but when you do, they are threatening.

TOLD YOU NOT TO TALK

YOU SHOULD HAVE LISTENED

The only way to stop them is to disconnect your phone and change your number, as well as your carrier. But you worry that somehow, he'll find your new number. He's a cop. Cops can do things like that.

Night is close and the clouds peel away from a dark grey sky. Night brings on the worst of your fears. The sun will be gone soon, easing the scorching temperatures that have been in the 90s for most of the month, but you won't leave your bedroom. You'll stay wrapped in a blanket, huddled against the wall. The air conditioning is cold but that's not what's making you shiver.

You know it is only a matter of time before there's another knock on the door or a text from an unknown number.

In the movies the good guys always win, but you know that's not the way it really is. Bad things happen whether you're good or bad. You want this nightmare to end but you cannot see any way out of it. On the TV shows you used to watch with your brothers there was always a good guy, usually a cop and sometimes even a superhero. Somebody who steps forward and comes to the rescue, but there's nobody like that now. Your rapist is one of the people who are supposed to protect you, and there is nothing you can do to stop him. You matter less than other victims.

Your life is in ruins. You can quit your job. Move to a different city. Start over again. Or buy a gun—in those same TV shows, vengeance was usually attached to bullets, but that's just a Hollywood ending. In real life—your life—the nightmare will end only when he decides to end it. The badge he carries gives him that kind of power and you're coming to that realization.

The statistics tell a familiar story. Numbers don't lie.

There is no happy ending.

EDITORS

S.A. COSBY (Guest Editor; @blacklionking73) is the New York Times national best-selling, award-winning author from Southeastern Virginia. His books include *My Darkest Prayer*, and *Blacktop Wasteland*, which was Amazon's #1 Mystery and Thriller of the Year and 3# Best Book of 2020 overall, a New York Times Notable Book of the Year, a New York Times Book Review Editors' Choice, Winner of the LA Times Book Award for Mystery or Thrillers, and a Goodreads Choice Awards semifinalist and the winner of the ITW award for hard cover book of the year, and won the Macavity for best novel of the year, the Anthony, the Barry, an honorable mention from the ALA Black Caucus and was a finalist for the CWA Golden Dagger. He is also author of the best-selling *Razorblade Tears*.

His short fiction has appeared in numerous anthologies and magazines, and his story "Slant-Six" was selected as a Distinguished Story in *Best American Mystery Stories* for 2016. His short story "The Grass Beneath My Feet" won the Anthony Award for Best Short Story in 2019. His writing has been called "gritty and heartbreaking" and "dark, thrilling and tragic" and "raw, emotional and profound."

ROGER NOKES (Editor-in-Chief; @McCaffery_write) writes fiction under the pseudonym Stanton McCaffrey. His short stories have been featured in *Guilty, Mystery Tribune, Vautrin, Shotgun Honey, Yellow Mama, Out of the Gut-*

ter, *Between Worlds*, and *Heater*. He has published two novels: *Into the Ocean*; and *Neighborhood of Dead Ends*. He works in communications with a UN agency.

ALBERT TUCHER (Contributing Editor; @AlbertTucher) is the creator of prostitute Diana Andrews, who has appeared in more than 100 hardboiled stories in venues including *The Best American Mystery Stories 2010*. Her first longer case, the novella *The Same Mistake Twice*, was published in 2013. In 2017 Albert Tucher launched a second series set on the Big Island of Hawaii, in which *Blood Like Rain* is the latest entry. He lives in New Jersey and loves NJ Turnpike jokes.

JAY BUTKOWSKI (Managing Editor; @jtbutkowski) is a writer of crime fiction and an eater of tacos who lives in New Jersey. His short stories have appeared in various online and print publications, including *Shotgun Honey*, *Yellow Mama*, *All Due Respect* and *Vautrin*. He is the Managing Editor and one of the co-founders of **Rock and a Hard Place Press**, an independent publisher of noir chronicling "bad decisions and desperate people" in short and longer format fiction, as well as in the flagship *Rock and a Hard Place Magazine*. He's also a father of twins, a doting fiancé, and a middling pancake chef.

LIBBY CUDMORE (Associate Editor; @LibbyCudmore) is the author of hipster mystery *The Big Rewind* (William Morrow, 2016) and The Wade Agency series in *Ellery Queen Mystery Magazine*. Her work has been published in *Tough*, *The Big Click*, *Hardboiled* and others, as well as the anthologies *Hanzai Japan*, *Welcome Home*, *Mixed Up* and *A Beast Without a Name: Stories Inspired by The Music of Steely Dan*. She is the hostess of the weekly #RecordSaturday live-tweet event on her Twitter account and the co-host of two podcasts, *The OST Party*, focusing on movie soundtracks and *The Shattered Shield*, where she discusses the FX cop drama *The Shield*.

PAUL J. GARTH (Associate Editor; @PauljGarth) is an editor for **Rock and a Hard Place Press** and *Shotgun Honey*. His short fiction has been published in *Thuglit*, *Tough*, *Needle: A Magazine of Noir*, *Plots with Guns*, *Crime Factory*, *Rock and a Hard Place Magazine*, and several other anthologies and web magazines. He lives and writes in Nebraska, where he lives with his family.

R.D. SULLIVAN (Associate Editor; @RDSullyWrites) is a writer of fiction, comedy and letters to the editor. She lives in Northern California with her family and three solidly mediocre dogs, where she runs, in no particular order, a corporate office, a winery, a subcontracting business, and herself ragged. Her own writing has been featured at *Fireside Fiction Magazine*, *Shotgun Honey*, and *Tough*, as well as in the *Killing Malmon* and *Murder-A-Go-Go's* anthologies. You can track her down over at govneh.com.

CONTRIBUTING WRITERS

(In order of appearance of work)

HECTOR DUARTE, JR. (@Hexpubs) is a writer/ educator out of Miami, Fl. He's published widely online and in print, like the recent anthologies *Pa Que Tu Lo Sepas: Stories to Benefit the People of Puerto Rico*, and *Shotgun Honey Presents Volume 4: Recoil*. In September of 2018, Shotgun Honey Books published his full-length short story collection *Desperate Times Call*.

JAMES QUEALLY (@JamesQueallyLAT) is a journalist, author, and general arbiter of fact from horse shit. He's spent the past 12 years writing about crime, policing and chaos: first in Newark, NJ for *The Star-Ledger* and currently for the *Los Angeles Times*. His debut novel, *Line of Sight*, was published by Polis Books in 2020 and received starred reviews from *Publisher's Weekly* and *Booklist*. The sequel, *All These Ashes* was published in October 2021. His short fiction has appeared in several magazines including *Thuglit, Crime Syndicate* and *Shotgun Honey*.

BOBBY MATHEWS (@bobbymathews) is a writer based in Birmingham, Alabama. His next novels—*Living the Gimmick* and *Magic City Blues*—are forthcoming in 2022 and 2023 from Shotgun Honey.

HILARY DAVIDSON (@hilarydavidson) is the bestselling author of seven crime novels, including *One Small Sacrifice, Don't Look Down*, and *The Damage Done*. Her fiction has won two Anthony Awards and a Derringer Award, and her short stories have appeared in *Thuglit, Ellery Queen's Mystery Magazine*, and *Mystery Tribune*. Her latest novel, *Her Last Breath*, has been named one of the best books of summer 2021 by *Parade Magazine, Travel + Leisure*, and the *Toronto Star*. Originally from Toronto, she moved to New York City in October 2001.

JOSEPH S. WALKER (@JSWalkerAuthor) lives in Indiana and teaches college literature and composition courses. His short fiction has appeared in *Alfred Hitchcock's Mystery Magazine, Ellery Queen's Mystery Magazine, Mystery Weekly, Tough*, and a number of other magazines and anthologies. He has been a finalist for the Edgar Award and the Derringer Award and has won the Bill Crider Prize for Short Fiction and the Al Blanchard Award.

KEITH ROSSON (@keith_rosson) is the author of three novels, including *Smoke City* (2018) and *The Mercy of the Tide* (2017). My story collection, *Folk Songs for Trauma Surgeons*, came out in February of this year. His short stories have appeared in *Ink Heist, Black Static, PANK, Outlook Springs, Cream City Review*, and others. He is also a legally blind illustrator and graphic designer—which certainly provides its own unique challenges and rewards—with clients that include Green Day, Against Me!, and Warner Bros.

TIM P. WALKER (@walkertimp) asks that you check out and consider supporting RAINN (Rape, Abuse & Incest National Network) and House of Ruth.

TRAVID WADE BEATY (@TravisWBeaty) grew up in Northeast Indiana, spent a good deal of his twenties in Los Angeles, and now resides in Washington, DC. While he's had a great many jobs, his favorites have included acting, teaching, and being a stay-at-home dad to two girls and three cats.

MIKE MCHONE'S (@mike_mchone) work has appeared in *Mystery Magazine, Mystery Tribune, Guilty, Sherlock Holmes Mystery Magazine*, the *Detroit News*, the *AV Club*, and *Ellery Queen* where he recently placed on their Readers Poll for his short story "A Drive-by on Chalmers Road?" He currently lives in Metro Detroit. Visit him online at www.mikemchone.com.

OLUSEYI ('Seyi) ONABANJO (@Seyi_Onabanjo) currently lives in New York City, has a BSc in Electrical Engineering from the University of Lagos, Nigeria as well as an MBA from Columbia Business School, New York. 'Ṣeyi worked in corporate IT for many years, but has been most recently employed as a project management consultant, in between bouts of tech entrepreneurship. 'Ṣeyi is currently completing the MA (Creative Writing) program at the University of the Witwatersrand, Johannesburg, and is using this experience to release the novel which has stuck in him for the past few years. 'Ṣeyi is prepping for a second hike up (and down) Mount Kilimanjaro, has an extremely patient wife, two ultra-cool kids, multiple bartenders, and hundreds of booksellers partly dependent on him for a living.

JEFFREY EATON is a retired pastor with an arrest record. He has numerous academic publications, and, thanks to **Rock and a Hard Place**, a couple of bits of fiction have also been published.

JAMES D.F. HANNAH (@JamesDFHannah) is the Shamus Award-winning author of the *Henry Malone* series; his most recent novel, *Behind the Wall of Sleep*, won the 2020 Shamus Award for Best Paperback Original. His short fiction has appeared in *The Anthology of Appalachian Writers, Rock and a Hard Place Magazine, Crossed Genres, Shotgun Honey, Only the Good Die Young: Crime Fiction Inspired by the Songs of Billy Joel, Trouble No More: Crime Fiction Inspired by The Allman Brothers*, and the upcoming *Playing Games*, edited by Lawrence Block.

Harlem native MICHAEL A. GONZALES (@gonzomike) is a cultural critic and short story scribe. His fiction has appeared in *The Book of Extraordinary Femme Fatale Stories* edited by Maxim Jakubowski, *The Killens Review of Arts & Letters, Dead-End Jobs: A Hit Man Anthology* edited by Andrew J. Rausch, *Black Pulp* edited by Gary Phillips, *Crime Factory, Brown Sugar 2: Great One Night Stands* edited by Carol Taylor, *Needle: A Magazine of Noir* edited by Steve Weddle and *Bronx Biannual* edited by Miles Marshall Lewis. He writes essays for *CrimeReads, Soulhead.com, Oldster Magazine* and *Catapult*.

PRESTON LANG (@LangReads) is a Toronto-based writer. He has written a number of short stories and at least two novels.

ANDREW CASE (@AClaudeCase) is the author of two novels, *The Big Fear* and *A Falling Knife*. His plays have been produced at Steppenwolf in Chicago, New Theatre in Miami, InterAct Theatre in Philadelphia, and others across the country. He spent ten years investigating police misconduct at the New York City Civilian Complaint Review Board and now serves as Senior Counsel at LatinoJustice, a civil rights organization that works to create a more just society by using and challenging the rule of law to secure transformative, equitable and accessible justice.

ZAKARIAH JOHNSON (@Pteratorn) plucks banjos and pens thriller, horror, and crime fiction on the banks of the Piscataqua. His stories have appeared in

Sherlock Holmes Mystery Magazine, *Thriller Magazine*, and elsewhere, exploring topics of class, loyalty, and bad decisions.

JEFF SOLOWAY (@jeff_soloway) won the 2014 Robert L. Fish Award from the Mystery Writers of America and is the author of the *Travel Writer* mystery series for Penguin Random's Alibi imprint. His short fiction has been published in *Ellery Queen Mystery Magazine*, *Alfred Hitchcock Mystery Magazine*, various MWA anthologies, and elsewhere.

RICHIE NARVAEZ (@richie_narvaez) is the award-winning author of *Roachkiller & Other Stories*, *Hipster Death Rattle*, *Holly Hernandez and the Death of Disco*, and *Noiryorican*. He lives in the Bronx.

MICHAEL DOWNING (@KMWriter01) is the author of *Still Black Remains*, *Lost Exit*, and *Nine in the Morning*, as well as two books in the *Fight Card* series: *Fight Card: Hard Road*, and *Fight Card: Can't Miss Contender* (written under pseudonym Kevin Michaels). His short stories and flash fiction (including a few that were nominated for Pushcart Awards) have appeared in a number of magazines, literary journals, and indie publications. Originally from New Jersey (with that same attitude, edginess, and love of Springsteen), he left the Garden State a few years ago to live and write in a small college town northeast of Atlanta.

"Racism is a visceral experience...It dislodges brains, blocks airways, rips muscle, extracts organs, cracks bones, breaks teeth. You must never look away from this.."

-Ta-Nehisi Coates